PRAISE FOR THIRSTY BY MIA HOPKINS

IR

ONE OF THE BE)F THE YEAR. "A po a motivation and a risk.

THE WASHINGTON POST

"*Thirsty* held me captivated from its first page to its last . . . A singular reading experience."

USA TODAY

"Bold and unapologetic."

SMEXY BOOKS

"A brilliant read. There are good writers, and then there are writers that just leave you in awe. And Hopkins has definitely left me in awe."

HYPABLE

"A sizzling, emotionally intense story that is both gritty and heartwarming, an addictive page-turner that will stay with me for a long time to come."

NEW YORK TIMES BESTSELLING AUTHOR CATHRYN FOX

"Sexy and soul-wrenching, with Sal's irresistible voice luring you through a living, breathing Los Angeles."

"An amazing read! I stayed up way too late to finish and haven't stopped thinking about the characters. Highly recommended!"

TRASHED

AN EASTSIDE BREWERY NOVEL

MIA HOPKINS

PROLOGUE

SEPTEMBER

A woman stands in the garden.

She's tall and dark, about my age. She walks the rows by herself, stopping every few steps to taste a berry or rub a leaf between her fingers and smell it. Her hair is tied up tight. No makeup. She wears a loose white T-shirt and striped black pants —some kind of uniform, I guess.

She doesn't notice me watching her.

I put my cigarette out in the ashtray by Rafa's door. I'm wearing basketball shorts, no shirt.

I've spent the last five years standing on nothing but concrete. When I step down, the dirt feels like heaven against my bare feet. When I look up, my eyeballs almost can't take in all the color and light. The morning sky is too blue. The plants in the garden are too green. And the woman—this woman—is so beautiful I can't stop staring at her.

Silently, I watch her through the leaves of the avocado tree. She bends down in the vegetables. Her dark, pretty hands pull back the leaves to examine the squash or eggplants or chilies growing in the shadows. She picks some *hierbabuena* and sticks the dark leaves in her mouth. I grab some and do the same.

Fresh. Green, alive—this is how she'd taste if I kissed her right now.

A single red berry hides under the last of the strawberry plants. She bends down, plucks it, and takes a bite. The juice stains her lips.

I'm fantasizing about kissing her again when it happens.

She falls forward and catches herself on her hands. From where I'm standing, her whole body shakes.

For a second, I hesitate. What do I do? There's no one to tell me what to do. No corrections officer, no shot-caller. I'm on my own.

For once, I have to decide for myself.

I take a deep breath, creep out of my hiding place and walk over to her. I kneel in the dirt, hold her shoulders and slowly pull her upright.

"Hey," I say. "Are you—are you okay?"

When she raises her head, I see her cheeks are wet with tears. She's crying—hard, silently—the kind of crying that comes from deep down inside.

"Are you hurt?" I check out her arms, her hands. No cuts, no blood, no bruises.

She rubs her nose with the back of her arm and for the first time seems to realize I'm here. She blinks and her dark eyes search my face. Teardrops hang on her long eyelashes.

"Is the caretaker here?" Her voice is rough from crying.

"No, Rafa's not here right now," I say softly. "I don't know where he went." I look around the community garden, but we're alone. My mind struggles to find a way to help her. "Would you...would you like a glass of water?"

She's confused by the question, but after a moment, she nods.

"Do you think you can stand up?" I ask.

She nods again.

I help her to her feet. I take her arm and put my hand on her back to help her balance. I can feel her shoulder blades through the thin cotton of her T-shirt. *Flaca*—so skinny. My heart is pounding a mix of blood and adrenaline. I tell myself to calm down.

Breathe, Trouble. Breathe.

We walk to the trailer and climb inside. "Uh, ignore the guy passed out on the sofa," I say quietly. "He's had a hard night."

We tiptoe past my older brother snoring under a blanket in the living room, and I lead her into the room in the back of the trailer. She sits down on the bed. I get her a glass of water. The bedroom is tiny, no other furniture, so I sit down next to her. The bed squeaks under my weight.

Being back in a small space makes me feel calmer. But as she takes a drink, her arm touches mine. Her skin is warm from the sun. It's baby soft compared to my skin, all tattooed and scarred and leathery. I have to concentrate to keep from jumping back—it's been so long since a woman has touched me. So fucking long.

When she's finished, I take the empty glass from her and put it on the bedside table. She sobs again and collapses against me. I jerk backward for a second, and my brain floods with panic.

I lecture myself. *She's crying. You're alone with her. She could accuse you of assault. Or worse. Shit. You'd be back behind bars before—*

She has no idea what I'm feeling. She rests her cheek against my chest. Her tears wet my skin. After I silently count to ten, I put my arms gently around her. A sound comes out of my mouth like a word in a language I learned a long time ago, but never use.

"Shh, shh."

While she cries, I close my eyes and take a deep breath. Her hair—it smells like cilantro from the garden. The bright, sharp scent takes me back, reminds me of late nights trashed with my homeboys, scarfing down tacos on the sidewalk. Of my family's garden, a million years ago.

Of East LA—of home.

Her hand slides up my back and hangs on my shoulder. I blink. Under her fingers, my skin tingles. She's warm and alive. Me? I'm frozen, barely breathing.

"Do you...wanna talk about what's bothering you?" I ask.

She sniffles and leans deeper into me. "No, not really."

"Do you want more water?"

"No."

I'm pretty good at reading people but I can't get a decent read on her. She's feeling all her emotions at once, and I don't know why.

She tips her head back.

I stay still as stone.

For the first time in five years, I kiss a woman.

No. Even better—a woman kisses *me*.

Her lips are full and hot, sweet with fresh herbs. My heart-beat races. Blood pounds through me.

Jesus.

I forgot. In my world of hard edges and hard surfaces, I forgot that anything existed as soft and sweet as a woman's lips.

With her kiss, she drags me into the dark heat, the hunger that's haunted me for so long. My world tilts sideways, but before I let myself enjoy it, I jerk back again.

I have to assess this situation.

One, she's upset.

Two, I'm horny as shit.

Bad combination.

"Wait," I say. "Hold up."

Up close, her eyes are deep, deep brown. "What?"

I'm speechless, caught in the moment.

"Don't you want this?" she asks.

"Yeah, 'course I do, but—"

She covers my lips with hers, and all the air leaves my lungs. She reaches for the metal clip holding her bun in place and pulls it like the pin of a grenade. Her black hair tumbles down, straight and shiny. I breathe deep. Heat pours through me, but I stop her again.

"Tell me your name, at least," I say.

She blinks. "Haven't you ever wanted to do something completely reckless?"

I can't help it. I crack a smile. If only she knew. "Reckless? Yeah. Sometimes."

She stands up and closes the bedroom door with a quiet click. I watch her trembling fingers lift up her T-shirt. Static crackles over her hair as she pulls the shirt over her head. My eyes drop to her simple pink bra, to her pretty tits, to the little belly that curves from her long body. She drops the shirt on the floor and goosebumps break out all over her beautiful brown skin.

We lock eyes. She's not afraid of me. She should be.

"Are you sure?" I ask.

She nods.

"But you look like a good girl."

She shrugs. "Looks can be deceiving."

This is crazy. I shake my head and laugh a little. "So...do you do this a lot?"

"Do what?"

"Fuck strangers?"

She doesn't flinch at the dirty word. "No," she says. "Never, in fact."

I watch, hypnotized, as she steps out of her black work shoes and takes off her socks. Her feet are long and pretty, toenails neat. No nail polish. She stands up straight. Just before she unbuttons her pants, her hands freeze on her fly.

"Condoms?" she whispers.

I'm dazed. "What?"

"Do you have condoms?"

"Yeah—yeah. I do." Cigarettes, a burner phone—these were my first purchases when I stepped off the bus from Delano. Before I left the counter of the liquor store, I bought some condoms. At the time, I felt stupid, too optimistic. But now, relieved, I reach into my backpack, take out the foil strip, and lay it on the bed.

She nods at me and takes off her pants. Her cotton panties are blue with little daisies.

I realize I'm holding my breath. That, combined with the rapid movement of blood to my dick, makes me dizzy. I force myself to breathe.

"Come on. Tell me. What's your name?" I ask.

Instead of answering my question, she leans forward and kisses me again. She runs her hands down my chest, over my scar tissue and the tattoos I got to cover up the ugly reminders of the night I got busted. I realize somewhere in my hazy brain that this is the first time I've messed around since the shooting. I was eighteen then, a player, a pretty face. I'm twenty-three now, a shadow. A nobody.

With her long legs, she climbs on top of me. I reach up and comb my hands through her cool, heavy hair. I stroke the back of her smooth neck, pinning her mouth to mine. She slips the tip of her tongue between my lips, searching me out. I cup the back of her head in my hand and kiss her deep, tasting her, finally giving her my tongue.

She moans.

The air leaves my lungs.

I'm lost.

There, in the tiny, quiet bedroom of Rafa's trailer, under the framed paintings of saints, La Virgen de Guadalupe, Santo Muerto, and a faded photo of Pope John Paul II, the gods answer my prayers. This beautiful woman lets me strip her naked. I remove her bra and panties and watch as she lies down on the bed.

For so long, my whole world was a cell, a day room, a concrete yard, and the nasty mess inside my head. Old-timers let me borrow their raggedy-ass romance novels to help me cope. Homies who had been in and out of the *pinta* warned me how good my first time would be when I got out.

But this.

This is better than *good*. Better than amazing.

I stroke the smooth skin of her face and dive deep into those dark eyes. I kiss her and kiss her. I kiss her until her lips are swollen, until I memorize her sweet flavor and drink it deep. I kiss her neck and massage her breasts. I put my hands on her hips, pin her to the mattress and suck her tiny nipples, swirling them with my tongue and grazing them with my teeth until she is trembling beneath me.

"Yes," she whispers.

After a long time, I put my hands on her thighs and spread them apart. She is natural but neat, with a triangle of short black hair above the most beautiful dark pussy I have ever seen. I take a deep breath of her, and every part of my brain blazes up.

"Why are you letting me do this?" I ask.

"Because."

"Because?"

"Because I need you to help me forget." She trails her long fingers over her body, offering herself to me. A gift—one I don't deserve.

"Forget what?" I ask.

"Everything," she whispers. "All of it."

ONE

FEBRUARY

At sunset, I ride across the bridge. Behind me is my hood. In front of me, beyond the river and the rail yards, downtown Los Angeles rises up with its tall buildings and cranes like giants.

For Valentine's Day, pink and red lights flash along the top of the US Bank Tower. I'm a romantic. You wouldn't know it by looking at me. My friend Rafa teased me before I left the trailer.

"Going to see your Valentine, Trouble?" he asked.

"Shit, I wish," I said.

My lonely ass passes warehouses and factories, homeless camps and fancy remodeled apartment buildings. In the jewelry district, traffic gets heavy, but I weave through the cars.

The place I'm looking for sits on the ground floor of one of the big glass skyscrapers. White light floods its sign, no missing it.

Giacomo's.

I ride my bike down a narrow alley until I find a pair of Dumpsters and a back door.

The cold wind between the buildings is so strong, I almost fall over when I stop. I catch myself and carefully lock my piece-of-shit bike to some exposed pipes. My ears are still ringing from the wind as I open the heavy metal door. It slams shut behind me.

I stand there, blinking in the bright lights.

I've never been in a restaurant kitchen before. It's big. Red tile floor. Everything is steel—countertops, shelves, refrigerators, ovens, pots and pans. There's an army of cooks dressed in striped pants and white jackets and aprons, cutting vegetables or butchering meat or mixing up weird-looking things in bowls as big as sinks.

I'm supposed to find the general manager. For a second, I study the faces of the staff. A couple of them are white, but most of them are brown. Are any of these guys the general manager?

I take another step into the kitchen. Some of the cooks raise their heads from their work. A few of them look surprised before they turn their faces away.

This reaction is nothing new to me.

I'm not exactly Mickey Mouse.

A cook pushing a cart full of boxes crosses my path. He's got a big black mustache and that ageless look the *veteranos* in my neighborhood sometimes have. He could be twenty-eight or fifty-eight—hard to tell.

"Excuse me," I say to him, "I'm looking for the general manager. Do you know where he is?"

"The GM? Dino?" The cook looks too busy to ask who I am or what I want with the general manager. "Check the office. Over there." He gestures to some doors on the other side of the kitchen.

The other cooks give me the side eye as I cross their territory and enter the swinging doors. On the other side across a hallway is a tiny office where a white dude in a navy-blue suit and a pink shirt sits at a desk.

"Hello?" I ask.

The man swivels in his chair. He's got narrow shoulders and

a little paunch. His gray hair is wavy and carefully styled. His reaction to me is exactly what I expect. He sits up straight and his eyes widen. We're alone in the office and he's scared.

"Can I help you?" he asks.

"Uh, yeah, hi," I say in a quiet voice. "My employment agency sent me. They told me you need a dishwasher tonight." I take my papers out and hand them over to him, along with my ID, just to save time.

The man looks at my ID and eyes me suspiciously. "Eduardo Rosas."

It's my real name, but I still feel weird when I hear it. "Yes, sir," I say. "Eddie."

He hesitates slightly as he puts his hand out to shake mine. "Dino Moretti."

We get some paperwork done together as I stand in the tiny office. I see shelves of binders, a corkboard pinned with receipts, and an old timecard machine. A split-screen monitor shows the six security cameras set up around the restaurant.

Dino studies me without trying to be obvious about it. What's he thinking? Has he hired anyone like me before? Do the tattoos on my neck scare him? From his reaction to me, they might.

Dino types my information directly into the computer. "Are you available to work full time?"

"Yes, I'm looking for full-time work."

"Are you able to lift twenty-five pounds?"

When I don't answer, he looks up from the screen and we make eye contact. I know he has to ask this question, but let's face it, I'm a gorilla. Six-foot-two, two-twenty. "Uh, yeah," I say, and for the first time, the guy cracks a smile.

"Emergency contact information?"

"My older brother. Salvador Rosas." I open up my cheap flip phone and find Sal's number. I read it out loud.

Dino taps in the number and clicks the mouse a few times. Then he turns back to me. "Let me tell you a little bit about us. Giacomo's is a fine dining establishment, open only for dinner. We do one hundred and fifty covers a night."

I don't know what that means so I just nod.

"We specialize in regional Italian food. My brother Giacomo is the executive chef. He's the head of the kitchen. When he is on a book tour or traveling to promote the restaurant, like right now, his sous chef Carmen Centeno is in charge." He looks sideways at me. "As a heads-up, her word is law. She runs a very tight ship. No slacking. No shortcuts. I've seen her throw staff out of her kitchen at the height of service. Understand?"

I nod. "Yes. Got it."

"Have you washed dishes in a commercial kitchen before?"

"Yes, sir." It's a lie, but I need this job.

"Good," says Dino. "The other gentleman you'll be working with is also new. He has never worked dish. You can show him the ropes. Go ahead and get set up."

With that, Dino turns back to his computer and picks up the phone. I stand there for a moment before I realize we're done.

When I find the employee restroom, I stash my bag and hoodie in an empty locker. I don't have a lock, but I don't have anything worth stealing either. I walk over to the dishwashing area and slip a plastic apron on over my head.

A kid comes toward me through the busy kitchen. He's white, a little younger than me. He's got plugs in his ears and a pierced nose. He's got tattoos too, dragons and flowers up and down his arms. His tattoos are the colorful, expensive kind, done in a shop. Compared with his, mine look rough and sloppy. But they should. They're prison tattoos.

"Hey," the kid says. "Are you the other dishwasher tonight?"

"Yeah." I pause, reminding myself to use my real name. "I'm Eddie."

"Nice to meet you," he says. "Boner."

"Boner?"

"Yeah," he says, like it's no big thing for me to call him Boner. "Dino told me you've done this before and that I should listen to what you say."

Because he's from my employment agency, I figure it wouldn't hurt to tell him the truth. I say quietly, "Listen. I haven't really done this before."

The kid's bright blue eyes get wide. "You haven't?"

"No."

"But—"

I fake a confident smile. "It's just washing dishes, right? We'll figure it out."

Together, we examine our station. On one wall, there's a sink with three sections. On the other wall, there's a bigger sink with a silver sprayer and a weird silver box-thing with two doors that slide down on both sides. I assume this is the dishwashing machine. A stack of plastic racks sits underneath on its own shelf. A conveyor belt slides through the machine, kind of like a mini carwash.

I'm pretty good with cars and fixing things, so after messing with the buttons, I think I know how this thingy works.

Boner and I make a plan. We figure he'll organize the dishes on the countertop as they come in. Then I'll stack them in the racks and run them through the machine.

No problem, right?

All of a sudden, the noisy kitchen goes quiet. Boner and I watch from our corner as an army of servers comes in through the swinging doors and stands in a circle by the line. They're dressed in black from head to toe. They're wearing long black aprons that fall down past their knees. Someone is standing in the middle of the group.

"Who is it?" Boner whispers.

"The chef, I guess," I say, but I can't see.

"Okay, here we go," says a woman's voice. It's deep, loud, and steady—the voice of a federal judge or the captain of a ship full of nuclear weapons. "Valentine's Day specials. Listen carefully and hold all questions until the end, understood?"

"Yes, Chef," the staff says.

She says something in Italian and then translates it to English. "Farmer's market vegetable salad, organic rose petals, pancetta, and vinaigrette." She says something else in Italian. "Seared scallops with blood orange and salsify." She says one more thing in Italian. "Wagyu beef two ways, served with polenta and roasted red beets." I hear a ruffling of papers. "Tonight's fresh pasta is tagliatelle with *sugo di carne* and parmesan. Special dessert, mascarpone *semifreddo* with crushed amaretti and candied flowers. Questions?"

The wait staff asks a few questions, and for some reason, I find myself zoning out, wishing I could listen to more of the chef's voice. It's sexy, a little rough.

Man, it's been a long time.

A long time.

Before my mind wanders back to that morning in the garden, the meeting ends. The waiters all clear out and the staff gets back to their stations. The chef has disappeared, the kitchen settles in. Boner and I watch as the cooks check all their ingredients and make sure all their equipment is in the proper place. They look calm and happy.

"See?" I elbow Boner. "They're chill. This'll be cake."

The kid smiles nervously and reties his apron. "Do you think we should ask someone, just to make sure we're doing the right thing?"

That would expose my lie and put me out of a job. I wave my hand, all casual even though I feel anxious too. "We'll be fine. Don't worry."

At that exact moment, the ticket machine at the end of the metal counter screams to life.

———

TWO HOURS LATER, Boner and I are in deep shit. Not only are busboys dropping off endless tubs of dirty dishes, prep cooks are dropping off stacks of sauté pans and saucepans faster than we can wash them. Our dish pit is a clusterfuck.

I'm cranking, but as soon as I put one rack through the machine, another five appear next to me. Boner is stacking the dishes as fast as he can, but the kid is in over his head. The machine takes a minute and a half but even that isn't fast enough to keep up.

A busser takes pity on us. With a disgusted look on his face, he shows Boner how to separate the plates and the glasses into the correct plastic racks. Then he has to go—he has his own responsibilities to take care of.

Goddamn.

What have I gotten us into?

All around us, the kitchen is a blazing hell of fire, food, knives, hot pans, and cooks busting their asses to get their dishes done. I can hear the female chef barking orders at her staff. "Two *sugo*, one branzino, fire four beef specials!" Each time she says something, all the cooks yell back at her in unison, "Chef!"

A busser drops off another tray full of dirty dishes. I curse under my breath. All of a sudden, the conveyor belt stops.

Boner and I look at each other.

"What the—?" There's absolute fear in his eyes.

I've been in prison riots. I've been pepper-sprayed and Tasered. I've had my balls kicked in by rival gangsters. Hell, I've even been shot.

Still, panic hits me when I realize the dishwashing machine has stopped working.

"You check what's going on. I'll clear off the dishes on the other side." Boner wipes his hands on his pants.

"Okay." I squirt some water on an extremely dirty sauté pan covered in what looks like fresh blood. The water hits a big metal spoon in the sink and sprays Boner's face. Now there's a huge puddle all over the floor.

"Shit, I'm sorry," I say.

"It's okay, it's okay." The kid wipes his face with his arm. He's a good sport, considering how I've fucked us both over in a big way. On the other side of the machine, he picks up a full tray of dishes and hauls it over his skinny shoulder.

Then it happens.

Like a palm tree in a hurricane, he bends to the right and bends to the left. He catches himself and a feeling of extreme relief hits me—until he takes one step backward, slips on the wet floor, and falls over completely. His feet fly up toward the ceiling.

The kitchen is loud, full of yelling chefs and clanking pots and pans. But when the tray of dishes crashes to the floor, smashing into a million expensive pieces, everyone looks up from their work at us.

I'm helping Boner to his feet when we both hear her voice cutting through the silence.

"What the hell is going on back here?"

Boner opens his mouth to say something, but I step out in front of him and cut him off. "It's my fault. I dropped the dishes, Chef."

"What?" Boner says. "No, it was—"

"My mistake." I put my hand on the kid's chest and push him behind me.

Everyone is staring at us. I notice the whites of the cooks' eyes as they watch from their stations, simultaneously working and enjoying the free show. My heart is beating hard. I am about to lose yet another job. But I can't let Boner take this fall. We're in this mess because of me.

I face the chef at last.

Tall and slender, she's got high cheekbones, full lips, and brown eyes that tilt upward at the corners. Her skin is smooth and dark, and her hair is tied up in a black, glossy bun.

Jesus Christ.

It's her—the woman in the garden.

The moment we recognize each other lasts less than a second. She blinks and I blink, and now we both have to make a decision about how to proceed with all these people watching. Acknowledge that we've met before? Or ignore that we have any history at all?

She makes the decision for both of us.

"What is going on back here?" she asks again. Her dark eyes ricochet between me and Boner before taking in the broken dishes, the dish pit, the broken dishwashing machine, and the dirty dishes piled up to heaven.

"What's your name?" She's looking straight at me, completely ignoring Boner, who whimpers like a puppy behind me.

"Eddie Rosas, Chef." I keep my voice steady. I try, anyway.

"Dino said you've worked as a dishwasher before." Her voice is icy and hard. "Did he lie to me?"

"No, Chef."

"So you lied to Dino."

Instead of saying anything more, I begin to take off the apron. It's about eight o'clock. I can be back at Rafa's before nine, get to bed early, and return to the employment agency tomorrow to see if any new assignments turn up.

"What are you doing?" she says. "You're not going anywhere." She points to the floor. "These dishes are from an artisan potter in Ojai. Unless you have a couple thousand dollars in your locker, you owe us some labor."

I look up. No way in hell is she going to admit she knows me, not in front of her troops. But when we lock eyes, her chest rises and falls sharply, like she's catching her breath.

And that's when I know.

She remembers. That morning—our morning.

The heat, the wildness.

I read the embroidery on the front of her white chef's jacket. Carmen Centeno, Sous Chef.

Six months I've been trying to find this woman. She never told me her name.

"Chef Centeno," I say in a calm voice, "I'm not the kind of person to run away from something I've done."

I'm taking a jab at her, and she knows it. She was the one who ran away after...well, after we did what we did.

When she narrows her eyes at me, my body catches fire.

"Okay, Eddie," she says. "So how do we fix this?"

TWO

Ten seconds of silence tick by. Still, I don't know what to say.

Without breaking eye contact with me, she yells, "Rigoberto!"

The Mexican chef with the mustache looks up from the cooktop where he's making what looks like six different sauces all at once.

"*Por favor*," she says, "can you show these two *payasos* how to do dish so that we can get caught up?"

"*Sí*, Chef."

Before I can say anything else, he appears at her side and she takes over his station. No pause, no handoff. It's like he steps out of his shoes and she steps right into them.

Rigoberto grabs a rolling cart next to the sink and piles the racks of clean dishes on it.

"You," he says to Boner, "put these away."

Boner stops trembling and rolls the cart away. As soon as the other side of the conveyor belt is clear, the dishwashing machine starts working again.

Rigoberto shows me the flap on the end that shuts off the machine if the belt is full. "Do you understand?"

I nod.

Next, Rigoberto fills the three-compartment sink. He adds different solutions to them and explains each one. "For pans and cooking equipment. One, scrub. Two, rinse. Three, sanitize. Four, air dry on racks. Don't wipe anything with towels. It's not clean. ¿*Entiendes?*"

I nod.

"Now watch me." Quickly, Rigoberto works like a beast through the backup of dishes. He organizes the pit and piles everything neatly in the racks. With the nozzle, he blasts loose food off the dishes and runs everything through the dishwasher. As soon as one rack is done, he takes it out and puts in the next one. He stacks the racks on another rolling cart. When that cart is full, Boner comes back with the empty cart and they exchange.

Rigoberto is fast and efficient, almost like a robot. The system he has is so smart, I regret that I pretended to know how to do this. The lie insults him.

"Clean this up," he says, pointing to the floor full of broken dishes. "The broom and dustpan are in the back by the mop sink."

Feeling humble, I do as he says. When I'm done, Rigoberto hands me the nozzle and watches as I try to copy him. I'm slow. My hands feel clumsy. But I see how easy it is to do the work when the workstation is clean. I see how fast I can go if I'm organized.

When he's satisfied with my limited skills, Rigoberto slaps me on the back. He's much stronger than he looks. "Okay?"

"Okay," I say. "*Gracias por enseñarme.*"

He washes and dries his hands. "Stay organized. Work fast. Questions? Ask. Always ask. Number one? Communication."

Rigoberto returns to the cooktop where he and Carmen

switch again. She shoots me a look of annoyance before taking back her place at the head of the line.

AFTERWARD, the general manager gives me and Boner a talking-to in the office. To our extreme surprise he tells us to come back tomorrow, same shift. I bum a smoke off the kid and we have a good laugh by the Dumpsters.

"The fuck?" Boner snorts. "They want us to come back?"

"Gonna take a long time to pay off those dishes." I take a long drag. I don't smoke much these days, but I enjoy it when I can.

"On these wages, yeah," Boner says. "Why did you take the fall for me?"

"Because I was the one who spilled water on the floor."

"Yeah, but I was the one who fell over."

"I was the one who told you I knew what I was doing."

He laughs harder. "I trusted you, you fucking liar."

In the privacy of the alley, we bust a gut. We keep talking as he lights up another cigarette. "I want to be a chef," he admits to me. "A big-time chef, like Gordon Ramsay or Emeril."

"A TV chef?"

"Sure, why not?"

"Do you know how to cook?"

"No, but if I hang around in a restaurant kitchen, eventually I'll learn, right?"

"Don't they have schools for that?"

He shrugs. "I'm not really a school-type person, you know?"

"Something we have in common," I say. To be honest, I hated school. I could hang in some classes. I liked math. But other classes? I felt so restless. Sitting still, being quiet, taking notes. I could never concentrate. The street—that's my class-room. People. Their stories. The things that make them tick.

After Boner and I finish our smokes, we bump fists and say goodbye. When I ride back over the bridge, the streets are empty and quiet. The wind has died down.

I park my bike outside of my friend Rafa's trailer, where I've been crashing on and off for the last few months. I wash up with cold water from a garden hose, then sneak inside. The couch is too short for me, so I lie down on the floor of the small, freezing living room.

At last, my thoughts circle back to the only place they really want to land.

Carmen.

It's kind of an old-fashioned name. It reminds me of black-and-white movies, high heels and stockings. Centeno. Why does her last name sound so familiar? Is she from the neighborhood? I don't remember her from school.

For days, I waited for her to come back. I searched for her on my bike, hoping to see her walking down the street. I could've asked around, but I figured she wouldn't want everyone in the neighborhood to know her business—our business.

For months, I've been thinking of her. Tonight I found her.

I turn her name around and around in my mind like a warm coin between my fingers.

Carmen.

Carmen.

Carmen.

THE NEXT MORNING, I ride my bike out to see my brother.

He's sitting in the kitchen of his girlfriend's house, eating toast and reading a schoolbook. His girlfriend Vanessa bangs around the kitchen and gets her daughter ready for school. The little girl is wearing two short pigtails that stand straight up. One side of her head is spray-painted red. The other side is spray-painted purple.

"What's this all about?" I ask, closing the back door behind me. Vanessa's asshole wiener dog barks at me as I pat the little girl's head. It's sticky with some kind of paint. "Who's this little punk rocker?"

"It's Crazy Hair Day, *Tío* Eddie!" yells Muñeca.

"Otherwise known as 'Make Mom Crazy Day' as I try to figure out what to do at the last minute." Vanessa cuts a sandwich into little triangles. "*¿Ya comiste?*" she asks me.

"Not yet."

"Sal, feed your brother." Vanessa puts the sandwich and an apple in a Hello Kitty lunchbox. She's dressed in office clothes, and her heels click on the floor. When my brother doesn't respond, she playfully slaps his shoulder. The wiener dog barks again. "Come on!"

"Jesus, woman. Haven't you heard? Violence is not the answer." Sal shuffles up and puts some bread in the toaster. "You want eggs?" he asks me.

"Sure."

"They're in the refrigerator. Pan's in the sink. You have to wash it." He sits back down to his book. Sal's in a brewer certificate program at Greenbriar University. On the side he makes and sells his own beer. Since he got out of prison last year, he's gone straight. School, work, Vanessa and Muñeca. His life is full. Today I'm here to help him and Vanessa deliver a few kegs.

Vanessa's grandmother comes out of her bedroom. I stop scrambling my eggs and greet her with a kiss on the cheek. "*Señora.*"

"Good morning, Eduardo." She's wearing a Dodgers sweatshirt, leopard-print leggings and bright blue sneakers. She glances back and forth between me and Sal. "Look at you two boys. So handsome. You don't happen to have a grand-uncle hiding somewhere for me, do you? Good looking, not too smart?"

"*Abuelita*," Vanessa says, "ready to walk Muñeca to school?"

"Baby, I was born ready."

The old lady and the little girl head out the front door. I scarf down my breakfast, wash the dishes, and put them away. By the time I'm finished, Sal has packed his own backpack and is dressed for school in a black shirt with long sleeves. He covers up his tattoos nowadays, and he's traded in his big pants for a pair of fitted jeans. Since leaving the gang, Sal has become a different person.

There's a pickup truck in the driveway, borrowed from a neighbor. I see the hand truck and the kegs piled in the bed. I squeeze into the cab with Sal and Vanessa. She drives, since both me and my brother lost our licenses a long time ago—one of the many results of our run-ins with the law.

We head over the bridge and make the rounds at a couple bars and restaurants in the Arts District. I roll out the kegs and pick up the empties while Sal and Vanessa greet the owners and managers. While Vanessa chats everyone up, Sal hands out free bottles of his latest creation. This week it's an amber ale called Forever Mine. He named it after his and Vanessa's song, "Forever Mine" by the O'Jays. It's a seasonal beer, made especially for Valentine's Day.

It would be easy for me to make fun of how lovey-dovey he's gotten over her, but as I watch them work together, they're genuinely happy. Any smartass remark on my part would just roll down that happiness like a raindrop hitting a windshield.

Sometimes I wonder if that kind of happiness is in my future.

But how?

Sal and me—we're brothers, but we're not cut from the same cloth. He figured out a way to walk away from everything: the gang, the past, our father. Me? I'm different. The past holds me in its grip. It won't let go.

Vanessa records the orders and takes care of billing. She's an accountant, and Sal is smart to leave all the details to her.

When the last keg is delivered, Vanessa makes the thirty-minute drive up to Glendale to Sal's university. When we arrive, I slide out of the cab to let him out. He slings his back-pack over his shoulder, and for a second, he looks like a normal college student instead of a formerly incarcerated ex-gangster who spent a serious chunk of his life in prison.

I shut the door and Sal walks around the hood of the truck. Through the open window, he gives Vanessa a kiss. I try to give them a little privacy. I make faces at my reflection in the side mirror. I fiddle with my stupid flip phone that never rings. When the kiss goes on too long, I finally say, "Okay, okay, I get it. You're into each other."

They break the kiss at last and laugh a little. "See you tonight," Vanessa says.

"Love you, baby."

"I love you too."

Vanessa merges back onto the freeway in the rattletrap. She's glowing like a heroine in a romance novel. There's nothing brighter than a woman in love.

"So it's 'I love you' now?" I tease her.

She smiles behind her sunglasses. "Are you surprised?"

I shake my head. "No. You're good for each other."

"How about you?" Vanessa asks. "Are you seeing someone special?"

"Me?" I shrug. "No, not really."

I stare out the window at the hills and houses. I want to bring up Carmen Centeno, but what can I say that wouldn't be weird? *I had mind-blowing sex with a stranger right after I got out of prison. I've been thinking about her nonstop for six months. I found her last night and oh, by the way, since the universe likes to play vicious practical jokes on me, she's my boss.*

"Your brother says you're not into relationships," Vanessa says.

I shrug again. "Never really had one."

"Never had a girlfriend? Why not?"

Obviously, prison. Before that, I was a wannabe player, too much of a hardass for relationships. In my heart of hearts, I want what Sal and Vanessa have, a real connection like the ones I used to read about in those old romance novels. But I can't bring myself to say any of this out loud. So to Vanessa, I say casually, "Never needed one."

She looks at me over the frames of her sunglasses. "Wait a second. 'Never needed one'? Jesus. You make us sound like can openers. What exactly is the purpose of a girlfriend if you 'never needed one'?"

Vanessa's fun to tease. "Oh, I don't know. Sandwich making?"

It's a bad joke. She smacks my arm with the back of her hand. "You're going to be making your own sandwiches for a long time with that attitude."

We hit a patch of traffic by Dodger Stadium, as usual. We're quiet for a long time until Vanessa finally says, "Listen, I probably shouldn't say anything."

I sit up straighter. "About what?"

"Sal—he's worried about you."

That's not news. I relax a little. "He shouldn't. I'm fine.

Look, I even got a new job. Downtown, a restaurant called Giacomo's."

She perks up. "Giacomo's? That's a great spot. I did some accounting for them, back in the day. What are you doing there?"

"Dishwasher." It sounds unimpressive so I add, "They like me."

"That's great!" she says. "How long have you been doing that?"

I clear my throat. "Uh, one night."

Vanessa's shoulders sag. She says nothing, and her quiet disappointment gets to me.

"But I'm going back tonight. It's a start," I say. "The other places—you know, those weren't the right jobs. This one—I like this one."

"That's good," she says. "I'm glad. Now, just focus on this job and don't let yourself get distracted by—"

I don't want her to say my father's name aloud, so I cut her off. "I won't, Vanessa. Don't worry about me."

"I'm not worried, it's just that—"

"Sal told me all this. Again and again." There's an edge to my voice that I don't like.

"I don't want to nag you. Sal and me, we both want to see you back on your feet. That's all."

"I know. Just—just let me get there on my own. Please," I say, as gently as I can.

We drive back to her house in silence. Before she drops me off and heads to work, Vanessa says, "Sal thinks your dad—he doesn't want to be found."

I climb out of the truck and shut the door. Through the open window, I say to Vanessa, "Sal's probably right."

"Then why? Why keep looking?"

For peace, I want to say. For penance. To somehow—

somehow—repair what's broken in my life, in my family. My father is alive, and I just can't leave him somewhere out there, alone.

Instead of telling her the truth, I shrug. "Guess I'm just stubborn," I say.

She shakes her head at me. "Guess so."

THREE

From Vanessa's house, I ride my bike a short way to St. Amaro's, our neighborhood Catholic church. It's recess, so the kids from the elementary school are in the fenced-off parking lot playing dodgeball and basketball. I park my bike by the church steps and attach the chain to the handrail. I keep out of sight, since the nuns and priests probably don't want a tatted-up felon circling outside the schoolyard gates.

I enter the church. I dip my finger in the bowl of cold holy water by the door and cross myself. I'm surprised the water doesn't hiss on contact.

Inside, the church is dark and quiet. It smells like incense, dying flowers, and wood polish. I find a pew in the back and quietly put down the kneeler. I kneel, cross myself again, and close my eyes. There in the dark I realize I can't remember the last time I actually prayed.

A minute passes.

I hear him before I see him. The jangling of his key ring, the strange slapping of his steps on the linoleum. That weird bouncing walk. He taps me on the shoulder and I open my eyes.

The church groundskeeper. His dark green coveralls hang

loose on his skinny shoulders. The patch on his chest says Miguel.

Without saying anything, I get up and follow him out the side door.

Across the concrete walkway is the convent. On both sides of the walkway, the nuns keep a rose garden. It's winter, so the branches are bare, but the reddish-brown thorns look bloody on the green stems.

I reach into my pocket for the envelope. It's fifty dollars, not much—the remaining wages from my last job framing houses for a construction company. I got fired from that job when I didn't show up for a shift. The reason? I was doing what I'm doing now—chasing a lead on my missing father.

Miguel takes the money from me and slips it into the pocket of his coveralls. He's nervous and twitchy even on good days. Right now, he avoids my eyes and looks back and forth between the church and the convent, as if someone is watching us from the windows.

"Okay," I say quietly. "What do you know?"

"Trouble, listen." He shuffles his feet. "You know I respected your father. He was a good guy. I hope they find him. I really hope they do."

I want to take Miguel by the shoulders and shake him. I want to tell him there is no *they*. There is only me. I'm the only one who's looking. Everyone else prefers Dreamer Rosas to stay dead and buried, all his troubles and secrets gone with him.

"Miguelito," I say, "thank you. I know it would mean a lot to my dad, you helping me out like this."

"*Sabes que,*" he whispers, "I don't want to start anything with the gang. *Varrio* Hollenbeck never gave me no trouble."

He has no trouble taking the money, though. Still, he's my only lead right now, so I have to be patient. "ESHB's got nothing to do with this. I'm just a son looking for his father. I'm not looking for anything else but answers."

"*Pues sí, pero*—"

"If your dad went missing, wouldn't you want to know the truth?"

"Of course, of course, but—"

I point to the tattoos on my forearm. "Miguelito, what does that say?"

His eyes finally settle on my ink. He looks genuinely nervous now. "Trouble, I—"

"ESHB," I say. "The gang is me. I am the gang. I put in the work, I did my time. I would never do anything to cross them. You know I bleed East Side Hollenbeck. So did my dad. You say you respect him? That you were his friend? If that's true, you'll help me like you said you would."

The word *friend* is a stretch. Before he spent some time in rehab, Miguel shot up with my dad.

I move my face in front of Miguel's when he tries to look away. I cast a shadow on him. I know I'm scaring him. But when conscience fails, fear can push people to make the right decisions.

Miguel swallows hard and puts a hand over the pocket that holds the money. "Okay, okay," he says at last. "Here's what I know."

I listen carefully.

"When you and your brother were picked up, that was it," Miguel says. "Dreamer had been using again for a few months by that point, but when you were both arrested, he stepped it up. The last straw was when your *abuela* and *tío* came to pick up Angel and bring him to Salinas. The house was empty. All three of his sons, gone." Miguel takes off his cap and rubs the bill between his fingers. "He felt like he didn't have nothing to live for. I'm sorry to say so, Trouble."

"And then what happened?"

"He started to get rid of everything. He pawned your mom's old jewelry. He sold the TV, all the furniture from the house. He sold his old junker. Broke into a couple of cars. Did a few burglaries, but nothing big. Nothing that paid out. Then he lost the house."

"I heard he was taking a secret cut from the dealers on the street." A dangerous game, and a good reason to get taken out by the gang.

Miguel looks confused. "Who told you that?"

Whispers and kites in prison. Rumors on the street. "Just something I heard," I say.

"I don't know about that. The big homies didn't really trust him to collect taxes anymore. Ruben took away your father's territory and gave it to Demon. At that point, Dreamer was too messed up to put in any work for the gang."

What?

That doesn't add up.

The story that got back to me and my brother was this: while we were locked up, our father's drug habit got so bad, he started taking a cut from ESHB's drug dealers without permission. The big homies in the Organization found out and put a hit out on him. Loyal to Dreamer, ESHB's shot-caller, Ruben, stepped in on my dad's behalf and stayed the green light. My father escaped with his life, but a few weeks later, he was seen in a bar mouthing off about ESHB. The green light was put back on, and there was nothing any of us—not even Ruben—could do. My dad disappeared a few days later.

Sal and I thought we knew the truth. No one came out and said it aloud, but ESHB has rules that can't be broken. Our dad had been killed, most likely shot and buried in a shallow grave somewhere in the Angeles National Forest.

A disgraceful death for a disgraced gangster.

That should've been the end of the story.

But two months ago, my brother found a phone number.

We called it. And Dreamer Rosas was on the other side.

He hung up on us. The number was immediately disconnected.

So here I am, digging up old skeletons. Sniffing around. Paying my way through as many informants as I can, even though I'm broke as hell.

Until I find him. My father, Dreamer Rosas.

"What happened when he lost the house?" I ask Miguel. "Where was he staying?"

"Here and there. At the crash pad, at the park. He'd stay with me sometimes. It got bad for both of us, Eduardo. We were using a lot. One of the nuns here, she had the rectory put me on leave. Your father's caseworker sent him to Narcotics Anonymous meetings. He brought me along."

"What?" This is news to me. "Where were the meetings?"

Miguel answers all of my questions as best as he can, but those were bad days for him too. I can see where his memory fails him. The picture I get is blurry at best—no details. Miguel went into an inpatient rehab program shortly after that and lost touch with my father completely.

"Did he make any other friends at the meetings?" I ask.

Miguel pauses. "I can't really remember."

"Think," I say. "Think hard. Anyone?"

He looks down at the bare rose bushes. "Wait—there was a woman."

"A woman?"

"Yes, a woman. *Era bonita.* She had a name like a flower. Rose? Lily, maybe? Something like that. Your dad liked her a lot."

I can use this information. "Do you remember her last name? What she looked like? Anything about her?"

"No, I don't—" The bell in the schoolyard rings, loudly enough that we both jump. Miguel looks panicked. "I have to go." Quickly, he puts his hat back on and wipes his hands on his pants. "I have to go," he says again. "I'm sorry, Trouble."

Before I can say anything else, he turns and hurries into the church.

WITH THE HELP of Rigoberto and the rest of the kitchen staff, Boner and I redeem ourselves. After a few hours in the dish pit, we get our technique down and fall into step. Rack 'em up, load 'em up, take 'em out, put 'em away. The work is not exciting, but at least Boner's a decent conversationalist, and a kitchen full of people is an interesting place to be.

Fuck.

Who am I kidding?

I can't keep my eyes off her—Carmen.

She can't be more than twenty-five years old. Without makeup, she looks like a teenager. But the entire kitchen staff treats her like a four-star general.

Dino was right—her word is law. As she stands at the head of the line, no plate leaves the kitchen without her approval. If I was feeling singled out yesterday, I shouldn't have. I watch her chew out a line cook and a dining room server with the same fireworks show she gave me. The thing is, she's tough but she's fair. A good leader.

I find myself wondering about her. How did she end up here? What drives her? And what drove her to sleep with me, a stranger and an ex-con, all those months ago, in a shitty trailer in a community garden?

As Boner and I finish cleaning up after service, she stops by our station. My heart starts beating like a subwoofer.

"Are you both settled in now?" She looks straight at Boner.

"Yes, Chef," we say in unison.

"Good."

Then?

Nothing. She walks away.

For days, I watch her, and she ignores me. I know she can see me—she sees everything in that goddamn kitchen, and probably everything in the dining room too. When it's time for the staff meal, both the front- and back-of-house workers gather together to eat. But Carmen makes a plate for herself and hides in the office.

On the down-low, I ask Rigoberto questions about her.

"How long has Chef Centeno been working here?"

"Maybe three years? Chef Moretti hired her after she graduated from culinary school, I think. She worked her way up. She's very good."

"Does she speak Spanish?"

"Yes. Spanish and English. And a little Italian too."

Okay, that's fucking hot. "Is she married?"

He gives me a sideways glare. Like the rest of the staff, he's defensive of her. "Not married. She lives with her parents."

"Boyfriend?" I pause. "Girlfriend?"

He shrugs. "I don't know. You're so curious, ask her yourself."

I'm curious but I'm not brave enough. Not yet, anyway.

Before the restaurant opens for the evening, I sneak into the dining room to see what customers see. The waitstaff is setting the tables with white tablecloths. The room is dark. Each table has its own little spotlight, as if dinner were a stage show. All of the servers are dressed in head-to-toe black with long black aprons that reach down to their shins.

The wall by the hostess stand is full of framed reviews about Giacomo's. Chef Moretti looks like Dino, just older and thinner.

He's smiling in every photo, dressed in his chef's jacket. On a shelf by the door are his cookbooks—big, hardback, shiny. Fifty bucks apiece. I wipe my hands on my pants, pick one up, and look through it.

I've worked here now for almost two weeks and still I've never seen Chef Moretti. Carmen runs this kitchen. She's nowhere in the articles, nowhere in the cookbooks—not even the acknowledgements. It's weird—this place would fall apart without her.

That night, Boner looks like hell. He has a cold. He looks pale and moves in slow motion. I ask Rigoberto to ask Chef Centeno to send him home early. She comes to the dish pit. For the first time since day one, she addresses me with a direct question. "We're three-quarters through service. Can you handle the rest of the shift by yourself?"

Her eyes are intensely dark. I'm speechless for a second.

"Yeah." I clear my throat. "I mean, yes, Chef."

Boner goes home. I get the work done by myself, even though it takes a little longer. By the time the last line cook leaves, the half-dark kitchen is clean as a hospital, quiet and still. I mop up my station, hang up my gloves, throw away my plastic apron, and go back to the lockers to get changed.

On my way out the door, I pass the office. The light is still on.

I pause.

Should I?

Now or never.

Before I lose my nerve, I approach the door.

FOUR

Carmen sits at the computer with a clipboard. A half-empty bottle of Tums and an empty bottle of Pellegrino sit by the keyboard. The clock on the wall says ten to one. The security monitors show everyone has gone home except for Dino—he's at the hostess stand looking over reservations on the computer.

Carmen has unbuttoned her chef's jacket. She's wearing a gray tank top, and underneath that I can see the edge of her purple bra.

God help me.

I knock gently on the doorframe. "Hey," I say.

"Are you finished?" She doesn't look up. I don't know why she's physically unable to look me in the eye. Is it because she wants to remind me she's a hardass? Or is it because she doesn't want to remember what happened between us?

"I, uh, wanted to check in before I left," I say, "to see if you needed anything else."

She shakes her head, her eyes still on the computer screen. "No, that's it. Have a good night."

I look behind me. There's no one in the kitchen. The small

hallway is empty. This is the first time we've been alone since I started working here.

Fuck, what do I tell her? I haven't really thought this through. To stall, I clear my throat again, and finally—finally—she looks up at me. Her dark eyes are blank.

"Anything wrong?" she asks.

"No. Nothing's wrong. I just thought I should, uh, say thank you. For the second chance. After that first night, I thought I was done. Gone. So thank you."

She scans my face. She's still wearing her Chef Centeno mask, but a tiny muscle in her throat flexes when I fold my arms and lean against the doorframe. She stops typing and reaches for the empty Pellegrino bottle. She puts it to her lips and drinks an imaginary sip. Her movements are nervous, a little jerky.

That's when I realize she's as uncomfortable around me as I am around her.

As an experiment, I flex my chest a little so she can see the muscles through my clothes.

She catches herself staring. Quickly, she puts the bottle down and smiles at me, a fake plastic smile that tells me only that she wants me to get out of her office, out of her personal space. "I can't take credit for that," she says. "Dino wanted you both to stay on. But I'm glad it worked out."

I stall some more. "Rigoberto is a good teacher. And Boner, he's a good dishwasher. He's coming around."

"Good. I'm glad." Her voice is flat.

"I know that Boner is interested in learning about cooking. I think he'd make a good prep cook, if you're looking for one," I say. "He works really hard."

"We're full up, but I'll consider him if a position opens." She turns back to her computer but when I don't leave, she looks at me again. "Is there anything else?"

Anything else?

Is she kidding?

Now I'm really pulling conversation points out of my ass.

"Uh, what are you doing?" I ask.

"What do you mean, what am I doing?"

I step closer and stand behind her. I point to the screen. "There, on the computer? What are you doing?"

Her deep voice wavers a little. "Just putting an order in to one of our vendors."

"Do you do that every night?"

"No, not every night," she says.

My heart is beating so hard I'm surprised she can't hear it. After six months, I feel like I'll go crazy if I don't touch her. As slowly as I can, I rest my hands on her shoulders. She jumps a little and freezes. Her breath stops.

"So, how do you know how much to order so that you don't run out?" I ask quietly.

She grips the edges of the clipboard but she doesn't move away. "We look at past data and t-try to make an informed estimate."

"Oh," I say. With gentle, firm pressure, I begin to massage her through the thick cotton of her white jacket. All of the tendons in her shoulders and neck are stiff with tension. With my thumbs, I massage the back of her silky neck. My fingers brush the sides of her throat. Her pulse races and her skin grows warm.

"Do you ever order too much?" I ask. "Or too little?"

"That happens." Her voice shakes. "Every now and then."

"Hmm." I look down at her tight black bun. It gives me a flashback. I see her silky black hair falling down over both of us as she rides me, grinding her way to a shaking orgasm on my cock. My throat is dry. "What happens then?"

"We have to find a way to improvise—to make something special with the leftovers, or to find a creative substitute." I find a knot at the base of her neck and circle it slowly with my thumbs. Her chin drops forward and she takes a deep breath. "N-Nothing can go to waste."

"Nothing?"

Her voice gets softer with each answer. "No."

I massage her. As if I'm back in a dream, she lets me. She groans softly when I rub the tight bands of muscle across her shoulders. But for the first time, the thought hits me—I don't know her at all. Not really. And I'm dying to.

"Carmen," I whisper in her ear. "I wondered what your name was. Did you know my name?"

"Yes."

"How?"

She says nothing.

Feeling braver, I whisper, "Say it."

"Trouble."

The word sounds all wrong in her mouth. "No," I say. "The other one."

"Eddie. Eddie Rosas."

"Is that why you ran off and never came back? Because you heard I was a Rosas brother?"

"No—"

"Because I'm in East Side Hollenbeck?"

"No." She turns the chair, breaking both the spell and my hold on her shoulders. When she opens her eyes, I see the real Carmen at last—that spark of the dark fire burning inside her. "None of that mattered to me."

"Then why? Why did you take off? That wasn't just hooking up, Carmen." I try to get under her skin. "That wasn't just *fucking*," I whisper, "and you know it."

"But that's *exactly* what it was." She looks almost sick as she says this. "I'm sorry that you read more into it, but that's all it was to me."

I stand up straight. I think of all the nights I jacked off rivers to my memories of her. "I don't believe you."

"I don't care if you believe me or not," she snaps back.

I'm silent.

This isn't going well.

When our eyes meet again, her frown fades a little. Jesus Christ. Am I wearing my emotions on my face? I concentrate hard on going neutral so she can't see the mixture of embarrassment and hurt I'm trying to hide, but I'm pretty sure it's too late.

"I'm flattered, really," she says in a quieter voice, "but for me, that was just hooking up. I wasn't looking for anything more. That's why I left before you woke up."

My mind races to bridge the empty gap between us. Before I got locked up, I thought I was a player. A homeboy with a reputation as a ladies' man. In reality, I was a horny teenager whose membership in ESHB made me an easy mark for neighborhood women who had a hard-on for gangsters. Any gangster would do, even me. Looking back, I wasn't special, even though I thought I was.

To top it off, when I got sentenced, my sexual development froze in time.

These days, I worry I'm awkward. I worry I'm this eighteen-year-old kid in a twenty-three-year-old body, acting stupid and believing I'm hot shit when I'm obviously not.

I'm so angry at my heart—for what, exactly?

For wanting closeness with her that I haven't earned.

With that thought, I take a step back from her and give her some space.

"All right," I say. "Okay."

Her shoulders relax. She takes a deep breath and lets it out slowly. I worry that I've scared her. In as gentle a voice as I can, I say, "Before I go, can I ask you something?"

"What?"

"What happened to you that day anyway? Why were you so upset?"

Carmen's dark eyes narrow at me. "Before I answer, can I ask *you* something?"

"You can ask me anything."

"I know who you are," she says. "But do you know who I am?"

"Besides your name?" I pause and study her face. She gives me nothing. "Uh, should I know who you are?"

"Yes. You should." She sighs. "The bakery. By the house where you grew up. My family runs it. Slim Centeno—he's my dad."

Now I understand why her name sounded familiar to me. The Centenos are one of the oldest families in the neighborhood. They've owned the corner bakery for three, maybe four generations. My family has been in the hood that long too, but our business is slinging and banging, not bread.

"I grew up in that bakery," Carmen continues. "I worked weekends and every day after school. You and your brothers used to come in all the time."

We did. Begging Slim for free stuff, shoplifting *chicle*, counting out our coins for day-old *conchas* and fresh sandwich rolls for our mom.

"You never noticed me," Carmen says.

"What?"

"You never noticed me," she says again. "Behind the counter, working at the register or baking in the kitchen." She sighs. "I had a crush on you."

I can't help myself. I laugh. It comes out like the bark of a dog. "You what?"

"Don't laugh at me. It's embarrassing." She shakes her head. "I had the biggest crush on you. But you were such a little shit. You never saw me. Never said hi."

This whole conversation has surprised me, beginning to end. I try hard to remember a little-girl version of Carmen on the other side of the bakery counter, but she's right. I guess I never noticed her. Too distracted by *pan dulce*, or by shoplifting, or by my own big head.

"So really, you weren't a stranger to me that morning in the garden," she says. "I knew who you were. And all of us in the neighborhood knew you'd just gotten out of prison." She fidgets in her chair. "I figured that would be my chance."

"Your chance?"

"To get with you. To finally make an impression on you. At last."

"What?" I say. "'An impression'?"

She doesn't say anything. She looks so embarrassed, I tell her the truth. "Carmen, I haven't been able to get you out of my head."

We look at each other then, a little shy. Which is weird, considering the insane sex we've had and the fact that we grew up together. Kind of.

"We got caught up in the moment," she says. "I was just your first after a long time. A piece of bread to a starving man. Nothing special."

"There's getting caught up in the moment," I say, "and then there's...I don't know. Chemistry. We had chemistry. Lots of it."

At last, I get a small smile from her. The corner of her mouth tips upward at the memory. She recognizes I'm telling the truth. We did have chemistry.

Cautiously, I step forward again.

As if to torture me, the memory of her taste suddenly appears in my mouth, in my throat, and my inner dog begins to bark. I imagine grabbing her and bending her over the desk. I have a flashback of sinking myself balls-deep into her, feeling that pussy crush me in its perfect grip. I imagine losing myself in her.

This is the effect she has on me. Wild. Powerful.

"Are you seeing anyone?" I whisper.

She looks me in the eye. After a second, she gives her head the tiniest shake.

I lean down and breathe her in. I touch my lips to her throat, just a brush, and I feel the delicate muscles in her neck tighten as she swallows.

"It was good between us, wasn't it?" I say softly. "Tell the truth."

She gasps, and her soft breath strokes my cheek. "Eddie—"

Out of the corner of my eye, I see it. Movement in one of the security monitors. Dino has disappeared from the hostess stand in the front of the restaurant. He reappears in the hallway monitor just outside the office. Panicking, I jump back a split second before he appears in the doorway.

"Chef?" His eyes dart between us. No doubt all of this looks wrong to him—the dishwasher in the office with the chef, both of them breathing hard. "I'm about ready to leave for the night. Is everything...okay...back here?"

Carmen is blushing bright red, but her voice is steady. "Everything's fine," she says so calmly even I believe her. "Eddie was telling me that the other dishwasher is interested in a position as a prep cook."

"Oh." Dino relaxes a little. "Boner, is it?"

"Yes," I say. "That's him."

Dino examines my face. "That's good of you to say so. We'll consider him when we have a position—that is, if Chef Centeno thinks it's a good idea."

"Uh, thanks," I say. I turn slightly so that Dino can't see my raging hard-on. "It would mean a lot to him."

Carmen switches off her computer and stands up. "How about we all head out together?" she says, too loudly, taking off her chef's jacket and replacing it with the black jacket hanging behind the door. "I'm exhausted. I can barely keep my eyes open." It's a lie. She's wired. So am I.

"Good idea," Dino says as reaches for the top drawer of the desk and takes out his phone and wallet.

Trying to calm down, I tune out their kitchen chitchat as the three of us take the service elevator to the underground parking garage. Dino drives a vintage Alfa Romeo Giulia, devil red. The thief in me whispers a reminder I could lift that car in my sleep. Carmen drives a twenty-year-old beat-up Toyota Camry, which seems weird to me considering the authority and skill she has at work. I pictured her riding around in a tinted Lincoln Town Car with a driver in a black suit who could karate chop me in half.

On the other side of the parking lot, Dino gets in his car and waits for Carmen to get into hers before he starts his engine. He's being protective of her. I don't blame him.

Carmen unlocks her door.

"Can I call you?" I ask under my breath.

She looks at me and sighs. "I don't know. It's not a good idea, with work and all."

I know she's right. But I can't ignore the spark between us, or the bonfire we started together once, not too long ago.

"Okay," I say. "What if you call me?" Quickly, I add, "Like, if you needed me to come in on my day off. Or something like that."

For a second, she looks me in the eye before giving Dino a sideways glance.

Hidden by her car door, she holds out her hand. Heart beating hard, I pass her my shitty phone. She quickly taps in a number, calls herself, and gives the phone back without saying a word.

Before I can embarrass myself by thanking her, Carmen gets in her car, starts it up, and drives up the ramp. Dino follows her, giving me the side-eye as he passes. When they're gone, I take the elevator back up to street level and ride my bike home with a goofy smile on my face.

FIVE

I lean my bike against the avocado tree. After I wash my face and brush my teeth, I sneak into the trailer as quietly as I can. Rafa will be up in a couple hours to work in the garden. His door is shut tight and I can hear him snoring softly in his bed.

I spread out two San Marcos blankets on the floor and crawl between them. I put one of the sofa cushions under my head, plug in my phone, and set an alarm for noon. Then I lie there shivering, turning the phone in my hand again and again.

I moved out of Sal's apartment last month. It's for the best. He's a neat freak, first of all. I'm not a pig, and I love my brother, but I couldn't deal with seeing him stress out about towels hanging crooked on the bar or cereal bowls in the sink. Also, he nags me, just like when we were kids. Most of all, he wants me to stop obsessing over our father. After I lost my last job, Sal and I had a big argument. That's when I left for good.

It's so dark in this trailer. Only the weakest moonlight makes it through the blinds.

I want to sleep, but nervous energy hums in my muscles. I put the phone down. I shut my eyes tight and try to stay as still as possible. Maybe sheer boredom will put me to sleep. But ten, twenty minutes pass and I'm still as awake as I was when I lay down.

My mind wanders to the only place it wants to go these days.

Silky, smooth, and cold.

That's how Carmen's hair felt in my fist.

I want to see her hair loose again, straight and heavy as a waterfall. I imagine the way she looked sitting in the chair, her face tipped toward me. Her lips were parted. Her dark eyes were even darker, dilated, like a junkie's. I could look straight down her throat and see her cleavage. I wanted to drop down into the shadow between those beautiful breasts.

Carmen's bra was purple tonight. I close my eyes and imagine it. Light purple.

Suddenly the living room goes from freezing to sweltering hot. With an annoyed grunt, I take off my T-shirt and roll onto my back. I throw off the blanket, and the air seems to lick my skin, teasing me.

I'm annoyed until I remember.

It's been one week since I jacked off.

Right. Okay.

I glance at Rafa's door to make sure it's still closed. It is, and his light is still off.

With a sigh, I lean back and close my eyes again.

Fuck.

Fine.

Let's do this.

I slide the waistband of my sweatpants down over my thighs. I'm hard as hell, on edge since I was alone in the office with Carmen. I take my shaft in my hand. Just that contact alone is enough to make my dick stand straight up. My balls are cold, already pulled up tight. I rub them with my other hand and take a deep breath.

I tighten my grip on my dick. My first strokes are slow, lazy, and light on the downstroke. I curve my fingers around the hot skin and pull, a little tighter each time.

I throw my forearm over my eyes and breathe deep. The only other sound I can hear is the sound of skin sliding on skin.

Now I'm back in that office, my hands on her warm, silky neck.

Chef Centeno is in control from the moment she wakes up to the moment she closes her eyes at night. But here, and now, Carmen is going to hand that control to me.

"Stand up and take off your jacket," I say.

Eyes on me, she stands up, slides the heavy cotton jacket off her shoulders and drops it on the chair.

I stare, taking in her smooth brown skin. "Take off your shoes and pants."

She does it. I watch her wiggle out of her shapeless work uniform, revealing her pretty hips and long, smooth thighs. Breathing hard, she waits for my next instructions, standing barefoot on the tile floor in her tank top and panties.

"Now take off everything else," I say with a smile.

I watch as she slowly peels off her shirt. She takes off her bra, and her skin breaks out in goosebumps. Her nipples are dark. She slides her panties down and steps out of them. I see that neat triangle of dark hair. Beneath it, shadowed between her thighs, the soft sweetness of her pussy. My eyes drink in every detail.

She's hugging herself lightly. She looks vulnerable. I'll comfort her, but not yet. Right now, I want to watch her drop all of her defenses—her poker face and the other, harder mask behind it.

"Carmen," I say. "How do you feel?"

"Nervous," she says.

"Why?"

"I've never felt this way about anyone."

"*Felt how?*"

She blinks. "*I don't know. Like I have no control.*"

I'm quiet for a long time. I let her stand there, naked and vulnerable. Her nipples harden, begging for my lips. "*Tell me the truth, baby girl,*" *I say at last.* "*Why did you let me make love to you that morning?*"

My mind races to form the words that will come out of her beautiful mouth. I grip my dick harder. Precome forms at the tip.

"*Because I wanted you,*" *she says.* "*I saw you in the garden, and I knew I had to be with you.*"

"*Why?*"

"*I knew you would take care of me.*" *She bites her lip.* "*I wanted to give it to you.*"

"*Give me what?*" *I ask.*

"*My body,*" *she whispers.*

My voice comes out as a growl. "*What parts? Show me.*"

She smiles shyly at me.

"*Show me,*" *I say again.* "*Tell me every part you want to give me.*"

She points to her bottom lip and strums the soft flesh with her fingertip. "*This,*" *she whispers.*

"*What's that?*"

"*My mouth.*" *She slides her hands down to her breasts and cups them in her slender hands. She scissors her fingers, lightly pinching her nipples between them like chopsticks.* "*These,*" *she says.*

"*What are those?*"

"*My tits.*"

I watch as she slides her hands down her stomach. With the tips of her middle fingers, she rubs the soft flesh on either side of her clit. "*This.*"

"*What's that?*" *I ask.*

"My pussy," she whispers.

My mouth waters. I speed up my strokes. *"Show me."*

She steps back and sits on the edge of the desk. She opens her legs and I watch, mesmerized, as she runs her fingertips along the sides of her pussy, but not over it. The tender skin gives in to her fingers. She's lean and tight everywhere else, but here, between her legs, she's soft and pillowy.

My dick grows harder and thicker in my hand. I'm struggling to breathe.

"I said, show me," I say.

Eyes on me, she puts those fingertips on either side of her pussy and spreads it open. The dark brown lips part, revealing a tiny, glistening opening, pink as a rosebud. Her clit is stiff. She drips down on the desk—just a tiny thread of clear liquid, but enough to make my balls twitch.

I step forward. I don't break eye contact with her, and her face softens as she submits to me, mesmerized by what I'm telling her to do.

"Good girl," I whisper. "Now open your mouth."

When she does, I slide my index and middle fingers between her lips. She sucks on them. I feel the rigid roof of her mouth and the soft, textured muscle of her tongue. She closes her eyes and sucks on my fingers like I dream she would suck on my cock, like I'm ice cream, like I'm candy, like I'm water and she's been wandering in the desert her entire life.

When my fingers are dripping, I pull them from her mouth, reach down, and slide them gently but firmly into her sweet, tiny cunt.

She grips me and groans.

"You like that?" I whisper. Slowly, I slide my fingers back and forth, dragging out the sensation.

"Yes."

She is wet and feverish. As I feel her stretching around me, I stroke her aching clit with the tip of my thumb, tiny circles. She is still holding herself open for me—good girl. Carmen follows directions as good as Chef Centeno gives them.

"Why do you want me to have this?" I ask her.

"Because you'll take care of it." Her eyes are watering with pleasure. "You'll take care of me."

"Damn straight I will."

"That feels so good."

"Does it, baby girl?"

"It feels perfect."

I curve my fingers and tap her G-spot. She grips me even harder. "So, am I taking care of you?"

"You're going to make me come."

My fist strains around my cock.

She whispers, "Oh God."

I reach down and grip my balls. My right hand works my shaft furiously. I open my eyes.

Instead of Carmen, I see darkness shot through with faint moonlight. I smell dirt and fresh herbs. A cold draft of air dances across my slick chest. My lungs are burning. I'm on the edge.

I hear her whisper in my ear. "Let's come together, Eddie."

My whole body flexes hard, bracing for the impact of my orgasm. When it hits, sensation floods my brain. Hot come shoots out of me, landing all over my abs, my chest, even my neck. It's a big one. All I can do is lie on the floor, paralyzed, every muscle contracting with pleasure.

In a daze, I wonder if Carmen ever thinks of me this way, if she ever touches herself and comes with my name on her lips.

When my orgasm subsides at last, I'm visited by that familiar mixture of relief and shame I always feel after I jack off.

The only sexual contact I have in my life right now is with my right hand. Five years behind bars, you know, you and your hand, you get close. You look out for each other. You develop mutual respect.

Even my right hand knows this is not healthy.

"Obsessed," I whisper to myself. "You're obsessed with her, you fucking creeper."

I find my T-shirt and clean myself up. I throw the shirt in a trash bag that holds the rest of my dirty clothes. I pull up my pants and readjust the blankets. Eventually, I fall asleep to the sound of my own breathing, alone. Like always.

———————

SAL and I work out at the YMCA near the park. He sometimes lifts at the health center at his fancy college, but because he feels sorry for me, he's agreed to meet me here three times a week. The weight room is a little run-down, but iron is iron. A hundred pounds is a hundred pounds whether you're in a fancy gym or a shitty one. All you have to do is lift it.

My brother has taught me to keep a notebook of my workouts. Like dorks, we both walk around the gym with pens behind our ears. I write out my weights, reps, and sets before putting my notebook down and taking my place to spot Sal at the bench.

Under the fluorescent lights, I see the dark shadows under his eyes. He's exhausted. Work and school and girlfriend and family have not left him a lot of time to recover. Add to that his growing business with Eastside Beer, and I know he's got a fair amount of stress.

"What's bothering you?" I ask when we set down the bar.

"Nothing's really bothering me. Just something I've been trying to figure out," he says. "We make these deliveries, right? All of them are downtown. Every day Vanessa's getting emails and phone calls from bars out in Hollywood, in Silver Lake, even the San Fernando Valley. They want Eastside Beer, but we can't get it to them."

"Why not?"

"We're making the beer all the way in Santa Monica. I can't afford to pay for delivery. With work and school, Vanessa and I can't drive it out there ourselves. On the other hand, I don't want to lose any of that business. People are starting to want our product."

"You sound surprised. You brew good beer, homes."

"I'm surprised by the growth," he says. "We haven't done any marketing at all."

An old *veterano* asks if we're finished with the bench. I tell him yes and wipe it off for him. He gives me a fist bump.

"You the Rosas brothers?" he asks.

"Trouble," I say. "That's Sal."

He gives us a little gangster nod. "I knew your dad, back in the day. My condolences."

And just like that, the ghost of Dreamer Rosas appears again.

"Thank you," Sal says.

We walk to the other side of the gym, leaving the old man behind. We get some kettlebell swings and lunges in. I don't want to talk about Dreamer and neither does Sal.

"What are you going to do about the beer?" I ask instead.

He shrugs. "I don't know. I'm in this program for the next twenty-two months. That's a long time. Until then, I can keep making the beer at Bay City Brews. But you know what would be cool?"

"What?"

"If I could somehow find the capital to open a taproom. Have people come to us instead of the other way around."

"A taproom? Like a bar?"

"Sort of. We'd sell our beer, no one else's. Maybe food. Beer and wine licenses are not cheap—that would be a big chunk of change, and there's no guarantee the city would grant us a new one in this 'hood. I'm not sure how it all works yet. But that would be tight, don't you think? An Eastside spot for Eastside beer?"

My brain cranks to life. I used to live for the hustle. "How much would something like that cost to start up?"

Sal snorts. "Why, you have a couple hundred thousand hanging around?"

"Hey," I say. "I'm poor but I'm sexy. No one can put a price on that."

A couple of neighborhood *chismosas* walk by, two grand-mothers on their way to water aerobics. To prove my point I give them a little smile and a wink. "Ladies, *buenas tardes.*"

"Looking good, *mi'jo,*" says the one in the flowery bathing cap. She returns my wink. "*Que chulada de hombre.*"

"So when is Trouble coming my way?" asks the other one.

Both of them bust up laughing.

SIX

At the top of my shift three days later, I lock my bike up and walk into the kitchen. The staff is standing around a workbench looking at a newspaper. Boner waves me over before I take off my hoodie.

"Eddie, come take a look at this."

A food critic has reviewed Giacomo's. He's written about Carmen's cooking as being both "refreshing and technically masterful at the same time." I reread the last line to myself. "Chef Centeno has been sous chef at Giacomo's for nearly a year and a half and a driving force behind the kitchen since her arrival three years ago. With cooking this playfully original, Centeno seems destined to step out of the shadow of a good chef to become a great one."

As I get ready for work, I think about the sign in front of the restaurant, lit up with floodlights. I think about the heavy cookbooks on the shelf by the hostess stand and the framed articles on the walls.

Chef Moretti has left his kitchen in Carmen's hands but has never given her public credit for it. When he returns—if he returns—I don't think this article will make him happy. It definitely doesn't make him look good.

Carmen arrives in the kitchen for the nightly meeting and brushes off any praise the cooks and servers try to give her for the article. As usual, she runs through the specials like today is any other day.

In the quiet period before service starts, I help Rigoberto by loading some produce into the walk-in. I open the heavy door and close it behind me. I rotate and stack the boxes neatly, making sure to mark each one so the cooks use the ingredients in the order they were received.

The fan inside the large walk-in is extra loud so I almost don't hear the door open and close behind me. I feel a breeze and turn around, expecting Rigoberto to give me more directions.

Instead, Carmen is standing there in her white chef's jacket. She looks as surprised to see me as I am to see her.

"Hey." I cap my marker and tuck it behind my ear. "Congratulations on the review. That was really cool."

She gives me a half smile. "Got lucky, that's all."

"'Got lucky'?" I say. "That food critic worships you. Even I know a review like that is a big deal."

She shrugs. "I suppose. We try to cook at that level every day, whether a food critic is in the house or not."

"Or whether Chef Moretti is in the house?" I ask. "I've been here two weeks and I still haven't seen him."

"He doesn't have to be here." She paws through a carton of Tuscan kale. The leaves are almost black.

"He doesn't?"

"No. His name's on the restaurant. He helped train me. He conceived of this place and found investors to help him build it. The recipes are his."

"But you run the kitchen that cooks them."

"That doesn't matter," she says. "His name brings people through the door night after night. Do you know how many restaurants start up in this city and fail? That open and close within just a few months? Giacomo Moretti might not be in the kitchen every day, but it's his brand that keeps us in business every night."

"But why doesn't he give you credit for the work you do? You take care of everything while he's away. I asked Rigoberto. Chef Moretti is in the restaurant maybe five days out of every thirty. He cooks at Giacomo's, what? Two or three times a year?"

She's annoyed. Her voice sharpens. "What do you want me to say? That it's fair? No, it isn't fair, but that's how professional kitchens work. Giacomo paid his dues. Right now I'm paying mine."

"Don't you want your own restaurant?"

With a sigh, she says, "Of course I want to run a kitchen of my own."

Now we're getting somewhere. "What would you make?"

She ignores my question. "One day, when the time is right, I'll move on. Until then, here I am. It's a good job. They pay me decent money to be here. So I show up."

"Every day?"

"Every day."

"But when will you know the time is right to move on?"

She shrugs. "I'll know."

"Why not now?"

"Stop," she snaps. "Just stop."

I've pushed her buttons. Time to back off a little. I stack up two more boxes as she continues to search through the cartons. "What are you looking for anyway?" I ask.

She bends down to reach the boxes on the bottom shelf. "Celeriac."

"What the hell is that?"

"It looks like celery with an ugly brown knob attached to it."

"You people eat the weirdest shit." I get down on my knees to search the same shelf where she is. We push and pull more boxes but still, no celeriac.

I'm closer to her now, and the fan masks what anyone might hear me say next.

I take a deep breath and shoot my shot. "Go out with me," I say.

She says nothing.

"Go out with me," I say again. "On a date." As if I had to add that.

"I don't sleep with coworkers. That's a hard rule."

I feel so awkward right now, my skin hurts. "I didn't ask you to sleep with me," I say. "I asked you to go out with me."

Her eyebrows shoot up. "Why would you ask me to go out with you if not to sleep with me? Isn't that why people go out with each other?"

"I don't know," I say. "Maybe people go out with each other because they enjoy each other's company. Because the other person is pleasant. Because the other person is a good listener, which you obviously are not."

She smiles a little bit to herself. I like the looks of that.

"Can I ask you a question?" she says.

"I told you, you can ask me anything."

"Why me?" She looks at me sideways. "You're Trouble Rosas. Everyone knows you don't have problems finding women."

My old reputation as a player is hard to shake. Most of the time it's useful. But how do I tell her that in six months there's been no one, not a single woman, since her?

I chicken out and tell a joke instead. "I'm tired of nice, normal ones. Thought I'd try you for a little while."

She makes a face at me and draws her hand back to slap my shoulder. I catch it and she laughs. I pull her close and the laugh disappears.

We're facing each other, kneeling on the floor of a giant refrigerator while thirty of our coworkers are rushing around outside.

My heart is punching its way out of my chest.

"Carmen," I whisper. I touch her face.

"Eddie—"

"You know I want you." My body temperature rises a thousand degrees. I stroke her cheek and run my fingertips down the side of her throat where her pulse is going haywire. "I want to kiss you, Carmen. I want it so much I think I'm going to die."

Her eyes are wide. "We can't do this here."

I'm caught in her spell. There is no *here* or *there* to me in this moment. Only her.

"I want to kiss you," I say again.

"That's a..." She swallows hard. "That's a bad idea."

"Some bad ideas are good." I can see her control slipping. I run my thumb over her bottom lip as lightly as a whisper. "I want you. You, Carmen."

That's when she jumps on me.

The pen behind my ear rolls under a shelf. Before I know it, I'm flat on my back and she's kissing me so hard I can't get a breath. Her mouth is hot and sweet. It's terrifying, seeing Chef Centeno lose control so completely like this.

But also—it's hot as fuck.

Carmen slides her cold hands under my T-shirt. When her fingers find the ridges of my abs, she moans and kisses me harder. Her wicked tongue goes deep, and somewhere in the haze, my brain wonders why she swings so hard between control and wildness.

There is no middle ground with her.

We are tucked between two shelves of cardboard boxes filled with produce. She's straddling me, unbuttoning her jacket with furious movements, like the jacket is choking her at the collar and she can't wait to get it off. When it's open, she gives a grunt of satisfaction, leans down and runs her hands up and down my chest.

Still, she won't look me in the eye.

She's breathing hard. I put my hands on her shoulders and push her gently away.

"Carmen," I say, warning her. "You know I want you. Do you really want me? Here? Like this?"

"Motherfucker," she whispers. "I want you *all* the time. Ever since you stepped into this kitchen."

"Could've fooled me," I say, because she did.

She leans down and smashes her lips against mine. I shut my eyes and slip back down into the sweet darkness with her at last. I wrap my arms around her and crush her against me. She arches her back and presses her hips down, aligning my hard dick with the heat between her legs.

I groan against her lips and pull away just enough to whisper, "Who are you?"

Underneath her jacket she's wearing a worn-out V-neck T-shirt. She's not wearing a bra. She leans back and, staring at my lips, lifts up her T-shirt, showing me her breasts.

Goddamn.

She's so beautiful.

I reach forward and cup her in my hands. So perfect.

She covers me with kisses—my face, my neck, my mouth. She grips my arms and squeezes me with her thighs. When she grinds against me, I hold still. I'm hard as hell. My dick strains in my pants, aching for her.

Eyes wild, she reaches down, unbuckles my belt and unzips my fly.

I lean back. My head thumps against the cold corrugated metal that lines the floor of the walk-in. "Carmen," I gasp. "Jesus."

She rubs my dick. "I remember this."

"Good," I say with a nervous laugh. "'Cuz it remembers you."

Carefully, she reaches into my boxers and pulls out my hard-on. I hiss as the cold air hits my skin, but that sensation quickly disappears when Carmen leans down and slides me into her hot, slippery mouth.

"I—you—ah." It's hard to form words when your fantasy woman seals her lips around your shaft and begins to milk your dick with the back of her throat. "I'm going to...just guess that you've been—ah, yes—thinking about that morning?"

She is too preoccupied right now to answer.

I thread my fingers through her hair and guide her head with my hands, slowing her rhythm. She draws a swirling, spiraling pattern with the tip of her tongue along the underside of my shaft. My body jerks forward. My ass flexes, lifting my thighs off the cold metal floor.

She slips off my dick and works my shaft with her hand. "Does that feel good?" she whispers.

"This is...irresponsible," I say.

"*You're* lecturing me on irresponsibility?"

"You have a point." I take my dick out of her hand and put it back in her mouth. Smiling around me, she takes hold of my hips and slides deep.

All of a sudden, we're back in the hot bedroom of Rafa's trailer, tearing into each other like vultures at the end of the world. Again, I wonder what kind of demons drove her to me that first time. What kind of demons are driving her to me today?

I've been a knucklehead most of my life. Locked up in juvenile hall, in jail, in prison. I know how to slide into my head when I need to, if I need an escape. But there's nothing in my imagination as good as being here with her, right now, losing ourselves like this.

Her hair is completely loose now. I brush the hair back from her forehead and hold it in place away from her beautiful mouth. I am so close to coming, I'm shaking with the effort of holding back. I'm breathing like a maniac, almost hyperventilating. The cold dry air in the walk-in burns my lungs.

"Yes," I gasp.

I'm drunk on her—completely trashed.

She grips the base of my dick and goes as deep as her narrow throat can take me. It's too much. My abs flex and my ears ring and my sense of control crumbles to dust.

"I'm gonna come," I say. "Carmen, I'm gonna come."

She moans and goes quicker, the universal signal for *I'm okay with you coming in my mouth.*

Fuck.

I pump my hips in time to her fist and mouth. I grip her hair gently and close my eyes. Jesus Christ, this is going to be a big one. Bigger because I wasn't expecting it, and bigger because we could get caught at any time. The old thrill of being bad—it's a rush I feel whenever I'm with her.

"Just like that, baby girl." I shut my eyes tight. I imagine my finger slowly squeezing a trigger. "Holy sh—"

Air rushes through the room.

Someone has opened the door of the walk-in.

Carmen jumps back like a scared cat and lowers her shirt. I sit up and yank my shirt over my aching dick. We are crouched in the shadows of the cartons but there is no mistaking what we've been doing. I zip up as quickly as I can.

Anybody in the kitchen staff would laugh this off. Rigoberto might hate me for a while, but what could he do to me? Dino would be furious, but if Carmen had my back, I don't think he'd give me the boot. I can handle a reprimand—that's nothing new. To be honest, all of this would be kind of hilarious if my balls didn't hurt so much right now.

I'm almost giggling when I look up at Carmen's face. The laughter fades as soon as I notice her eyes are wide with shame. She's pale and pasty, as if she's going to be sick.

I turn around.

It takes me a second to recognize him. Gray hair. White chef's jacket. He looks like Dino, but leaner and meaner.

Standing in the doorway is Giacomo Moretti.

SEVEN

Boner runs out into the alley as I unchain my bike.

"Service is about to start," I tell him. "You better get your ass back in there."

"What is going on?" he says. "Chef Centeno is still in the office with the big boss. No one will tell me what's happening."

I'm not going to narc on Carmen. "I have no idea what he's telling her."

"But what did Dino tell you? He seemed upset when he came back inside."

"He gave me my paycheck and told me I was done here." I wave my hand as if losing this job is no big deal, even though it is. "We had a disagreement. I was careless. He's sending me home."

Boner looks panicked. "For good?"

Even though I'm not feeling confident about my ability to find more work, I say, "Shit, I was looking for a job when I found this one, right?"

"It's not right, Eddie," Boner says. He's wearing his plastic apron. The wind whips it back and forth. "This is messed up.

They can't just fire you for disagreeing with them—no write-up, no warning. It's not fair."

It's perfectly fair considering what I was just doing, but I don't mention that. Instead, I readjust my backpack. "How long has Chef Centeno been talking to Chef Moretti?" I ask. I hope she's okay. She looked really shaken up.

Boner nods. "More than thirty minutes. We don't know who's going to expedite tonight."

Carmen always stands at the front of the line, handing each dish off to the servers. Someone else will have to step up. Maybe even Chef Moretti will have to do some work in his own kitchen. Whatever the case, it's no longer my problem.

"You better get in there." I tip my head toward the door. "They need you."

Boner adjusts his ball cap and rubs his face. He looks disappointed and angry on my behalf. "Listen, Eddie. You take care of yourself."

"All right, homes. You too."

We bump fists and do a half-hug. I haven't known this dude long but something about the kitchen has helped us bond. Maybe that's what happens in kitchens—people bond a little closer than they should.

I let go and walk my bike out to the driveway. I wince a little —my balls ache like they've been kicked. Boner shuffles to the back door of the kitchen and disappears inside. When the door slams behind him, a feeling of frustration washes over me.

I didn't love this job, but I didn't hate it. I liked my coworkers, and I made friends. I know I should take ownership of all my dumb decisions, but a part of me wishes I could get a pass on this one. When it comes to Carmen, my brain doesn't work right.

I don't know what I'm going to do next for money. My

savings have all gone toward finding my dad. I kick Rafa a few dollars for the bills. What little I have left won't last long.

I'm about to take off when Carmen drives out of the underground parking lot in her Toyota.

I get off my bike and lean it against one of the Dumpsters. I walk up to her car and she lowers the window. She looks just as sickly as she did when we were caught, but now she also seems lost and tired. Her eyes have a faraway look.

"Are you all right?" I ask.

For a second I'm afraid she'll be angry. Instead, she's sad. Her shoulders hang loose like all the fight has been drained out of her. "I'm all right," she says softly.

"But what happened with Giacomo?" I ask. "Boner said you were in the office for a long time."

A loud beeping noise interrupts us. A trash truck enters the opposite side of the alley. It's slowly heading our way.

"We should get out of here," I say. "Are you driving home?"

She shakes her head. "I can't go home just yet. I can't face my parents like this."

"Then where?"

"I don't know." She sighs. "I was just going to drive around for a while. Clear my head."

I look her over. Hollow eyes, a slouch. She looks emotionally wasted. I don't want her to be alone right now.

"Can I go with you?" I ask.

Instead of answering, she stares at me. I blow out a breath. If she leaves now, I don't know when I'll see her again. Maybe never. I'm not ready to face that reality yet.

That's when she unlocks the passenger door.

"Get in," she says.

IN SILENCE, we drive through downtown, through China-town, and up into the hills. We pass the fire academy, the police academy, and end up on a flat hill in Elysian Park overlooking the city.

The lot is deserted. Carmen parks the car. I open the windows and let the cold breeze blow on my face. For a moment, I put my problems on pause, take a breath, and take it all in—downtown's skyscrapers. The different neighborhoods that make up my city. The mountains to the east. The airport and the ocean to the west.

Locked up, I missed this feeling—the wind on my skin, the whole world in my eyeballs. For five years, all I saw were the walls of my cell, the walls of the yard, the same faces, day in and day out. Playing cards. Watching TV. Listening to the phone ring, knowing the calls were never for me.

And now here I am. Above the city—no, a part of the city, parked in a car with a very pretty but very sad girl.

Man.

This is all kinds of messed up.

"I lost my job, Eddie," Carmen says at last. "Chef Moretti fired me."

Her news punches me in the gut. "But the kitchen—it doesn't run without you."

"It only seems that way." She sighs. She taps the pink glass rosary hanging from her rearview mirror and it swings back and forth. "To be honest, it's a good team. It existed just fine before me and it'll exist just fine without me."

"Does the staff know?" I'm surprised they didn't threaten to burn the restaurant to the ground unless she's rehired.

"No," she says. "Giacomo told them I'm taking some personal time off. He'll probably tell them tomorrow I'm not coming back." Her face crumples at last. A tear slips from the corner of her eye, races down her jaw, and drips off the point of her chin. She's not wearing her chef's jacket. She's wearing black pants, clogs, and her white T-shirt. Her hair is in a loose ponytail, still messy from my fingers. Without the jacket and bun, she no longer looks like the imposing Chef Centeno. She looks like Carmen, only lost and heartbroken.

"Oh, man," she says. "I fucked up."

I reach over the center console and awkwardly take her in my arms. To my surprise, for the second time, she holds on to me and sobs against my shirt. The sound is tiny, almost inaudible, and I grip her tighter. I don't know what to say.

She pulls back and sniffles. There are teardrops in her long, dark eyelashes. "I've always been a good worker," she says. "That's something my family taught me in the bakery—work is life. Always put all of your heart into your work, and never do anything half-assed. I've never lost a job before."

"Lucky for you, I've lost lots of jobs." I wipe away one of her tears with my thumb. "I can give you tips on how to cope."

She doesn't smile. "I don't know what I was thinking. I wasn't thinking."

As I stroke her hair, I think about how some people seem to keep their heads on all the time. I've never been one of those people. Every now and then my emotions take control, and I let them. Lots of problems in my life come from this one thing.

"This is my fault," I say. "I ruined everything for you."

"No, Eddie. This is one hundred percent my fault." She looks out at the city. "My choices. My actions. I was your superior, and what I did was so, so wrong." She groans. "I was the perfect employee. I did everything right. Until today. I've never lost control like that. Ever."

I can't stand to see her hurting. "To be fair, I am extremely sexy. I mean, I don't blame you."

Carmen shakes her head and smiles sadly.

I want her to laugh a little, but I also know how much this

job meant to her. Maybe one day she will find this situation funny. But not today.

"What did you do before you started working at Giacomo's?" I ask.

"I went to cooking school," she says. "Three years. Napa Valley."

"That sounds fancy."

"Oh, it was fancy, all right." She sighs. "I have the fancy student debt to prove it."

"And before that?"

"Panadería La Golondrina. Of course."

Her family's bakery. La Golondrina—it means "swallow," the bird. I remember the old glass cases filled with pastries. I remember the smell of baking bread filling the neighborhood, making my empty stomach growl. "Can't you go back?" I ask.

"No. I can't." When she looks at me, her eyes are so sad I feel her pain take a seat inside me.

"But why not?" I ask.

"It's closed. For good."

"What? Why?"

She's quiet for a moment before she says, "It's complicated." Before I can respond, she starts up the engine and says, "Come on. Let's go."

I don't like how she dodges my questions. I'm hungry to learn more about her, but she keeps shutting me down. "Do you want to hang out a little while longer?" I ask. "We could go to the garden."

She purses her lips. "I don't know if that would be a good idea."

The trailer—she's thinking about the first time she was alone with me. "Rafa's there now," I say to reassure her. I look at the time on my phone. "We could get something to eat."

That works. "Okay."

CARMEN DRIVES out of the park and merges onto Sunset Boulevard. She drives east and before long the street changes names. Now we're on Avenida César Chávez. The Eastside.

She parks just outside the gates of the garden in the shadow of the hospital. As we walk through, I greet some of the regular gardeners, old-timers from the neighborhood and lots of mothers, recently emigrated from Mexico or El Salvador, tending to their plots. It's still winter, so not much is growing, but they're preparing the soil for spring, always planning ahead. Always looking toward the future.

Rafa is done working for the day. I open the door of the trailer for Carmen and she climbs cautiously inside.

"Viejo," I call, *"¿dónde estás?* We have a visitor."

Rafa comes out of his bedroom. Smiling, he takes Carmen's hand and kisses it. He may be a leathery old hippie, but Rafa always surprises me with his moves.

"Lady Chef," he says. "I was hoping I'd see you again."

While Rafa and Carmen talk in the trailer's tiny kitchen, I get rid of my mess in the living room and clear off the coffee table. Rafa has decorated his place with dried herbs and flowers, candles, paintings, and statues of saints. There are also images of holy figures and symbols somewhat outside of the jurisdiction of the Catholic church, indigenous spirits and orishas that Rafa treats with equal respect. He's told me he comes from a long line of *curanderos*—native healers—so he follows the old ways of doing things.

I take three bottles of my brother's beer out of the refrigerator and open them. Rafa carries out three plates of steaming food and Carmen carries the tortillas wrapped up in a clean kitchen towel.

"Where?" she asks.

"Right here," says Rafa, putting the plates down on the coffee table.

Carmen takes a seat on the sofa. Just like he does everyone else, Rafa has calmed her down. She smiles at him as he reaches over to flip on a boom box that's older than I am. Classic soul music crackles out of the speakers—lowrider oldies, the soundtrack of my childhood. After Rafa says a long prayer, we dig in.

"I'm nervous. I've never cooked for a chef before," Rafa says.

Carmen takes a bite. "Is this *cochinita pibil?*" she asks. Slow-roasted pork.

"Yes," the old man answers.

"*Que rico,*" she says. "It's really good."

As we eat, Carmen and Rafa talk in Spanish about his story. He was born and raised in East LA. Back then, the gangs were not as dangerous as they are today. He spent his time riding bikes with his friends. "The most trouble we ever got into," he says, "was stealing oranges from our neighbor's tree."

He turned sixteen during the hippie psychedelic movement. He started experimenting with drugs, and out of frustration, his parents sent him to live with relatives on a ranch in Mexico.

"My grandfather was a *curandero,*" Rafa says. "He taught me indigenous farming methods. I studied horticulture in the university. When I was finished, I got a job here as the caretaker of this community garden. That was more than twenty years ago."

Carmen looks back and forth between us. Rafa and I couldn't look more different. "How did you meet?" she asks.

"Rafa hooked me up back in the day," I say. "We've been friends ever since."

Carmen is smart. It doesn't take her long to put two and two—or four and twenty—together. She turns to Rafa. "You grow weed here? In the community garden?"

Rafa laughs. "Not anymore, Lady Chef. A friend and I have

a hydroponics setup in Hacienda Heights. Totally legal. Times have changed."

I watch Carmen's face as she studies Rafa. "There's a lot more to you than meets the eye, isn't there?" she says.

He looks between us. "That's true of all of us, isn't it?" He flashes her a white smile that matches his hair. "Would you like seconds?"

EIGHT

When the meal is done, Rafa retreats to his bedroom while Carmen and I clean up. She kills her beer. "This is good." There's no label on the bottle. "What is this?"

"My brother made it," I say.

Carmen's eyes light up. "No shit."

"He's studying to become a brewer. That one is called Forever Mine. It's an amber ale." I go into the spiel I heard Sal give a dozen times yesterday morning to the different bartenders. "His company is called Eastside Beer."

She puts the empty bottles on the counter. "Tell him it's amazing."

We take a walk together in the garden just as the sun goes down. She's cold, so I give her my hoodie. Something grows warm in my chest when I see her zip it up. It's so loose on her narrow shoulders.

"Do you live here?" she asks. "With Rafa?"

"Sort of," I say. "I'm kinda...couch surfing at the moment." This sounds a lot cooler than admitting I'm technically home- less. "I lived with my brother for a while." I remember the arguing and nagging, the hundreds of annoyances. "This setup works a little better," I say.

She hesitates on the next question. "So are you still...active? With East Side Hollenbeck?"

"Sal found a way to leave the gang. Since then, they've kept their distance from our family." This is not a lie, but I don't answer her question. In my heart, I've left the gang. But in reality, they still own me.

Carmen digs her hands into the pockets of my hoodie. "What did you go to prison for?"

Not everyone is brave enough to ask this question.

"Grand theft auto and carjacking," I say. "My brother and I got caught stealing a car together. The owner came after us and shot me. My brother beat him up trying to get the gun away. On account of our records and our gang affiliation, we got five years. I served my sentence. I'll be on parole for three more years."

She's quiet for a minute, absorbing this information. Regret washes over me. Everything went to hell the night Sal and I got arrested. If I hadn't been careless, I wouldn't have been shot. My brother and I wouldn't have gotten locked up. My father wouldn't have started shooting up again or gotten into trouble with the shot-callers—and I wouldn't be on this stupid, fucking impossible mission to find him. A heroin needle in a haystack.

Carmen says something.

"Huh?" I ask, distracted by my own baggage.

"I said, 'Where did you get shot?'"

"You didn't see my scars?"

She shakes her head.

I look around. Everyone has packed up their tools and left the garden. There's just enough sunlight left to see.

I lift my shirt over my head and sling it over my shoulder. I show her the scars on my upper torso and along the underside of my arm. Shotgun scars are fucking hideous. They make you look like a monster. So I got tattoos—heavy ones, big ones—to disguise them. A huge *placa* across my chest—Trouble, my gang name. Our Lady of Guadalupe on my arm. I got tattoos to honor home-boys who passed away. Spiderwebs and skulls, flames, fire, and smoke. Last but not least, I have a big rose tattoo. My brother and I got those when we were younger—for Rosas, our last name.

Carmen's eyes wander over my bare skin. She lifts her hand and with the tip of her finger, traces—just barely—the rough skin of my scars, hidden by ink.

"Damn," she says under her breath. "That must have hurt."

"The ink? Kinda. Not really."

"No, the gunshot wounds."

"I was in the hospital for three weeks."

Gently, she runs her fingers up and down my chest. The gesture is half curious, half sexual. As she touches me, I can feel her trying to read the story written on my skin.

When I was a kid, I always looked up to the older home-boys. They looked so badass, so powerful. Their ink and scars and muscles marked their identity as gangsters.

But now I know the deeper meaning. The truth is, I didn't grow up in a safe environment. Many things could've killed me. So I put on muscle. I got scars. I covered them with ink. I grew my own armor, and now I wear it whether I want to or not.

"Trouble," she says quietly. "Your nickname—it suits you."

"I never really liked it."

"Why not?"

That question is too complicated to answer right now, so I shrug. I look around, trying to change the subject. We're standing in the broccoli and the cabbage.

"Hey, I know your secret," I whisper to her.

"What?"

"Vegetables."

"What do you mean?"

"Vegetables turn you on. That first time here, in the garden. In the walk-in. And now. You have a vegetable fetish. Just admit it. Ain't no shame in it. I won't tell anyone."

"You're so stupid."

"Broccoli...celery. Eggplant." I wiggle my eyebrows at her.

She shakes her head at me even as she lets me take her in my arms. "Jackass."

"Kiss me."

Hesitating, she leans forward and studies my face up close.

What does she see?

Tatted-up gangster hoodlum?

Trouble the player?

Or does she see Eddie—whoever that is?

I kiss those sweet lips, and her eyes close slowly. We kiss until the sun completely disappears and we're standing in the middle of the garden in the dark. It's still too cold for crickets, so the only sound is the traffic on the street on the other side of the hospital.

You'd think it would be too cold for me to be out here without a shirt on, but in Carmen's arms, I feel her dark fire. I think to myself that I'll never experience cold again, as long as she's near me.

For all the kinky shit we did together, just standing here kissing like a rated-G movie might be the most intimate thing we've shared.

We walk hand in hand back to the trailer, and I feel accomplished. I've made her feel better. I've cheered her up. And I got a kiss—not bad. I'm feeling pretty proud of myself.

"Listen," I say. "Call me. Any time you feel like talking. Any time you want moral support. If you want company. If you want to...you know, hang."

I hear her laugh in the dark. "Hang?"

"Yeah."

"You're so cheesy."

"Guilty as charged. Come here."

In the shadow of Rafa's trailer, I kiss her again. I bend her back a little bit and she squeaks, caught off balance. She melts against me, and her sigh makes me feel all warm and tingly inside.

On the real, though.

If I were slightly less of a gentleman, I could take her out back behind the trailer or bend her over the hood of her car or find a tree stump to hump her against.

I'm thinking about all of these things, to be honest.

But there's an emotional rawness to Carmen right now. She's had the shittiest of shitty days. The least I can do is rein in my own horndog urges until she's in a better place.

I don't think that makes me a hero—my dick definitely doesn't think I'm a hero right now.

I open the car door for her. She gets inside and I close it gently.

She rolls down the window. "Eddie."

"What's up, Lady Chef?"

Her smile could light up a million dark nights. "Thanks," she says.

"You're welcome."

I watch her as she drives away.

THE NEXT MORNING, I take the bus to Giacomo's nice and early so I won't run into any of the staff. I had high hopes my bike would still be by the Dumpster in the alley where I left it. As usual, my luck and my hopes don't match up. Someone's stolen it. More likely, it's been taken away by garbage collectors who mistook it for trash.

I'm angry at myself for being careless. I always lock it up, but I guess I got distracted when I saw Carmen upset. This is bad timing—I can't afford a new bike right now.

Time to beat feet. I tighten the straps on my backpack and start walking.

When I arrive at my parole officer's office for my regular check-in, my face feels frozen. After all the usual BS, I tell him about losing my job at Giacomo's. As usual, he shakes his head at me.

"So you're going back to the agency, right? Today?" He speaks to me like an impatient mother might talk to a three-year-old.

"Yeah, I'll go."

True to my word, I walk the four miles to the employment agency. On my way there, I pull down the sleeves of my hoodie and try to stay inconspicuous. This is another gang's territory. We're not currently beefing with them, but you never know who didn't get the memo.

Rain starts pissing down just as I enter the office. My case manager's a young woman with glasses. *Chichona*, cute as hell. I look at the big jar of candy and the photos of her dogs on her desk. I've been working with her for the past six months. I sweet-talk her because I want to stay on her good side, but also because she has no idea how sexy she is—none. Which in itself is a type of sexiness.

"Hey, Sugar," I say as I sit down. Sugar's not her name but she seems to like it.

"I was hoping not to see you again so quickly." She's annoyed. "What happened at Giacomo's?"

"You won't believe this," I say. "Downsizing."

She looks at me over her glasses. She really is cute. "Down-sizing?" Her voice is flat.

"Yeah." I open the jar of candy and take out a handful of jellybeans. "They decided to downsize their dishwashing staff by one. Last night. Right in the middle of my shift. I can't explain it. It seemed really unfair." I put the jellybeans in my mouth, chew, and swallow as Sugar mad-dogs me. "So how are Meatball and Funfetti doing?" I ask. "Is that new shampoo working for Meatball, or is he still itchy all the time?"

"Eddie." The tone of her voice tells me that she is done with my *pendejadas*. I knew this would happen sooner or later. "I warned you the last time that if you lost this job, I wouldn't be able to find you a replacement right away."

"Sugar." I lean forward. "It wasn't my fault this time. I swear."

"Right." She pushes her glasses up with her pen. "I don't have anything for you at the moment. Check the computer in the waiting room. If you don't find anything there, come back in one or two weeks. I might have better news for you then."

"One or two weeks?" I say. "You've got to have something in your back pocket for me. You always do."

"You've burned through three jobs in the past six months. I can't help you if you don't help yourself."

I want to tell her that I honestly did my best at this job. I learned everything Rigoberto taught me, and I showed up on time every day. I worked hard and got along with people. "You know I've got my GED, right?" My voice is a little desperate. "I told you that, right?"

"Yes. First time you came to see me." She sighs. "At this program, we have a limited number of job openings sent to us by employers. You're only one of many, many clients I have to find placement for. And I just don't have anything for you right now."

"Did you get new glasses? They look really nice on you."

"I'm not kidding, Eddie. You need to start taking this seriously. It's time for you to commit to something. This is not a game."

I sit in the waiting room of the employment agency and scroll through the beat-up computer for positions I'm unqualified for. Some of the listings are old, almost six months. Others are for positions outside the boundaries of my parole—I can't leave the county without permission. The only ones that pay a decent wage are union jobs—electricians, linemen, ironworkers. I don't have any of that training.

Now the rain is pouring down hard outside. I'm counting out change for bus fare back to Rafa's when my phone rings in my pocket.

Carmen.

I'm so relieved to see her name on the screen I'm speechless for a second.

"Hello?" she says shyly.

"Yeah, I'm here, I'm here."

"Are you busy?"

I log off the computer and shut it down. "No. What's up?"

"There's something I need to do," she says, "and I was wondering if...you could come with me."

After the morning I've had, she could tell me to literally punch myself in the head and I'd probably do it. "Sure. Where do you want me to go?"

"The bakery."

"You want me there right now?" I ask.

"I'll be there in an hour. Can I meet you?"

"Yeah. Sure. Okay."

When I hang up with Carmen, I suddenly don't feel so shitty.

My case manager takes pity on me and gives me an umbrella

from the lost-and-found box behind the front desk. It's a purple Dora the Explorer umbrella. I click it open over my pathetic head and start back over the bridge.

The Centenos's bakery is a few doors down from the house where I grew up. A new family has bought the house and fixed it up. As I walk past our old place, I don't look at it. I can't. It hurts too much to think about the times I spent there with my family. We were happy, once. The first twelve years of my life were good—pretty good, anyway.

I stop at the corner. This is it—Panadería La Golondrina. The memories come flooding back. Back when he had a good job, my dad would sometimes come home at the end of his shift with a plastic bag full of fresh, sweet bread.

But this isn't the place I remember either. The mural on the side of the building, *La Virgen de Guadalupe*, is faded and peeling. The windows are all boarded up. There's a handwritten sign on the door that says *Closed for Remodeling*.

I stand in the doorway of the bakery where I'm sheltered from the rain. I fold up my new Dora the Explorer umbrella and lean it against the wall where it can dry off. The arms of my hoodie are soaking wet but the hood is dry, so I put it on over my head and wait.

I'm starting to feel giddy about seeing Carmen again when I spot the car.

NINE

A gray Monte Carlo. Its tinted windows and nice rims can't distract from the dents or patches of primer.

Slowly, like a lazy shark, it pulls up to the curb in front of me. My feet are concrete blocks as I walk up to it.

The passenger-side window rolls down. I look inside.

The driver, Spider, is the shot-caller for our clique. Fresh from the barber shop with his shaved head and sharp goatee, he gives me a nod. He's dressed in a loose flannel and an oversized Ben Davis jacket. He's strapped, no doubt.

I'm about to say something when the back window rolls down.

Ruben—my father's best friend, our former shot-caller before he disappeared six months ago. No one knew where he went—that's why Spider took over. Spider and my brother have some kind of arrangement. Spider is the reason why Sal has been able to leave the gang, and the reason I've been allowed to lay low since I got out.

But with Ruben back, my standing in the gang is unclear. Who is the shot-caller now?

I look between Spider and Ruben and realize the truth.

Chauffeur and boss—it's Ruben.

Ruben is dressed in a Pendleton with sharp creases along the sleeves. The old cat wears a pair of Locs—dark sunglasses—even in the rain. He takes them off and stares at me, hard.

"Long time no see, Trouble." Ruben's deep voice sends a shudder through me. I'm afraid of him. He knows more about my father than he pretends. I know a man doesn't survive thirty years in ESHB without having a steel spine and a dead heart to match.

"*Oye,*" Spider says, and I catch a flash of regret in his eyes. He's been demoted—he can't protect me from Ruben, and we both know the score. "We have a special errand. Ruben thinks you're the right one for the job."

"Okay," I say, because that's what you have to say.

"Noon tomorrow." Spider continues. "At the place. Be there."

Before I can respond, the car windows roll up and Spider and Ruben drive away. I go over the message. The place—one of the gang's many crash pads, an abandoned house by the freeway that also serves as our arsenal. An errand—but what?

I've been doing my best to stay away from the gang. With all the heat ESHB has been drawing in the last year, it hasn't been hard to lay low. But now Ruben is back. He's issued the order, so I have to show up. I have to do what he says.

A sick feeling bubbles up in my stomach. Rain slides down my neck and I shiver, but this has nothing to do with the cold.

I'm still on the sidewalk when Carmen pulls up in her car. She parks and turns off the engine. When she steps out of the car, she goes straight to the covered entrance of the bakery.

"Why are you standing out in the rain?" she asks.

I blink and turn my attention on her.

She's wearing jeans, tennis shoes, and a dark sweatshirt. Her hair is in a long braid and she's wearing a Dodgers cap over it. I blink. This is the first time I've seen her in civilian clothes. The jeans show off her long, muscled thighs and pretty hips. I've seen this woman butt naked, but for some reason, seeing her in her own clothes turns me on and I'm hard by the time she says, "Eddie? Are you all right?"

The rain is still pouring down on me. I snap out of it and go to her. "Yeah, yeah. I'm fine."

She's putting keys in the door when I bend down and kiss her lips. A quick peck—but it warms me from my head to my toes. I feel better immediately, and I push my problems aside for now.

"Good morning, Lady Chef," I say quietly.

She smiles a little and turns the key in the lock. The glass door swings open. We walk inside and my eyes adjust to the darkness. With the windows boarded up, the only source of light is the open door.

We walk over the worn-out tile floor. The glass cases are all empty—no bread, no *conchas*, no *elotitos*. Tongs and trays are piled on the counter. In the large back room, the ovens are cold. The equipment is covered with sheets of clear plastic.

Carmen bends down to pick up the junk mail that has piled up on the floor by the door. "My dad told my mom not to come back here. When the cops finished their investigation, my dad was still in the hospital. That's when she and I snuck back and cleaned everything up."

"Hold up," I say. "What happened to your dad?"

"You don't know?"

"No."

"I guess I assumed everyone in the neighborhood knew what happened." She walks behind the counter and flips a few switches. The fluorescent lights flicker on. "He was beaten. Badly. In the parking lot."

I'm confused. This is East Side Hollenbeck territory.

Nothing happens here without us knowing about it. If something goes down without our permission, we break heads. People pay the price. "What the fuck? By whom?"

She sighs. "Las Palmas."

Las Palmas is another gang. Their territory starts just across the avenue. It's a longtime rivalry—even my grandfather beefed with Las Palmas. But the avenue has been our border for generations. We don't cross it, and neither do they. At least, that's my understanding—the reality might be different.

"They'd been harassing him for months," she continues. "Trying to collect taxes. They threatened him. He told them again and again he was under East Side Hollenbeck's protection. He told every homeboy in ESHB who would listen. He even called the cops. But nothing changed. Last October, a couple of guys from Las Palmas cornered him and beat the shit out of him in the parking lot after closing time. One of his employees scared them off with my dad's handgun. If he hadn't..." She trails off. "The employee who witnessed the crime was afraid to be interviewed—he left town without telling anyone. He was undocumented and didn't want the police to hand him over to ICE. The detectives in charge of the case took their sweet time following up. The investigation went nowhere. So no one was arrested. No one was prosecuted."

I can feel the bitterness in her as she tells me the story. But everything about what happened to Slim feels wrong. What really happened here? Did Spider know about this? Did Ruben?

"Is your dad okay?"

"Sort of." She looks away from me. "Anyway, the last few months before all this, investors visited regularly to see my dad about selling the building. Rich people with expensive cars. There's a lot of money pouring into this area, ever since the Metro station opened."

That's something I noticed as soon as I got out of prison—

old buildings coming down, new ones going up. There are tons of fancy new condos just across the river on the downtown side. It was only a matter of time before all that money began to flow eastward, gathering around the new train station in Mariachi Plaza.

"My dad held out," Carmen says. "This is our family business. Our 'bread and butter,' he called it. He had hoped I'd take it over, eventually—but I wanted something different. When I went to cooking school, my mom and dad decided to work here until they were old enough to retire, then pass it on to one of their employees. But after my dad got hurt, he said, 'Get rid of that place. I never want to see it again.'"

There's a little dust on the glass refrigerator that used to hold the cakes and cupcakes present at every *cumple*, baptism, and graduation in our neighborhood. Carmen traces her fingertip over the glass the way she touched the tattoos on my chest, as if she's trying to learn something she can't see with her eyes alone.

A car pulls up outside the front door. Automatically, I stand in front of Carmen and reach for the gun I don't have. Then I feel stupid—Carmen's story and my run-in with Spider and Ruben have put me on edge.

I turn my attention back to the street and notice that the car is a late-model Mercedes Benz with tinted windows. Two men come out. I can't tell what race they are, but they're dressed in expensive suits. The license plate holder is from a car dealership in the San Fernando Valley. One holds an umbrella for the other as they approach the door.

"The guy on the left is one of the investors who's interested in buying the property. The one on the right is his accountant," Carmen says to me. "My parents wanted me to see them today."

"Why am I here?" I ask quietly.

"Moral support," she whispers. She looks at me sideways.

I'm a head taller than her and twice as wide. At last I get it—she wants muscle. Backup. Okay. That I can do. I tip my head back and put on my best gangster mug.

As soon as the two men walk in, Carmen stands up straighter and her eyes get hard. There she is—Chef Centeno. She shakes their hands and introduces me as her business associate, Eduardo Rosas. They don't tell me their names.

The men begin to ask her questions about the bakery.

"How long has your family owned this place?"

"Since the forties," she says. "It's been continuously owned and operated until we went on hiatus last October."

"Why are you interested in selling now?"

"My father has decided he'd finally like to retire."

She leaves out the part about gangsters and extortion. Wise move.

As Carmen easily handles the buyer, I walk slowly around the bakery, taking it in. Plastic trays and tongs are stacked by the front door where customers could pick them up. They'd choose whatever rolls and sweets they wanted, then bring them to the cashier to pay. The back room is enormous with high ceilings, multiple vents, and industrial fans. There's a giant mixer in the corner, big enough to prepare cement for a driveway. Baking pans are stacked inside tall rolling carts.

I run my hand over the beat-up workbench where all that bread was made, year after year after year. If I close my eyes, I can still smell the bread baking.

I look through the small pass-through window between the kitchen and the front of the bakery. That window was for sand-wiches—Slim made delicious Mexican *tortas*. I remember. He sold them at lunchtime along with ice-cold beers and sodas from the little refrigerator by the cash register.

I stop.

Wait a second.

Beer.

Holy shit.

The bakery has an existing beer and wine license.

"Has Slim considered renting this place out instead of just selling it?" I ask, interrupting Carmen's conversation with the investors.

Carmen looks at me with a confused expression. "What?"

My brain is humming now. "Instead of selling it, why doesn't your father rent it out?"

The two men glance at me as if I'm a fresh turd they've both accidentally stepped on.

"My parents and I haven't discussed that possibility," Chef Centeno says. "We've only discussed selling." Her voice is cold, a warning.

"You should think about renting."

"Why?" she asks.

"If it were me, I'd hang on to the property a little longer. Think about it. Fifteen years ago, everyone was investing in downtown LA, buying up property left and right. Now downtown is too expensive for most investors, so they're moving east, across the river. It only makes sense that would happen here too, right?"

"I don't follow," Carmen says.

"It's simple." I direct my smile toward the investors. "Just wait a little. These gentlemen are here because they're counting on bigger buyers coming through in a couple years. Am I right?" When the umbrella-holder mad-dogs me, I add, "What's the word? Gentrification? Yeah. That's it. They're counting on gentrification."

When Carmen frowns at me, I back down. I walk into the kitchen and sit up on the workbench, flashing my smile at the investors whenever I catch their eye. When they shake

Carmen's hand and leave, she storms into the kitchen. I'm ready for her.

"Don't be mad, Lady Chef." I hold up my hands in a gesture of *don't shoot.*

She smacks the counter with her hand. The sound echoes against the high ceilings. "Why can't you act normal, just for a few minutes?"

"I don't know. Because I'm a gangbanger?"

That riles her up. "Eddie, I swear—"

"They're one of many offers, right? If they don't buy, others will. It doesn't matter. We owe them honesty, not good manners."

She growls at me—straight-up growls, like a Rottweiler. "We don't owe anyone anything. We choose to show good manners because we're courteous, professional people." She throws up her hands. "I don't know why I'm lecturing you. It's not like you're even listening to me. *Travieso.*"

Travieso—troublemaker. There's a little smile mixed in with her frown, so I think she's only playing at being angry.

"I *am* listening to you," I say calmly. "I just have an alternative for you and your folks, if you'll hear me out."

Her chest rises and falls as she takes a deep breath and lets it out. "Okay. What?"

Carmen folds her arms and listens as I tell her about Sal and Vanessa's delivery route, and my brother's struggles to balance expansion, production, and rising demand for Eastside Beer.

"Where does he make the beer now?"

"At his mentor's brewery, Bay City Brews, all the way out in Santa Monica. He has something called an alternating proprietorship, meaning two different breweries share the same facilities. Vanessa borrows an old pickup to deliver the kegs. I help them out with deliveries twice a week."

"You do?"

"Yeah." I repeat Sal's most common complaint about selling his beer the way we do. "The beer is good—you've tasted it. But we're competing for tap handles and shelf space with breweries that have a lot more resources than us. If my brother had a larger place to brew and store the beer, and if we had a spot to serve it and introduce it to new customers—here, on the Eastside—I think that would help us get ahead of the pack."

Carmen nods, absorbing what I say.

"Even if it doesn't work out for my family," I say, "your family can hold on to the building a little bit longer and sell when prices are even higher than they are now." I smile. "What do you think?"

As I speak, Carmen moves closer and closer to me, as if she can't resist what I'm telling her. To be honest, I can't resist it either. It sounds so good, I can't believe the idea is coming out of my mouth.

I take her hands and pull her forward until she's standing between my knees. She tips her head back to look at me from under the brim of her baseball cap. Her dark eyes narrow as she studies my face.

"Are you really serious about this?" she asks.

I rest my hands on her shoulders and run them down her arms. "We have to look at the numbers. I don't know if it will work," I say, "but I know two people who can tell me if it will."

TEN

I call Sal, but he doesn't pick up. He's probably in class. I call Vanessa. She answers on the first ring. She's at her office downtown—I can hear people talking quietly and phones ringing in the background.

"Hey, can I come over tonight for dinner?" I ask.

"What?" She sounds busy. "Why are you even asking?" She pauses. "Why are you acting weird?" I never had an older sister, but I imagine she'd be just like Vanessa.

"I'm not being weird," I say. Carmen watches me. I wink at her to reassure her. "Listen, there's someone I want you to meet."

Vanessa squeaks. "Wait, is it a girl?"

Bait taken. "Yes."

"Oh my God, Eddie! That's awesome. Of course you can bring her over." She pauses. "But I didn't clean the house—and I didn't buy food. The house is a rat's nest and she's gonna starve to death. Couldn't we take her to a restaurant instead? This is really short notice."

"Are you kidding?" I snort. My brother is slightly obsessive compulsive about cleanliness. I know—I used to live with the motherfucker. "Sal keeps your place spotless. And as for food, don't worry. I'll bring us all something to eat."

"What? You? Bring food...to our house?"

"Yeah. What's wrong?"

She's quiet for a second. "Sorry, I just had to look outside the window to see if there were any pigs. You know. In the sky. Flying around."

"Ha-ha," I say in a sarcastic tone. "What time should we come over?"

"We'll all be home at five."

"Okay. See you guys then."

I hang up the phone. Next task. "So, one day out of the kitchen. You must be missing it," I tell Carmen.

"What do you mean?"

"I mean, you must miss being in the kitchen, cooking. Giving people joy through food."

Carmen stares at me. "Are you...did you...just volunteer me to make food for your family?" She shakes her head. "The balls on you. I swear."

"Be honest, Carmen. Doesn't cooking bring you joy? I mean, you *are* a chef, after all. This is your life's work. Your calling."

She rolls her eyes at me. "How many people?"

"Including you and me, five adults. One kid."

"How old is the kid?"

"I don't know. Little?"

"Eddie, I hate cooking for kids. Kids are picky."

"You don't even blink when you cook for a big-time food critic but cooking for a kid has you shook? Really?" I slide down off the counter and take her hand. "Come on. Let's go to *el super*."

With a fat chunk of my last paycheck, I buy everything Carmen wants. We load the groceries from the cart into her car and drive to Vanessa's house. We arrive at five on the dot.

Vanessa opens the door and greets Carmen with a big hug as the evil wiener dog barks his damn fool head off. Vanessa's grandmother and daughter crowd Carmen as I carry all the bags into the kitchen and unpack everything.

"Where's my brother?" I call out.

Nobody answers me because they're too busy falling in love with Carmen.

The Lady Chef enlists their help and soon the kitchen is full of loud laughter and delicious smells. Carmen even gives Vanessa's daughter something to do. The little girl sits at the table crumbling a big chunk of white cheese with her fingers.

I pop open a bottle of beer and sit on the couch, not because I'm feeling particularly lazy, but because it's fun to eavesdrop on them as they cook together. Women's voices are full of energy. I didn't hear many when I was locked up. Your ears begin to miss that sound. The laughter. The music and the way they shape sentences. And Spanglish—bouncing back and forth between two languages to create something new. The language of home.

My brother walks in through the front door. He looks exhausted, but his face lights up when he sees me in the living room. He puts his backpack down and runs his fingers through his hair. He's taken a cue from me and grown it all out, along with a beard of his own.

He's wearing a T-shirt from his school, Greenbriar University, and an unzipped sweatshirt from Bay City Brews, the host brewery where he makes his beer.

Muñeca runs out of the kitchen and throws her arms around him. Sal picks her up and kisses her cheek as she laughs with pure happiness. She calls him Sal, not Dad—her biological father died before she was born—but their strong connection is obvious. I have a flashback to our little sister but I shake off the memory before the old pain of her loss can catch up with me.

Sal sits down on the couch next to me as Muñeca runs back

to the kitchen to continue helping. I bump my brother's fist and we pull each other into a half hug. We may not be able to stand each other as roommates, but after five years in separate correctional facilities, we never take for granted the time we spend together now.

"So Vanessa sent me a long crazy text about a girl," Sal says. "What's this all about?"

"Her name's Carmen," I say. "She's a chef. She's in the kitchen right now with everybody."

"A chef?" Sal looks at me sideways. "*The* chef? You found her?"

Of course he'd remember that morning in Rafa's trailer. He saw Carmen's walk of shame through the garden. He saw the stupid little hearts in my eyes after she walked away.

"Don't be weird," I say.

He elbows me, hard, in the ribs. "Look at you."

"Ow, fucker." I rub the spot as we laugh a little. But there's important news I need to tell my brother, even if he probably doesn't want to hear it. "Hey, listen." I lower my voice. "I have to tell you something."

"What?"

"It's about ESHB."

Again, the tiredness drops over my brother's face like a shadow.

"Eddie, I told you to lay low," he says.

I cut him off before he can start the usual lecture. "You need to know this. Ruben's back."

"What?"

"Yeah. I ran into him and Spider this afternoon." I don't tell Sal about the special job they have for me—he would be furious.

"Did Ruben say where he's been?"

"No."

"This is not good." Sal grows quiet as he rubs his beard. "Watch yourself, okay?"

I nod, but I don't say anything else.

"Vanessa says you got a job at some restaurant downtown," Sal says, changing the subject. "She says that it's been good." He punches my shoulder. "That's the kind of thing I want to see you doing. None of these *tonterías*. None of the old bullshit."

He is my older brother. I owe him my life. But I hate it when he tries to boss me around. He's tried to step into our father's shoes since we were little, and it always rubs me the wrong way.

"Yeah, so," I say, swallowing down the irritation in my voice, "that job...it didn't really work out."

"What?" His smile fades again.

"Carmen and me," I say. "We both got fired."

"What the hell did you do?"

I shrug. "Nothing." He looks skeptical. I add, "For reals. I swear. It just kind of happened."

Sal is about to unleash more judgment on me when Vanessa calls from the kitchen, "Dinner's ready!"

My brother gives me a dirty look before we get up and walk to the dining room. The table is almost set. Vanessa's grandmother is showing Muñeca where the forks and spoons go. At each place there is already a bowl of hot soup, bright green and steaming. We sit down and bow our heads while Vanessa says a quick prayer.

I look from face to face to face at the table and have another flashback. Our house—back when we were whole. Sal was there, but so was our younger brother, Angel. Our mother and sister were still alive, before the accident. And our father—Dreamer—sat at the head, proud of his family, proud of the food he put on the table with legit money.

"Amen," Vanessa says.

I blink and I'm back in the present.

"*Crema de verduas.*" Carmen announces the dish just like she did in the restaurant. But this time she adds, "Vanessa made this."

"Sure, with your help," Vanessa says.

We eat. The warm soup tastes like an entire vegetable garden in my mouth, but smooth and creamy. I look at everyone's faces as they eat. They are caught in different states of ecstasy, all from a spoonful of soup. I look at Carmen and smile. I love how she has done this—made everyone so happy.

We chat about everyday stuff, work and school and bingo, regular *chisme* about the neighborhood including the three families on the block who recently decided to sell their houses.

"They didn't even have to put up for-sale signs," Vanessa says. "Buyers come knocking every week."

"Things are definitely changing," her grandmother says.

I clear the plates and Carmen brings out the main course. "*Mole verde,*" she says. "This was made by me and Muñeca. Muñeca cut the herbs from the garden for me."

The little girl's smile is so big, it cracks me up. We dig in. The taste of tomatillos and fresh herbs fills my mouth.

Third course. It all unfolds like a story, chapter one, two, and three. "It's Lent, so I decided to make my father's favorite, *capirotada.* Chinita helped me with this one," Carmen says.

The old lady points to her granddaughter. "And Muñeca helped with the cheese."

Again, the little girl smiles big. I ruffle her hair.

Capirotada is a bread pudding made with eggs and brown sugar. There's cheese and raisins in it, and it tastes like the best of my childhood in one bite.

In prison, I would have done unholy things for a home-cooked meal like this. Carmen put it together without much thought, and she got the family to participate and make it their own.

I turn to my brother. "Sal, Carmen is Slim's daughter. Her family owns La Golondrina Bakery."

Sal looks at Carmen, and a kind of sad understanding shadows his face. "I was sorry to hear about your dad," he says quietly. "How's he doing?"

"Better." Carmen puts down her coffee cup. "A lot better."

"Is your mother taking care of him?" Vanessa's grandmother asks.

Carmen nods. "A home healthcare worker helps her in the afternoons."

The table is quiet for a moment. I didn't know the extent of Slim's injuries, and the news makes me slow down as I realize the difficulty of what Carmen had to do today. That bakery was her family's business for generations. Her father was badly beaten in the parking lot. Her mother is home taking care of her father. Without siblings, Carmen must look after the business and tie up all the loose ends alone. I've seen her handle pressure—she can do it, no problem—but when I realize what she's going through behind the scenes, I can feel the weight of her burden.

Muñeca asks for a second helping of *capirotada*. Her mom gives her one more spoonful.

"I wish you could cook like this, Mommy," the little girl says.

Awkward, but honest—Vanessa is an awful cook.

"Mommy wishes she could cook like this too." Vanessa leans over and blows a raspberry on Muñeca's cheek as the little girl squeals.

We clear the table. Vanessa's grandmother takes Muñeca upstairs for bedtime. Vanessa pours us some fresh coffee as we all sit down in the living room. I take a look at Sal, who's staring at me with a look that says, *What is about to happen?*

Carmen takes out her portfolio with all the information about the bakery.

I clear my throat. "So, remember how we were talking at the gym about how much you wished you had your own place to sell Eastside Beer? Carmen and I have a proposal."

To start off, Carmen talks about the property. Then I talk about the possibilities of a taproom. In my own ears, I sound like a combination of a slimy used car salesman and a kid standing in front of a classroom giving a book report for a book he didn't actually read. But as I talk, Sal and Vanessa listen—really listen—to what I'm saying. So I get overconfident and say, "Carmen, she can even make food."

Lady Chef barks, "Wait, what?"

I ignore her. "We can have food and beer together. It'll be just like Bay City Brews, but over here in the hood. A place to hang out, get a bite to eat, introduce people to the beers. What do you think?"

Sal leans back and folds his arms. "I don't know. This neighborhood—it's not wealthy like Santa Monica. Who's going to spend money on fancy beer here?"

"Think bigger, dog," I say. "That tide of dollars is coming. You can see it in the housing prices, the investors. Nothing is going to hold that money back. And we can be here to catch it when it comes."

He looks skeptical.

"If you're worried about selling out," I say, "ask yourself, wouldn't you rather we opened this business than some *gringo*? The white folks are coming, Salvador. You know it. It's going to be homeboys versus hipsters in a couple years. Whose side are you on?"

Sal shakes his head. "You're so dramatic."

"Eddie," Carmen says, "there's more to the picture than that."

"What do you mean?" I ask.

"The younger generations born and raised here, they're going to school," Carmen says. "They're becoming professionals. Soon, they'll have disposable income." I realize she's talking about herself, her own aspirations. "Craft beer, it's a luxury I'm betting they will want. If the product is local, even better."

"You were looking for an opportunity," I say to Sal. "Here it is. Keep Eastside Beer in the community. Build it at home." I turn to Vanessa. "What do you think?"

Vanessa stands and picks up her laptop where it's sitting on the kitchen counter. She comes back to the living room, opens it, and starts it up as we watch.

"Only one thing that matters here," she says, "and that's the numbers."

We watch as Vanessa plugs numbers into formulas. She runs some weird models and asks Carmen a million questions about the property, most of which Carmen knows the answers to. Sal and I sit back and watch the ladies in action. They are both smart, practical women at the top of their game. Sal's a scholarship whiz kid and his beer is amazing. I'm a *payaso* surrounded by three goddamn geniuses. I look at them all closely, hoping a few brain cells will rub off on me.

"Do you really think this is possible?" Sal asks Vanessa.

"To be honest, I've been thinking about the business a lot," she replies. "Making the beer at Bay City Brews and transporting it here is not cheap. A big initial investment in a home for Eastside Beer would pay off over time."

"We can call it Eastside Brewery," I say. "It's perfect."

"No, it's nuts." Sal's eyes study the numbers on Vanessa's screen. "I'm still in school. I barely make enough to pay my bills. With my record, what bank is going to extend a loan?"

Vanessa looks at him. "Take your brother's advice. Think bigger."

"What do you mean?"

"Me. I have the money."

We all stare at her. I wouldn't say we're in shock, but we're close.

"What?" Sal says again.

"There's a reason our neighbors are selling their houses left and right," Vanessa says. "My grandmother bought this place in the sixties. It's paid off, and its value has gone through the roof. If Carmen's parents' price is right, the equity will cover rent, remodeling, and equipment—at least for a little while."

Sal shakes his head. "I can't let you do that, *hermosa*. I can't take your money."

"You're not taking it. I'm not giving it to you, stupid." Vanessa reaches over and takes my brother's hand. "In case you've forgotten, I'm an accountant. I don't throw my money away. I invest it. And I want to invest it in you." She looks around the table at all of our faces. "In *us*."

ELEVEN

Carmen drives me back to Rafa's. I'm amazed and giddy at what's happened today. Vanessa has agreed to create a business plan. It'll take a few days. Then we can present the idea to Carmen's parents and see what they think.

None of this was in motion yesterday. And now it is—because of me. I had the idea, and I made it real.

I'm feeling pretty proud of myself.

Carmen slaps the dashboard with her hand and brings me back down to earth. "Are you even listening to me?"

I jump. Obviously, I was not listening, but I don't admit this. "What? What's the matter?"

"You're such a bully."

"What are you talking about? Me? A bully?"

"I don't appreciate being made a part of your crazy plans."

"What plans, Carmen?" I look at her. She's fuming. "Why are you so mad?"

"You said to them, 'Carmen, she can even make food.'" She drops her voice down low in the way women do when they repeat the things men have said that annoyed them. "And this afternoon, you assumed I'd make dinner for your family. I'm not a short-order cook, Eddie, and I'm not your maid. I have a career. I may have gotten fired from Giacomo's, but that doesn't mean I want my next gig to be frying tater tots and jalapeño poppers for a bunch of drunks."

"Oh, so it's beneath you? Making food for regular people?" I'm teasing her. I know I shouldn't, but to be honest, I'm planning ahead. If I make her mad enough, I can apologize. Then maybe we can have really good make-up sex.

"At the risk of sounding like a pretentious ass, yes!" she yells. "Yes, it *is* beneath me. I'm not going to act like my three years in culinary school and three years in a top restaurant don't mean anything. I can get a new restaurant job in a heartbeat, and I don't need your weird form of charity to do it."

"You're right," I say. "I didn't say you couldn't get your own job—that's not what I meant at all. I just got excited about the whole thing. My imagination went wild. I got carried away." I want to explain to her that I don't *ever* have good ideas—at least good ideas that everyone else agrees are good too. But this isn't about me, it's about her. "Obviously, we can't afford you. You're like, the Ferrari of cooks. We'll get us a Ford Pinto. It'll be fine."

That calms her down a little bit. I watch her out of the corner of my eye, testing out her reactions.

"Real talk. Did you see how much they loved your food? That was amazing, how you did that without really thinking about it. Even Muñeca gobbled everything up."

Carmen's shoulders relax, and I keep going.

"When I was locked up, I would've done anything for a meal like that." A bad taste comes into my mouth along with a bad memory. "Have you heard of the brick?"

"No. What's that?"

"When I first got to prison, I had a hard time adjusting. I got in trouble. So they put me in the box. The prison guards called it the SHU—secure housing unit. Solitary confinement, basi-

cally. I was there for three months. An attitude adjustment—
that's what they said I needed."

I keep my voice light, but the SHU was nothing to laugh
about. I was alone in a windowless cell for twenty-two-and-a-
half hours a day. I got to walk the corridor and exercise in a
small yard for ninety minutes. Alone time like that? It fucks
with your head. I had to fight myself to stay sane.

"The worst thing of all was the food," I say. "When you piss
off the guards enough, they put you on a special diet. They
called it the brick."

She makes a face. "I'm afraid to ask, but what the heck
is that?"

"It's like, they take vegetables, old bread, and the cheapest
meat they can find, and grind everything to a paste. Then they
bake it like meatloaf. You get two slices a day. There's no salt, no
flavor. It tastes like absolutely nothing."

"Is that even legal?"

"It has the required nutrition, but I wouldn't call it food." I
shudder a little bit. "Imagine. The same thing. Day after day
after day. I would close my eyes at night and dream about
real food."

"Like what?"

"My mom's *pozole*. Fresh salsa, red and green. Mangoes
with *chamoy* and chili powder. Fuck, a French dip sandwich
from Philippe's. Tears—like, literal tears—would form in my
eyes. I'd wake up straight-up sobbing, like a baby."

She's smiling a little now, and I feel better. She pulls up to
the curb in front of the garden.

"When your world is tasteless, your mind tries to recreate
flavors. Smells. It's a way to stay alive." I have a flashback of standing
with Carmen in the garden. I remember how her lips tasted the first
time I kissed her. I remember the sensation of her body against

mine, like every craving I had ever had, focused in that moment. "What you made tonight was the meal of my dreams, no exaggeration," I say quietly. "I know you've spent years of your life in the kitchen. For you, it's just work. But don't forget that it's special."

"Lots of people can cook."

"No, it's not the cooking that's special."

"Then what is?"

"It's the ability to give happiness." In the dark car, I reach up and touch her neck, as lightly as I can. "To give pleasure."

She takes a sharp breath. I massage her for a long time until her cool skin turns warm under my fingers.

I lean over to whisper in her ear. "Come inside with me, baby girl."

When she looks up at me, my inner dog begins to howl.

Sweetly, she says, "No."

"No?" I brush my fingertips down toward the neckline of her T-shirt and stroke her collarbone. "Why not? You know you want to."

"Rafa's in the trailer. I can see his truck parked in the driveway."

"That *viejito* doesn't care. He drinks two beers, smokes a fatty, and falls asleep like a rock."

"I'm not going to...do what we did...with someone else in the trailer."

"You didn't care when Sal was there."

She pushes my hand away. "That's because I wasn't thinking straight." Her voice has an edge to it. She's annoyed.

I sit up straighter, but I don't make a move to leave the car. "Take me home with you, then."

"You're crazy. I live with my parents."

"That's okay. I know how to sneak into windows."

"Don't be gross, Eddie." She turns on the dome light of her

car, not really ruining the mood as much as sending a message that she's not interested.

My mind races to solve this puzzle. I have a little money left from that last paycheck. I can afford a room, but not a very good one. Carmen's a tough cookie but she deserves more than some fleabag motel room off the freeway. She definitely doesn't deserve *piojos*. How about her car? We could drive somewhere secluded, climb into the back seat, find a little Marvin Gaye on the radio...

"I know what you're thinking," she says. "You're trying to come up with a solution."

Would a direct approach work here? I give it a shot. "Of course I am trying to come up with a solution. I want to sleep with you."

She snorts. "I'm sure you do. But this conversation is not actually about sex."

I'm confused. "It's not?"

She turns to face me. Her eyes are shaded by her ball cap, but her beautiful lips are in full view. I want to kiss them so badly, I'm almost shaking. I'm smuggling a baseball bat in my boxers. I force myself to sit still.

"If we're going to work together to see this through," she says, "you can't just steamroll me like you did today. I didn't like that you made decisions for me. I'm willing to help you out, but tell me what you need. Tell me what you're planning and let me decide. Don't decide for me."

"To be honest, I don't really plan things out," I say. "The words—they just kind of rush out sometimes. I don't even know what I'm saying half the time."

She rolls her eyes. "Yeah, well. You need to work on that. You're a grown-ass man."

Point taken. "Okay."

"I'm serious."

"So am I. You're right. I wasn't being fair. I'm sorry."

"Don't do it again."

"I won't."

"Good."

I study her lips some more. Her top lip sticks out a little more than the bottom one. "So," I whisper, "wanna smash?"

She presses the button on her door that unlocks mine. "Good night, Eddie."

———

IN THE MORNING, Rafa gently kicks me awake. "Rise and shine, *joven*," he says. "*Camote* and *calabaza* today. Let's get started."

Grumpy and half-asleep, I wash up, get dressed, and drink the hot hippie concoction the old man has made me. I think it's green tea, but with Rafa it could be anything. We go out into the garden. We plant rows of sweet potatoes and squash, putting each little plant in the ground like tucking in a baby.

I'm cranky, but I have to admit, the dark soil feels good against my hands. We water the new plants. The air smells like fresh, clean dirt. Healthy. Pure. Rafa has me water the rest of his plot while he harvests some radishes and broccoli. He'll set aside a few of the vegetables for us. The rest he'll sell to neighborhood housewives for a little pocket change.

"Hey, tell your *hermano* I'm running low on beer," he says.

"*Borracho*." I'm joking. He's not a drunk. He's a stoner. "Which one do you want? I'll tell Sal to bring me some the next time we go on a delivery."

"What was it called? Eastside Pride. That one was really good."

I know from my beer lessons with Sal that Eastside Pride is

a wheat beer, a *hefeweizen*. It's his most popular brew. "You got it, *viejo*."

After chores, I go for a long run around the neighborhood and finish with some old-school calisthenics in the park. Push-ups, sit-ups, burpees. All the stuff I used to do when I was locked up. Hot and sweaty on top of dirty from the morning's gardening, I wash up behind the trailer, out of sight of the neighbors who've come to tend their community garden plots. Shivering, I towel off, put on some clean pants, and walk out from behind the trailer.

One of the mothers in the neighborhood watches me out of the corner of her eye. She's cute. Short hair. Lipstick—to go to the garden?

I give her a half smile and a nod, the standard gangster greeting for females. She turns her attention back to her two toddlers in the garden. She's got dimples. She looks at me one more time, really quick, then smiles to herself.

I jacked off hard last night after Carmen left. I jacked off a second time in the middle of the night. You'd think that would be enough. Nope.

I'm still fucking horny.

Back in the day, before I got locked up, it would've been easy for me to go over there, get Dimples's number, give her a call, and arrange to meet up later for a good pipe-down. I used to like hitting on moms. With shit to do, places to be, they never gave me the runaround, provided they wanted what I had to give—specifically, a good time, no strings attached.

But.

That was then. This is now.

Once again, I think about Carmen.

Her lips. Her heat.

I know all about cravings. I know about wanting something

you can't have—I lived it for five years. But I also know how delicious it feels to finally get exactly what you need.

I take one last look at Dimples and go back inside the trailer to finish getting dressed.

WHEN I'M ready to go, I take a deep breath.

Before I can second-guess myself, I slide my backpack under the couch where it can't be seen. I leave the trailer and hide my phone and keys in a little hole in the avocado tree where no one will find them. When I wave goodbye to Rafa, I have to swallow down the fear that rises up in my throat. I leave the garden behind me before I lose my nerve.

I walk through ESHB territory, laying low and avoiding the major streets and patrol cars. Twenty minutes later, I reach a familiar alley.

I stop for a moment at the rusted gates.

Jesus Christ. This bullshit again.

If I could leave this life behind, I would. In a heartbeat. But this gang owns me—Ruben owns me—and if I want to continue breathing, there's only one choice I can make.

I step between the rusted doors of the heavy gate where I can't be seen from the street. I follow this alley to where it ends at the retaining wall that separates the freeway from the neighborhood. I turn and follow a second alley parallel to the wall. Freeway traffic speeds by on the other side.

So much in the world has changed in the five years I've been away, but this alley is exactly the same. Weeds grow between the cracks in the old asphalt. There's litter of every kind, abandoned shopping carts, old mattresses. A beat-up Dumpster overflows with fresh trash. Behind it, the wall is scorched where a fire has blackened it.

There's a rain-warped plywood board leaning against a chain-link fence. I move the board and crawl through the hole cut in the wire.

I walk through one yard, hop a low fence, and walk through another. It's risky to do this in broad daylight, but there's an advantage—no one is home right now. Kids are in school, and for the most part, everyone is at work. When I was a *mocoso* doing home burglaries with older homies, we hit in the middle of the day. They brought me along because I was small and could climb through windows.

I reach the third yard. I walk across hard dirt, clumpy dead grass, empty beer bottles and cans, and hundreds of cigarette butts. There's a dirty sliding glass door with a broken lock. I open it and step inside.

TWELVE

The abandoned house smells like ass. I look down—the floor is piled with trash. Rotten food fills the kitchen along with fat, lazy flies. *Varrio* Hollenbeck graffiti covers every wall. All the windows facing the street are covered with aluminum foil. The only source of light comes from the dirty sliding door at the back of the house.

This is one of ESHB's crash pads. When homeboys have nowhere to go, they hide out here. It's a place to sleep, get drunk, get high, get laid. The house also serves as our meeting place and arsenal. Stolen guns are hidden in the attic and all the closets.

I step over a pizza box when Spider walks out of the hallway to greet me.

"Trouble," he says. "Good to see you, brother." We bump fists.

A kid is sitting on a bare mattress in the middle of the living room. Seventeen or eighteen, he's lighting up the bulb of a long glass pipe. I watch him take the hit. Spider kicks him.

"Show some respect, you little shit."

The kid stumbles to his feet. His eyes are all pupil, no iris. He's breathing hard. "Hey, 'sup," he mumbles. "I'm Lalo."

I watch as Spider pulls a Glock 9mm out of the hallway closet, checks the chamber, and slides it into the waistband of his khakis. He hands another to Lalo, who does the exact same thing.

Spider raises his eyebrows as if to offer me something out of the closet. I shake my head—I already hate that I have to do what he says. I don't need to make things worse by playing cowboy today.

"I'm good, homes," I say.

"Sure?"

I nod.

The expression on Spider's face is puzzled. He reaches into the shadow of the cabinet and pulls out a brand-new knife in a leather sheath. He shows me the blade. It's wicked looking, serrated on one side—some kind of hunting knife.

"Take this," he says. "Just in case."

I know enough not to argue with him. Without a word, I slide the clip of the sheath into my pocket.

We leave the crash pad. There's a Honda Civic parked in the alley with dealer plates—stolen, no doubt about it. Spider drives. I climb into the shotgun seat and Lalo, shaking and sweating, jumps into the back seat.

Spider pulls out of the alley and heads east.

We don't talk. All I can hear is the rattle of Lalo's uneven breathing.

Every bone in my body wants to jump out of the car and run, but I can't.

East Side Hollenbeck is dangerous, but it's nothing compared to the Organization, the powerful prison gang that oversees us. The Organization's big homies are all housed in Pelican Bay, the supermax prison in Northern California. They call the shots—everyone, including Spider and Ruben, follow their orders.

The benefits? The Organization provides protection to our homies in the *pinta*—Organization inmates made sure I was safe while I was locked up. Outside of the penitentiaries, it provides a connection to the Mexican drug cartels and stability between street gangs—retaliatory drive-bys and random shootings are forbidden without a green light from above.

In exchange for this? The Organization demands only two things. Number one, fifty cents of every dollar we make. Number two, immediate and complete obedience.

So when ESHB tells me to do something?

I do it.

If I don't?

Green light. Every homeboy from San Diego to Salinas declares open season on me.

As Spider drives slowly into the hills east of Hollenbeck territory, I struggle to stay calm and clear-headed. The road climbs into El Sereno, a residential neighborhood that overlooks the freeway.

Most things don't shake me, but as the road narrows and twists up between the houses on the top of the hill, my stomach cramps up. I don't know what Spider has planned, but I can't shake the feeling we're rats heading into a trap. A getaway would be impossible up here. The road is only wide enough for one car to pass through—anyone could box us in.

Spider parks the car and turns off the engine.

"Okay, listen up, both of you." He points out a light-blue house four driveways down. "That's that *pinche chavala* Ochoa's house."

My brain races. Who is Ochoa? I've been out of the game too long.

"The dealer?" Lalo pipes up.

"He pays taxes to the Hillside Locos," says Spider. "Last week Ruben heard him mouthing off about having a grip of handguns. Ruben offered to buy some but Ochoa refused. So today we're here to take them."

I make a fist that Spider can't see. My nails bite into the palm of my hand. Robbing a fucking drug dealer? That's the errand? I've been out of the life since I was eighteen and now he's throwing me back into the pool headfirst.

"I'll pull up in front of the house and keep the engine running. Lalo, do as we always do. Front door, guns blazing. Don't give anyone a chance to react. Trouble, you find the guns. Lalo will cover you. We had one of the kids case the house. Ochoa lives with his mom. She's at work, so he's alone during the day. His lazy ass is probably still in bed. Get in, get out. Understand?"

"Got it, *carnal*," Lalo says. He takes the gun out of his waistband and checks the chamber again, this time with lots of drama like some kind of Hollywood action star. He's sweating through his shirt. This is exactly what I need today—a teenage meth addict running point for me on an armed robbery.

Spider drives past the blue house, makes a Y-turn in the narrow street, and pulls up next to the driveway. He doesn't turn off the engine. "Okay," he says, "go now."

Lalo and I run directly to the entrance. Adrenaline pumps through my body as I strike the ball of my foot in the middle of the door. The lock breaks away from the frame and the door flies inward.

The TV in the living room is on. I spot a few balloons of black tar heroin on the coffee table. Lalo goes directly to the person sitting on the sofa, a kid with a shaved head wearing a stained T-shirt and boxers. Lalo grabs him and shoves him to the ground. He puts a knee in the kid's back to pin him down. He shoves the barrel of the gun against his neck. The kid tries to reach for something under the coffee table but Lalo grinds his knee down. "Don't be fucking stupid. We're East Side Hollenbeck. Where are the guns?"

"Guns?" The kid grunts, trying to get a breath. I can see from here that he's got some kind of buzz on. His reactions are slower than normal. "Ain't got no guns!" he says again.

"Piece of shit." Lalo grinds down harder. "Where... are...the guns?"

"Ow! Fuck! What guns? I ain't got no guns!"

With the top ridge of his Glock, Lalo smacks the side of the kid's head.

He whimpers. "I don't have none, I swear, I swear!"

While Lalo presses Ochoa, I search the closets and cabinets of the house. I check the kitchen. As fast as I can, I check the floors for loose boards and kick area rugs out of the way, looking for any kind of hidden compartment. In frustration, I flip the mattresses. All I find is a whole lot of nothing.

I go back to the living room, lean down, and put my face in Ochoa's face. He's young, maybe seventeen. His eyes are dazed, but there's fear in them—he's sober enough to know we could kill him easily if we wanted to.

"Where are the guns you were bragging about?" I ask him in a calm voice. I'm playing good cop today. "Give them to us, and we're out of here. That's all we want."

But the kid doesn't want to play. "Fuck you!"

Lalo pistol-whips him again. Now Ochoa is disoriented on top of being high.

"You don't want trouble," I say. "Where are they?"

Tears form in the corners of his eyes and drip down to the wooden floor. Lalo presses his full weight on Ochoa's back, making it hard for the kid to get a full breath. "I lied." He begins to sob, which is embarrassing for all of us involved. "I lied. I thought—I thought—if I-I said I had an arsenal, no one would come here. No one would bother me."

Lalo and I exchange a look of frustration. Annoyed, and without any real purpose, Lalo smacks the kid again. Ochoa howls with pain. "Stop, please stop." The sticky, unmistakable smell of urine fills the living room. He's pissed himself. I feel sorry for Ochoa in the way I feel sorry for all people who've made bad decisions thinking they were good ones.

Angry, Lalo pulls his arm up to pistol-whip the kid one more time, but his swing goes wild and he smacks me in the eye with the grip. The pain is sharp.

"Fuck!" I yell. My hand goes to my face. "What the hell is wrong with you?"

"Shit, shit, shit. I'm sorry, dog." Lalo turns his attention back to Ochoa. "Look what you made me do, *culero*."

My ears are ringing with the unexpected blow. My left eye goes blurry. "Leave him," I say.

When Lalo gets up, the kid doesn't move. I watch him carefully as Lalo sweeps the dope on the coffee table into his pocket.

"ESHB!" Lalo shouts. He waves the gun in the air. He has no idea how stupid he looks. "Don't forget who did this to you, you piece of shit." He taps the side of the gun against his chest like Denzel Washington in *Training Day*. "*Varrio* Hollenbeck, motherfucker!"

I was expecting a tragedy. Instead, I'm standing in the middle of a bad comedy.

"Come on. Let's go." I feel a black eye starting to form along with a killer headache.

We run back to the car, jump in, and Spider speeds away.

BACK IN THE GARDEN, I take another shower to wash off my experience in El Sereno.

I run over the details in my mind. After we got clear of the hills, Spider drove us back to the alley behind the crash pad. Lalo took the car to our usual chop shop to get gone. The drugs amounted to a couple hundred dollars, nothing dramatic. Spider took the dope with him. Before I left, he slapped me on the back.

"This didn't go as planned," he said, "but Ruben and me, we're glad you're back, Trouble."

I nodded and swallowed down the words I wanted to say.

When I was younger, the gang was my purpose. Lots of people think gangs are a new thing, a simple problem that needs to be solved. They have no idea how deep the roots of many LA gangs are. My grandfather was ESHB, way back in the sixties. My dad followed in his footsteps. For a while, my dad left the gang and went straight. Then bad luck hit us hard. Dreamer Rosas lost his job. My mother and sister died in a car accident. Looking for refuge, Dreamer went back to the gang. He brought his sons with him.

School bored me. The teachers who weren't burnt-out wrecks tried to push me in the right direction, but they had no idea what my life was like or how to connect with me. I mouthed off. I got Fs. I got into fights. I was a pain in everyone's ass.

In those days, the only place I felt at home was with my homeboys. I got everything from them. How to talk. How to walk. How to dress. How to behave. How to get girls. How to make money. How to survive.

Along with that, I got other things, things I wasn't completely aware of. How to accept Trouble as your name. How to alienate yourself from others. How to make stupid decisions.

How to be the kind of person who laughs out loud when the judge gives you your sentence.

I turn off the shower and get dressed again. In one of Rafa's feng shui mirrors, I examine my face and see it—the ugly purple shadow of a black eye.

"Fuck," I whisper.

I pull my backpack out from under the sofa. I take my keys and phone out of the hole in the avocado tree and replace them with the knife Spider gave me. The hole is hidden in the trunk behind a thick branch of leaves. No one would find the knife here unless they knew where to look.

Before Rafa comes home, I put on my backpack and leave the garden again.

THE SUN IS SETTING when my bus arrives at the stop. It's full of commuters either getting off work or heading out into the night to start their shifts. There are a couple of students in hoodies and backpacks, scrolling through their phones. There's a homeless person or two, keeping to themselves, quiet and waiting for a stop that never comes. People give me the side eye as I walk down the aisle. I pull up my hoodie.

I find an empty seat and stare out at the traffic and sidewalks of Whittier Boulevard. This is East LA's most famous street, a main drag where car clubs show off their restored vintage cars on weekends. On weekdays, it's a regular street. Local businesses cater to working-class people and recent immigrants. Check-cashing offices. Pawn shops. Meat markets. Discount stores that sell school supplies, party supplies, cleaning supplies, international phone cards, and the occasional luxury. Leather cowboy boots. Cheap perfume. CDs of music from home.

But I see some changes mixed in. New strip malls. New

bank branches. At the stop where I get off, there's a brand-new Starbucks with a drive-thru. It looks like it used to be a Burger King.

Across the street is a big stucco building with glass windows. Medical offices—they look new. I check the address again. It's correct. I walk through the glass doors and follow the signs marked with arrows and the word *Recovery*.

When I arrive at the conference room, the meeting has already started. As quietly as I can, I slip in through the double doors and take a seat on a folding chair. There are about fifteen people in the room, all different races and different ages, seated in a circle.

The facilitator of the meeting is a big homegirl in a flowered T-shirt and red ball cap. She addresses a woman sitting near me. "How about you?" she asks. "Would you like to say something today?"

The light-skinned African-American woman is wearing a black dress with white polka dots. Her hair is in a neat bun on the top of her head. I notice she's curvaceous, with a small waist —the kind of hourglass body my mother and all my dad's girl-friends had.

I remember Miguel the church groundskeeper's description.

"Yes, a woman," he had said. "*Era bonita.* She had a name like a flower. Rose or Lily. Something like that. Your dad liked her a lot."

"Hello," she says in a clear voice. "My name is Daisy."

THIRTEEN

After the meeting, everyone mingles by a table set near the door. On the table, there's a box of donuts, some cups, and an ancient coffeepot.

Some people introduce themselves to me. I shake their hands and tell them my name, but I don't share more.

I attended these meetings in prison, twelve-step programs for criminals and gang members that were run exactly the same way. I know the drill.

Without being too obvious, I make my way through the group until I'm standing close to the woman named Daisy.

Her story was short, but good. I can tell she's had lots of practice telling it. She moved here from a small town. She was lonely and lost until she met a man who introduced her to drugs. For six years, addiction stripped away her sense of self to the extent that she didn't know how to leave her abusive relationship. Each rock bottom gave way to a new rock bottom until a judge sentenced her to drug court, which eventually led her to these support meetings.

Ten years later, she has a job as a receptionist. She has a small apartment and a cat named Pringles.

For her, and no doubt for other people who are working toward recovery, this meeting room is a safe place. I don't insult her by trying to pretend I'm not the person I am.

"Daisy," I say. "My name is Eddie."

She shakes my hand and examines my face. She takes in the black eye, the tattoos, my height. Something flickers in her eyes and I know she knows who I am before I explain.

"Nice to meet you, Eddie," she says.

"Can we talk?"

She's still for a moment, considering her answer.

"Okay," she says.

We walk across the street to Starbucks and I buy her a cup of hot chocolate. We sit in a quiet corner away from the groups of teenagers sucking on their Frappuccinos.

"I'm guessing you know why I'm here," I say. "You knew my father. Dreamer Rosas."

She nods. "Who told you where to find me?"

"Miguel."

"Of course." She sighs in the graceful way a long-suffering woman sighs when nothing really surprises her anymore. She's younger than my dad, for sure—maybe in her mid-thirties. I know twelve-step programs like this discourage romantic relationships and flirting. But things happen. With my dad, things happened all the time.

Daisy takes her time but during our talk, she opens up to me. She tells me Dreamer sometimes talked about me and my brothers—his two older boys locked up in prison, and his youngest boy, stolen from him by his in-laws.

"He was ashamed," she says. "He felt he hadn't done enough for you and Sal. He regretted he had messed up his chance to raise Angel."

Hearing her say my brothers' names out loud makes this

experience feel more real. I wonder how much more truth Dreamer shared with her woven in with the inevitable lies.

"Were you my dad's girlfriend?" I ask.

Daisy takes a sip of hot chocolate and stares across the room at nothing in particular. "I don't know. It was complicated with Dreamer. At first I was supposed to be his sponsor." She gets a dreamy, sad look in her eyes. "In the end, we both disrespected each other's boundaries." She looks back at me and says slowly, "I was sorry to hear what happened to him."

I nod.

Here's where things get tricky.

Daisy is intelligent—one minute with her and anyone would be able to tell that. But how good is she at lying? Does she know the truth about my dad being alive? Does she know where he is?

I decide not to give her the chance to lie to me.

For this to work, all I know is everything I say to her right now has to be true, or she will see right through it and never trust me again.

"I was his favorite," I say quietly. "Middle kid. Trouble-maker. My teachers hated me. My mother—she didn't know how to deal with me. My older brother was always bossing me around, telling me all the things I was doing wrong. But my dad —my dad was my buddy. He said I reminded him of himself when he was little."

Deep inside me, I feel a small, hidden spot in my heart warm up.

"When I was six or seven, my mom and dad had a big argu-ment. Over what, I had no idea. The next day, my dad took me to the flower district downtown. Five o'clock in the morning, we drove over the bridge. It was still dark, but the wholesalers were all open. The sidewalks were wet. Buyers and florists walked around the warehouses, making their deals. And here I was, this dumb kid, following my dad like a puppy."

Daisy watches me. I can't read the expression on her face. I continue. "I remember the smell of roses surrounding me. In my mind, the only flowers in that market are roses, because that's what my father bought for my mother—two dozen long-stem red roses, her favorite. He knew one of the wholesalers who cut him a deal in exchange for some meat that 'fell off the truck' at the slaughterhouse where he worked. He paid half price for the flowers. When we walked back to the car, he let me carry the bouquet."

I haven't told this story to anyone. Suddenly I'm that little kid again, standing proudly at my dad's side.

"I remember my arms filled with red roses. The thorns poked me through the clear plastic, but I never complained, never said one bad thing about the experience because I wanted him to bring me with him wherever he went. I wanted to be a part of his adult world more than anything. I never stopped thinking—Sal isn't here. Angel isn't here. He's bringing me. His favorite."

My empty hands are folded on the table. I look down at them. I only had enough money for Daisy's drink, not one for me. "When I look back, he was teaching me how to say sorry." Something occurs to me after all these years. "That's what I was holding. A big bouquet of his sorries, all tied up in a bow. In his world, as long as you knew how to say sorry, you never had to take responsibility for yourself. You never had to change." I look up at Daisy. "Do you have a pen?"

She takes one out of her purse and hands it to me. I write my phone number on a napkin and slide the pen and napkin over the table.

I look her in the eye. "I want to hear my dad's voice again," I say slowly. "To tell him I tried, and to tell him, 'Dad, I'm sorry. For everything.'"

The words hang in the air between me and this stranger. I

push my chair back from the table. The story has made me more emotional than I had expected. All I want to do is leave this place, get away, hide.

"Eddie," Daisy says.

I look up.

"Sometimes," she says, "what we want and what we get are two very different things. Sometimes it's not up to us."

I nod. I know—fuck, I know.

"Thank you for talking to me," I manage to say. "I have to go."

MY BUS HOME is almost empty. I sit in the back seat with my hoodie up. When the stupid tears finally stop, I wipe my face with my sleeve and take out my phone. I stare at it for a minute. Then I dial Carmen's number.

She picks up. "Eddie? It's late."

"I want to see you," I say quietly.

I hear a TV in the background. I hear her walking down a hall and closing a door. "What? I can't. We're all settled in for the night. I'm in my PJs." When I don't say anything she adds, "What's wrong?"

What can I tell her? What can I say? My chest aches. I'm raw with feelings I usually keep on lockdown. I wipe my face again.

"Wait. Are you drunk?" she asks.

"What? No, I'm not drunk."

"Are you in trouble?"

"No. I just...I want to see you."

She hesitates. The bus stops at a red light. That's when it dawns on me. Why am I dragging her into this mess? She deserves better than this—better than me.

"You know what?" I try to make my voice lighter. Less weak. "I'm sorry. I didn't realize how late it was."

"Where are you?"

"Don't worry about it. I'll call you tomorrow, okay?"

"But—"

"Good night, Carmen."

I hang up, turn off the phone, and put it back in my pocket.

I stare out the window. The bus passes closed storefronts behind security cages and all-night taco joints.

My chest aches. I hate how I feel.

I want to get a buzz on. To be honest, I want to get trashed. Rafa's out of beer, but he might have something good lying around for me to light up.

Anything to get me out of my head tonight—I'll take it.

At the bus stop by the hospital, I get off and walk down the dark street to the gates of the community garden. I fish my keys out of my backpack. I'm turning the corner when I see it— Carmen's car, parked at the curb in front of the garden gates.

Her parking lights are on. In the darkness of the car, I spot the flare of her phone screen as she scrolls through it.

I walk up to the driver's-side window. She's wearing a ball cap, a hoodie, and pajama pants. She rolls down the window and turns on the dome light.

"Jesus, what happened to you?"

I forgot about my black eye. "Nothing," I say casually. "Just a little tune-up." I try to pretend that my heart isn't beating faster at the sight of her. "What are you doing here?"

She looks skeptical. "I was worried," she says. "You didn't sound so good. I tried calling you back but it went straight to voicemail. I took a chance that you might be here, but the gate was locked."

"So you were just going to wait out here all night?"

She shrugs. "Like I said. I was worried."

"What about your parents?"

"They think I'm in bed."

I crack a smile. "Oh, yeah? With who?"

She rolls her eyes and unlocks the doors. "Just get in."

Carmen drives up Soto Street. She turns the radio down low and switches from the news to an old-school station. "Whittier Boulevard" by Thee Midniters comes up from the speakers. Cruising in a beat-up Toyota, with Carmen by my side, I suddenly feel like the king of the boulevard.

"Where are we going?" I feel lighter than I have all day.

"Have you eaten?" she asks.

"No."

"Okay. Let's get food."

We cross the LA River. On the radio, Thee Midniters leads to Mary Wells, the Temptations, and Ralfi Pagan. Old ghosts ride in on the songs and swirl around me. My dad and his old homeboys, smoking and joking on the sidewalks. My granddad and his original gangsters, holding their corners in zoot suits with razor-sharp creases.

I look out the window and see Twin Towers. The county jail. How many homies do I know in there at this very moment? Probably a lot.

"Where are we going, anyway?" I ask.

"Be patient. You'll see."

We reach Union Station. When we turn onto Alameda I see where she's taking me.

"Oh my God. You serious?" I want to kiss her. I mean, even more than I usually want to.

"You said you missed it." With a little smile on her face, Carmen pulls into the half-empty parking lot of Philippe's.

While Carmen maneuvers the car into place, I take out my wallet on the sly and try to count my remaining money out without her seeing me. There's a ten, a five, and three ones. I jingle my pocket. Two dimes and a quarter. I push the thought away that this is the last money I've got until I find another job.

After Carmen parks, we enter the restaurant and shuffle over the sawdust-covered floor. My stomach growls louder—it's been years since I've had one of these sandwiches, and I can't wait. It's fifteen minutes until closing time. We get in line to order.

"So?" Carmen says as we wait.

"What?"

"What was it that you wanted to talk about? When you called me?"

Seeing Carmen, taking a drive, listening to music, and now smelling the scent of my favorite sandwich in all of Los Angeles have worked together to take me away from the anxiety I got after my meeting with Daisy. Carmen has driven away the dark shadow that's followed me all day. I don't want to call it back.

"Well?"

"To be honest, I wasn't planning on talking." I lift an eyebrow at her.

FOURTEEN

Carmen nods slowly. "So it's like that?"

"Like what?"

"You're going to make a joke to keep from being real with me?"

"What do you mean?"

Her voice gets edgier. The words come faster. She's annoyed. "You call me with your voice shaking. You hang up on me. I come see you and you've got a fucking black eye."

A couple customers turn to look at us. Carmen doesn't care. "Your face is all puffy," she continues. "Something is wrong, but you don't want to tell me what it is. Why not?"

I'll do anything to keep from answering these questions. I look down. Her pajama pants are pink with little pink flamingoes on them. "Did you really climb out of your bedroom window?" I ask quietly.

Her voice is pure acid. "No. I snuck out the back door."

I have to keep her talking to keep her from asking me more questions. I can't tell her about what happened in El Sereno. I can't tell her about my dad. "Let's save my drama for later. Right now I want to talk about you. What did you do today?" I put my arm around her shoulders and pull her in.

She sighs but leans against me.

"Tell me," I say.

"I called some friends," she says. "Asked around to see if there were any new restaurant openings in the area. I helped my mom clean the house. Then I went to the drugstore to pick up my dad's prescription. After that, Sal and Vanessa called me. They said they'd completed their business plan and wanted to set up a date to meet with my parents about leasing the bakery."

"Wait. What?"

Sal, Vanessa, and Carmen made a date for a meeting and didn't tell me? I was the one who brought them together, and they didn't think it was important for me to know about the meeting? I'm annoyed. It's an ugly feeling.

"So did you set up an appointment?" I ask.

"Yeah. Tomorrow. Sal and Vanessa are coming to my house."

"Why didn't you guys call me?"

It's a dumb thing to ask and both of us know it. Carmen looks at me with a puzzled expression on her face. "You know, if it goes through, the contract would be between your brother, his girlfriend, and my parents, right?"

We get closer to the front of the line. My emotions sag again, like helium balloons losing their air. A part of me wishes I had no feelings at all—especially today. Sal and Vanessa left me out of their meeting, and I feel like an outsider.

Carmen is studying my face. "For what it's worth," she says, "all I did was set up the meeting. I'm not part of the decision-making process either. My parents send me to take care of their business but when there are any real choices to be made, they take it right out of my hands. Like I can't be trusted. Like I didn't run one of the best kitchens in the entire city for three years. That means nothing to them."

Before I can say anything, it's our turn to order. When I ask for a plain French dip, Carmen looks at me funny and says, "I'll have two beef double dips with Swiss cheese. Side of coleslaw. Side of macaroni salad. A Coke, and a slice of blueberry pie."

The server in her old-fashioned uniform makes the sandwiches and packs them up to go. I'm mesmerized by her hands flying over the food as she prepares it for us. I hand over my portion of the bill and Carmen pays for the rest with her debit card.

We get back in the car and find a quiet side street in an industrial area of downtown. All the warehouses here are closed, so the sidewalks are empty. Carmen turns off the engine and turns up the radio again.

We get our grub on. That first bite is so good I chew it slowly to make the sandwich last.

"Good?" she asks.

"Better than sex," I say. I pause. "I mean, sex with other women. Not sex with you. It's not better than that. Not that I... have sex with other women. I mean, I have, but not recently."

She rolls her eyes again.

Time to change the subject again. "So. Chefs like this stuff?"

"I'm a chef, and I love it." She examines her French dip like a jeweler looking at a diamond. "A good sandwich is a beautiful thing, isn't it?"

I smile. "Tell me something. Why did you want to go off and become a chef anyway? Your parents had a business for you. Why didn't you just do that? Why didn't you just run the bakery?"

"I worked with them. I lived with them. I'm an only child, so they put a lot of pressure on me to take over. I love my parents, but I just got restless. I wanted to see the world, to see what else was possible." She takes a bite of her double dip. "I used to watch the Food Network when I was a kid. I've always wanted to be a chef, to have my own place."

This makes me smile. "Your own restaurant? Really? Would it be a fancy one, like Giacomo's?"

She grins back. "No. Nothing like that."

"Then what?"

"Mexican comfort food," she says. "I love to make family-style stuff. Stews, big pots that bubble away on the stove at home, smelling good." Her eyes get this happy, faraway look. "And after all this time, even though I was in denial, I still love to bake bread. Everything about it. The kneading, the rise, the magic. I love the way bread dough feels in my hands." She takes a drink of Coke and rubs her tummy. "You know what? I ordered too much. Can you finish this for me?" She offers me her sandwich. She's only taken two bites.

"Really? Are you sure?"

"Yeah."

I take it and dig in. "Have you told your parents about this? Your dream to have your own restaurant?"

She shrugs. "When I was a kid. They didn't take me seriously."

"But how about now?"

"I don't really bring it up. They have a lot on their minds right now." She looks away from me, as if I've gotten too close to a sore spot. I watch as she takes a bite of her coleslaw and pushes the container across the dashboard to me. "Oh man. My eyes are too big for my stomach. Can you finish this too? I don't want to throw it away."

I look at the coleslaw and back at her. She's sweet—much sweeter than she lets on. "You think you're so slick, don't you?" I say.

"What do you mean?"

"Buying all this food you weren't planning to eat."

"I don't know what you're talking about." She's smiling. "Just eat. Let's not waste it."

I lean over and kiss her cheek. "Tell me something. If you wanted to see the world, why did you move back home after you graduated?"

"Financial reasons. I wanted to pay off my student loans as quickly as I could—culinary school wasn't cheap. By saving on rent, and working in Los Angeles where wages are a little higher, I paid off as much as I could. Still have a ways to go, though. That's when I can think about starting my own business." She takes another sip of the Coke. "Living at home—it's not an ideal situation. But my parents have been generous enough to let me stay."

I take this opportunity to dive deeper. "What about a social life?" I ask. "What about...boyfriends?" I try not to sound creepy. I fail. I totally sound creepy.

Carmen plays with the ring on her Coke can. "I've had a couple since I got back. Didn't work out."

"Were they assholes?" I ask hopefully.

"Not really."

"Did you break up with them because you're married to your job?"

"Ew, no. It was never like that." She makes a face at me. "I work a lot, sure, but for the right guy, I can make time."

Like a starving man, I polish off all of the food. I gather up the trash, then walk it out to the trash can by an empty bus stop. I return to the car, feeling full and happy. We're still alone on the street.

"Do you have to get home?" I ask. "Sneak back in?"

She shakes her head. "They're asleep now."

We put the seats back. Carmen turns off the dome light and opens the sunroof. Even though it's cold and there are no stars to see tonight, it feels good to look up. The sky is big, dark, and endless.

After a long time, I say, "You said for the right guy, you could make time."

"Yeah. I could—I can."

I'm hot and cold. I hold my breath and shoot my shot. "How about me? Can you make time for me?"

When Carmen doesn't answer me, I look over at her. She's staring up at the sky.

Goddamn.

She's beautiful.

I used to be angry at fate. When I was younger, fate piled problem after problem on me until I thought my life was some kind of practical joke. I responded with recklessness. I just stopped caring what happened to me. If the universe didn't care about me, why should I?

But things have changed.

I'm not angry at fate right now. Fate brought Carmen into my life right after I got out of prison. Fate brought her back to me. Like lightning struck me twice.

Not only has Carmen fed me without making a big deal of it, she's snuck out of her parents' house for me. Me—an ex-con with absolutely nothing to offer her. Nothing to give.

"Tell me something," I say. "You have your shit together. You're a good girl. School, career, big dreams. Why are you fucking around with me?"

"I told you. When I saw you in the garden, I wanted to prove to myself that I could do it."

"There's more to it than that. You were upset that morning. You still haven't told me why."

She snaps the ring off the empty Coke can and drops it inside like a coin in a piggy bank.

"You can tell me," I say.

"The morning you got out," she says slowly, "was the morning after my dad got beat up."

I blink. Shit. That makes sense.

"I'd been at the hospital all night with my mom," Carmen says. "She made me go to work. She said it would be good for my head. So I did. I went on the produce run. I stopped at Rafa's garden. I was a wreck, just trying to pull myself together. That's when I spotted you."

"Did you recognize me?" I ask.

She snorts. "I don't forget a face. Unlike you."

I smile. "So, I wasn't a stranger to you."

"No," she says. "Your brother was back in the neighborhood. The *chismosas* were gossiping about how you would be out soon too." She looks at me. "You weren't—you aren't—a stranger to me, Eddie. I know who you are."

I put my hand on hers. I trace her long, hard fingers and the faint burn marks on the back of her hand—the scars of a chef.

"I was an emotional mess that morning," she says. "I was tired. I was angry. And you were the perfect distraction. That's all there is to it."

"A distraction? That's all I was to you?"

She starts to pull her hand away. "Every time I think about that garden—"

"Forget the garden for a second," I say, holding her hand tight. "Now. Why are you here right now?"

She's quiet for a long time.

"I'm not sure," she says at last.

What do I want—what do I need—to hear from her?

Let's be real. I have no right to desire anything. I'm lucky to be in her company. My heart is so hungry for nice words that I forget for a moment, just a moment, what the rest of me is hungry for.

On the radio, "Tell It Like It Is" by Aaron Neville rises up, slow and sexy.

She's not sure why she's here with me.

Time to make her sure.

Gently, I take off her ball cap and throw it into the back seat. I lean over the center console, put my hands lightly on her cheeks, and stroke her smooth skin. I look at her face in the dark. I imagine the shape of her beautiful eyes, the shape of her nose. I can feel her warm, soft breath on my hand as I touch her.

"Is this okay?" I ask.

She whispers, "Yes."

I lower my lips until there's a millimeter between us, the thickness of a piece of paper. I'm as close to her as I can get without actually kissing her. Tremors of anticipation run through me, turning my spine into a fault line.

"Put your seat down as far as it will go," I whisper.

She pulls the lever and slides back. I lower the zipper of her hoodie. She's trying to stay calm, but her chest is rising and falling like she's running a race. My lips stay close to hers, but we're still not touching. I slide my hand under her T-shirt. She's not wearing a bra.

We're in a desolate part of the city. No one will sneak up on us here. The street lamps above us don't work—broken by hoodlums or burnt out from neglect.

In the dark, I can feel Carmen's beautiful eyes staring at me. I imagine her pupils are huge, trying to drink in as much light as they can.

"Lift up your hips," I whisper.

She does it. Gently, I pull down her pajama pants and panties until they're down around her shins. I don't take them off all the way—we need to get dressed in a flash if someone sees us.

In the darkness, as slowly as I can, I slide my hand over her hip, along the side of her torso, and around the curve of her right breast. When I cup her in my hand, she whimpers. I massage her, and her skin burns like fire beneath my fingers. I brush the sensitive tip with my thumb. Her nipple hardens.

"Eddie."

At last, I kiss her lips. She tastes sweet, like her Coke. Kissing her feels like taking a hit of a strong narcotic. She enters my bloodstream. Pure pleasure flows from her, slides into my body, and takes hold. We kiss until the kissing takes over. We kiss until we're nothing but two drowning people pulling at each other's clothes, gasping for air.

"Do you want me?" I whisper against her lips.

"Yes," she says.

"Is that why you came out to see me tonight? Because you wanted me?"

"No, I came out because I was worried about you."

"I'm a hardass, Carmen. I can take care of myself."

"I don't think you're as hard as you pretend you are."

If there is anything left inside me that can be called a gentleman, it leaves at this very moment. It flies out the window back over the river where I'll catch up with it again later, after Carmen and I do the kind of shit you don't even confess to your priest.

"Baby girl, I'm not pretending." I take her hand and rest it on my dick.

FIFTEEN

She undoes my belt and zipper and slides her hand into my underwear. When she curls her long fingers around my cock, I melt into the seat.

Suddenly, a little light fills the car. I look up. Above, I see the moon. It's shaped like a strange round teardrop, and it lights the broken leftovers of clouds beneath it. The clouds look like fingerprints on glass.

The clouds—that's where I'm floating while Carmen strokes me.

I touch her dark hair. It's so soft. "The last time we played this game, we both got in a lot of trouble for it."

"Don't talk about that right now," she says.

"Why not? It's true." I smile in the dark. "The last time, you went down on me so good, I almost came in your mouth. Right there, at your job." I pause, trying to slow down my breathing. "Why? Why would you break all the rules to do that with someone like me?"

"Because," she says, "you're different. The rules don't apply."

Okay, now fate is fucking with me.

I take my heart and shove it behind my rib cage. My chest tightens. I know exactly what's happening—my emotions are gearing up to do something extremely stupid, like fall in love. I blink. To distract myself from this line of thought, I turn toward her and say something raunchy.

"Are you wet, baby girl?"

Carmen likes dirty talk. I know this because she whispers, "Yes."

I slide my chair back. "Come here," I tell her. "Face the windshield."

Carefully, she climbs over the gear shift and sits on my lap in reverse cowgirl. I reach under her T-shirt and stroke her smooth, hot back with my fingertips.

"Bend forward," I say.

As she balances there, I pull the condom out of the pocket of my backpack, rip it open, and slide it on. When I'm fully covered, I take my shaft in my hand and swipe the head of my cock against the crack of her ass, back and forth. I press against her pussy. Soft. Hot. Her head rolls forward and she moans, so I do it again and again until she's so wet, I can feel her dripping down over my fingers like hot wax from a candle.

"Do you even know how sexy you are?" I sit up. "Use me, Carmen. Use my dick to get off."

She reaches between her legs and takes my dick. She works it gently into her pussy. In the shadows, the fit is tight and perfect. Her muscles stretch around the crown. When she squeezes, we hear her slick muscles tighten, and we both moan, turned on by the sound.

In the tiny space, she balances by holding on to the "oh shit" handle above the passenger side door. One hand grips the handle and the other balances on my hip. She slides up and down my dick, jacking me off with her tight pussy until I can hardly breathe. Still, I hold back. When she sinks down lower, I groan.

"Do you like this?" she whispers. "Do you like fucking me in the car?"

I kiss the back of her shoulder. "Yes, baby girl. You're doing so good."

I reach forward and slide my fingers through the wetness that's pooled at the base of my cock. This girl is driving me crazy. She's gorgeous and eager and as horny as I am. I didn't think women like her existed, much less wanted anything to do with me.

When my fingers are lubed up, I reach for her clit. It's swollen and hungry for attention.

With the softest touch, I glide the tip of my middle finger in a tiny circle where her clit rises to meet me. Carmen freezes, then clenches up, crushing my dick. My balls tighten. I take two hard breaths and get myself under control again.

"It's too much," she whimpers. "I'm too sensitive."

I know she doesn't want me to baby her. "Ride me," I say. "Make that hungry little pussy come."

She balances her hands flat on the dashboard and slides herself down my dick a little more. She pulls herself up and glides down again, resting deeper and deeper each time. Soon my fingers are swimming, and her slick little clit swells like a tiny stone against my fingers.

"You're too big."

"Fuck yeah. Say that again."

"You're too big. I can't take all of you."

"We both know you can."

As if all she needed was encouragement, she slams down hard, taking every last thick inch inside her. Fever blazes inside me, lighting up every nerve in my body. Sweat drips down my temples. She's sweating too. Her skin is slick.

Each time Carmen slams down on me, I have to fight back. Warm come swirls in my balls. I force it to stay down. I want this girl to come, and I want her to come hard. I want to see her shaking, her mind blown from how good it feels to be with me. I want her to feel about me the way I feel about her—amazed.

She arches her back. Her moans turn to grunts. Her thighs slap mine and now she's taking us home, both of us, at a hard gallop. I stroke her faster and she whimpers as I build the orgasm inside her, teasing it out, torturing her.

"Baby girl, do you like this?" I gasp. "Tell the truth."

"Yes."

"You like being bad, don't you? You like breaking the rules with me. It turns you on."

"Yes."

"Why are you like this, Carmen? Why do you have to be bad to come so hard?"

With my other hand, I give her tight little ass cheek a quick spank, grab the flesh in my hand, and squeeze. Between her legs, she's drenched. Gently, I slide my thumb over the tiny, slick star of her ass. She clenches me even harder. While she grinds down, I stroke her clit and her ass at the same time. Even though I'm barely touching her, my gentleness is pulling out the wildness in her. It's driving her crazy, the way I can control her body like this. The way I hold her climax just out of her reach.

"Eddie," she says. "Please. Make me come."

"I will. When I'm ready."

"Oh, fuck. Please." She lets go of the dashboard and starts to play with her tits. I wish I could see her, her shirt tucked up under her chin, her pretty hands pinching those hard brown nipples. My balls twitch, threatening to blow. I throw my head back, close my eyes, and wrestle my orgasm down. It paces back and forth inside me like an animal in a cage.

I brace my feet on the floor and push my shoulder blades into the car seat. I grab her hips in my hands and pin her in place. I thrust hard, my dick high and deep. She makes a surprised little sound halfway between a gasp and a sigh. I begin to fuck her like this, from below.

"Play with yourself," I growl. "Come all over me."

I can feel her fingers as she rubs herself. Her pussy is blazing hot. I speed up my thrusts. The friction builds even more heat. We're going to melt the condom. We're going to fuck right through it.

That's when I feel it—a ripple of muscle inside her, deep and quick. She freezes.

"Eddie," she whispers. "Oh God. Oh, fuck."

The orgasm whips through her. When she arches her back, she pushes her sweet ass against me and crushes my dick in her cunt. I feel the contractions, sharp and powerful, and the extreme pleasure I feel is balanced out with pride—I gave this to her. I'm making her come like this.

When she's finished, she slides off.

Shaking, I move her body until she's sitting on the passenger seat and I'm facing her. Dazed on sex, she pulls off her pajama pants completely and braces her feet on the dashboard. She puts her legs on either side of me and spreads them apart, nice and wide. In the dark, I can smell her pussy, wild and sweet. My dick points straight up, aching to be back inside her.

Now I can see her beautiful face. I kiss her neck, tasting the sweat on her skin. I suck on her nipples and squeeze her breasts in my big hands. When I lean forward and kiss her lips, I pin her arms to the seat, and move my hips until the head of my dick rests in the dip of her hot, swollen cunt.

Our kisses are hungry. Her little tongue in my mouth drives me wild. I break the kiss and grip her arms tighter.

"Yes, like that," she moans. "Be rough."

I rest my forehead against hers, take a deep breath, and thrust into her as hard as I can. She howls and for a moment I'm terrified I've hurt her. She's tight. I'm big. I should be more careful.

I'm about to apologize when she whispers in my ear, "Perfect."

For a moment, the word swirls around in my brain. Months have passed since we slept together. I know now I'm not crazy. My mind didn't play tricks on me. Being locked up didn't warp my sense of pleasure, and my memory is good, not bad.

I was right.

That morning with Carmen was the best sex I'd ever had.

Until tonight.

Heat licks up my arms and legs and gathers at the center of my body. I'm so hard, I ache. Struggling for air, I pull out halfway and thrust again. Pleasure blazes in every cell in my body.

"Trouble," she whispers.

"Say my name." I kiss her once more. "My real name."

"Eddie."

I thrust again—five times. Ten times. A dozen. I let go of her arms and brace myself above her. I place one hand lightly on her neck and stroke her throat with my thumb. I kiss her as gently as I can. But below the belt, I'm fucking her like a machine, stretching her sweet pussy to its limit around me.

She slides a hand between us and strums at her clit. I dip my head, suck one of her nipples into my mouth, and twirl the tip of my tongue against it.

Her second orgasm grabs her so suddenly, she screams. The

sound pulls me over the edge. For a moment, I can't breathe. I release her nipple and shut my eyes tight.

When it hits me at last, every muscle in my body locks up. Neck, back, shoulders, legs. It drowns me. I fight back and fuck her through my climax, pulling the last drops of pleasure from both of our bodies until there is nothing left.

Through it all, Carmen strokes my arms and chest. Her hands are cool against my hot skin. I collapse on top of her, and she embraces me, running her fingertips up and down my back.

When I can breathe again, I kiss her temple.

"Come home with me," I whisper. My voice is broken. "Please. Just come home with me."

She looks into my eyes. Darkness in the darkness.

"Okay."

ON THE FLOOR of Rafa's living room, I spoon Carmen close. She's back in her pajamas. I'm dressed in boxers, even though I don't want to be. We're cuddling between two thick blankets. Her soft, sweet ass nestles against my dick and before long, I'm hard again. I'm feeling warm and happy and to be honest, pretty proud of my dick.

Carmen says something.

"What, baby girl?" I say.

"I said tomorrow at the meeting with my parents, Sal and Vanessa are going to present their business plan and ask to rent the bakery. But I've been wondering..."

"Yeah?"

"Vanessa has a daughter and a full-time job. Sal won't be able to be at the taproom all the time—he's working and going to school. It's going to be hard for them."

I yawn. "Yeah, I was wondering about that too."

"A lot of taprooms in LA are only open on weekends. But even then, lots needs to get done during the week. At first, construction. Meetings with inspectors. Setting up. Receiving orders. And deliveries—those still need to happen."

"I can help them with the other stuff, but I don't have a driver's license."

"Yes, but I do."

"What are you saying?" My voice slurs. I'm warm and high, here with her in my arms.

"I could help you guys out."

This surprises me. "What about finding another restaurant job? I thought that's what you wanted."

"I still want that. But I can help you guys out until I get hired somewhere else."

We're hooking up. It's good. We're getting along. But something doesn't add up to me. "Why? Why do you want to get involved in this?"

She strokes my arms where they're locked around her. "I can be of use. I have experience with the day-to-day requirements of operating a business."

"You do," I say. "Between you and Vanessa, you have the experience and the knowledge to make this work." I'm quiet for a second. I'm not a businessman, but I know numbers. "It'll be a long time before Eastside Beer can sustain itself. You have to know that at the very best, they'd be able to pay you minimum wage."

"Yeah. I know."

"So really, why do you want to do this?"

She sighs softly. "It's going to sound cheesy."

"Just tell me."

"Don't laugh."

"I won't. I promise."

"Part of me wants to work in this community again."

"That's not cheesy. Do you miss working at the bakery?"

"Maybe. A little. I don't know." She pauses, her brain working. "You remember what our kitchen at Giacomo's looked like, right?"

"Yeah."

"Three-quarters of Chef Moretti's kitchen staff is Mexican or Mexican-American. I've worked in kitchens where the entire staff in the back of the house was brown and the entire front of the house was white. All the restaurant owners I've worked for have been white. But brown hands made that food. Brown hands built those businesses, built that value." She strokes my hand where it rests on her tummy. "I hated working in the bakery when I was young because I wanted an escape. An adventure. What I didn't appreciate at the time was that my family owned and operated the bakery for generations. Now I've been out in the world, I can see what an accomplishment that was."

"So why not just take over the bakery?"

She shakes her head. "It wouldn't be sustainable. The neighborhood is changing. The newcomers won't have the context to appreciate La Golondrina the way the old-school families did. The new residents—they'll want gluten-free cupcakes, not *bolillos*."

"That's a tragedy," I add. "*Bolillos* are delicious. The more gluten the better."

"But you know what both the old-school families and the newcomers will appreciate? A brewery. Your brother's brewery. A place to grab a beer and relax."

I'm slowly waking up to the things Carmen is telling me. "What keeps us from being just another hipster business? Just another sign of gentrification?" I ask. "Sal took me to the brewery in Santa Monica where he makes his beer. It was hipster central. Lots of money. Plus, old neighborhoods like

Hollenbeck—they've always been suspicious of change. The residents will accuse us of being sellouts. *Pinches vendidos.*"

"Maybe," she says. "But I'm guessing most of them won't. They know this is our neighborhood, Eddie. It always was."

I kiss the top of her head. She's right. The Centeno family has operated La Golondrina for three generations. The Rosas family has been banging in Hollenbeck for three generations too.

"You're right." I say. "This is our neighborhood."

"For what it's worth, we're royalty here," she whispers.

Carmen's ponytail has come loose. I slide off the elastic and run my fingers through her cool, smooth hair. I'm awake now, and so is my body. She turns around to face me.

"Royalty, huh?" I whisper.

"Yes."

"Come here, *mi reina.*"

One kiss turns to two, five, ten. Soon my boxers are off. Her T-shirt disappears next. Now her pajama pants. Now her panties.

Under the blanket, I feast on her body. Her nipples are sweet and tender between my lips. Between her legs, the intoxicating smell of her pussy fills my senses, and I lose myself in pleasing her. I lick up and down her swollen lips. I dip the tip of my tongue inside her to lap up her sweetness. When I've had my fill, I suck on her clit until she opens to me. I press a finger into her and she grips me, pulling me deep.

She's silent. I measure her pleasure by the speed of her breaths and the temperature of her skin against mine. When I lick her to the edge of her climax, she grips the blankets in her fists and arches her back off the floor. Quickly, I slide a second finger into her and fuck her in time with the strokes of my tongue. She comes for the third time tonight, her legs locked around my shoulders, her pussy soaking my face and beard.

In that moment, she's a queen, and I'm the king who serves her.

Royalty—that's what she called us.

I roll another condom on.

"I need you," she whispers. She grabs me and puts me inside her. "Eddie, I need you."

SIXTEEN

Carmen shakes me.

"Hey. Wake up!"

I open my eyes. I'm buck naked on the floor of Rafa's trailer. The windows are open. Bright sunshine fills the living room. I blink and look around. Rafa's nowhere to be seen. Carmen is dressed in her pajamas and she's pulling on her sneakers like the trailer's on fire.

I reach for my phone to check the time. It's dead—I forgot to plug it in last night. Next to a tangle of blankets and pillows, I spot three condom wrappers. Despite last night's marathon, I've got serious morning wood, and it's pointing straight at her.

"What time is it?" I'm half-awake.

"It's noon."

"What?"

"We're late for the meeting. It started at eleven thirty. I was supposed to introduce Sal and Vanessa to my parents. Oh, Jesus. My mom's gonna kill me." She tosses my boxers at me. I catch them and slip them on over my aching hard-on. "We both forgot to set an alarm last night."

Last night. The memories rush back to me. In spite of her

panic, she is beautiful in the bright sunlight. I can see her nipples through her T-shirt. No bra. I stand up and try to take Carmen in my arms, but Chef Centeno slaps me away.

"Are you crazy?" she hollers. "We have to go now."

"Jesus! Okay, okay."

I take a piss behind the trailer—Rafa said not to do this, but I'm pressed for time. Quickly, I wash my hands and face and brush my teeth with water from the garden hose. I get dressed and hop in the car just as Carmen screeches off.

On the road, Carmen freaks out even though I try to calm her down. I tell her my brother Sal is anal-retentive, so they probably arrived early and introduced themselves without her, no problem. I tell her not to worry, because Vanessa is a businessperson who knows exactly what she's talking about. Her parents will recognize that. I tell her to relax because Sal and Vanessa probably brought a selection of beer with them. They'll probably all be drunk by the time we arrive. The worst case scenario I imagine is nothing like the one that's playing out inside her head. Nothing I say seems to make a difference.

"You don't know my mom," she says again and again.

She and her parents live in a nice small stucco bungalow with a neat lawn and those tropical flowers that look like birds' heads. We walk up the driveway, and she tries to comb her hair where it escapes from under the ball cap. She folds her arms over her chest—no bra under her T-shirt. She's still wearing her flamingo pajama pants. We couldn't find her panties in the living room—I think they're under Rafa's couch. Her lips are swollen. There's a small hickey on her neck just under her ear.

Anyone can see she's been up to no good.

And I'm the cat who's dragging her in.

With a sigh, I check out my reflection in the front window as she unlocks the door. My black eye looks worse today than yesterday. I take in the tattoos, shaggy beard, and messy hair.

Carmen's right to be nervous. Not only is she bringing home a gangster ex-con, I look the part.

We enter the living room and Carmen closes the door behind us. Connected to the living room is the dining room. Papers are spread out on the table. Sitting there are my brother Sal and Vanessa, both of them looking clean and professional. Sal's eyes meet mine. His face is serious but I know he's laughing at me on the inside. I keep my expression frozen to keep from cracking up.

Sal and Vanessa sit at the table with Carmen's parents. I remember her father from the bakery. Slim was always a chubby guy—someone gave him that nickname when he was a kid, and it stuck.

"Eduardo," he says. "Hello. Long time no see."

When he stands up to shake my hand, I notice he's using a metal cane. He's dressed in khakis and a polo shirt. His hair is combed neatly. But something is wrong with his eyes—he looks past me, not at me, and I'm reminded that Carmen said after his beating he wasn't the same man as he was before.

Slim takes his seat again. I turn to Carmen's mother, but she's not paying any attention to me. She's sitting straight as a crowbar in her chair. She's tall and slender like Carmen, but her hair is slicked into a bun and her face is pulled back just as tight. She's wearing a sleeveless navy-blue dress and pearl earrings. She's staring at her daughter with murder in her eyes, taking in the wrinkled clothes and messy hair. Her jaw is squared and her bottom lip sticks out, like a boxer with a mouthguard.

"There you are, Carmen." Her voice is ice. "Your father and I have been waiting for you all morning."

I look at Carmen. She seems to shrink into herself. It's strange to see her this way. I don't like it.

"Excuse me," Carmen says to everyone at the table. "I'm sorry I'm late. I'll join you in a minute."

She turns and walks into the hallway. Sal glances at me and tips his head slightly toward the empty chair next to him. I sit down.

"Where were we?" Vanessa says. "I believe we were discussing the lease term?"

As Vanessa organizes the notes in front of her, I notice Carmen's mother has turned her attention on me. Anger—that was the emotion she showed Carmen. For me, she has nothing but disgust. When Vanessa and Slim start talking about the monthly rent, Carmen's mom tips her head back slightly and looks down her nose at my tattoos, my beard.

I keep still. It's obvious what she's thinking—I'm the piece of shit who's ruining her daughter's life.

A part of me wants to blurt out, *She's not a child—she's a grown-ass woman.* I smile to myself. *Yeah, your daughter's a grown-ass woman who gave it up to me three times last night.*

Carmen's mom's eyes flash as if she can read my mind too.

"Excuse me," she says suddenly.

Vanessa and Slim look up as the woman stands up, walks down the hall, opens a bedroom door, and slams it behind her. I can hear the muffled voices of Carmen and her mother as they argue, their anger soaking through the plaster walls.

Slim shakes his head and looks at us apologetically. "I am sorry about this. My wife—she has been on edge all morning. Forgive us." He shuffles the papers. "I can see you have done all of your homework, Ms. Velasco. Can I keep these and look them over?" He gestures vaguely with his hand. "I need a little more time to understand everything. The old brain—it's a little slower now."

"Of course." Vanessa puts everything in a folder and hands it to Slim. "Take all the time you need. I've written my cell phone number on the back of my business card. It's inside the folder. Call me if you have any questions."

As usual, Sal is quiet—when it comes to negotiations or business of any kind, he lets Vanessa take the wheel. It's wise—she's a smart cookie.

The door to the bedroom opens and Carmen and her mother appear in the hallway. Carmen has combed her hair. She's wearing a skirt, a sweater, and sandals. I've never seen her in clothes like this—she looks like her mother has dressed her. Her eyes are puffy, like she's cried and wiped her tears quickly away.

Vanessa glances at me and Sal and quickly zips up her briefcase. She stands up. Her voice is calm. "Mrs. Centeno, it was a pleasure to meet you. Thank you for sitting down with Sal and me to discuss this. I've left all of the paperwork with your husband so that you can both look everything over on your own."

Slim walks us slowly to the front door and shakes our hands. Carmen stands behind her mother like a shadow, avoiding eye contact with me.

"Any questions, please ask," Vanessa says again as we stand on the doorstep. "When you've made your decision, if you think you'd like to work with us, please call me. I'll contact a third-party broker to draft the lease agreement."

I walk down the driveway behind my brother. I climb into the back seat of Vanessa's car and look out the window. I see a slice of Carmen's face just for a moment before her father shuts the door.

I let out a deep breath. One motherfucker of a headache is rising behind my eyes. "Did we—did I—just screw that up for you guys?"

Vanessa lowers her sunglasses and glances at me in the rearview mirror. "We made most of our points before you two arrived, so I think we're okay."

"Jesus." Sal shakes his head. "Mrs. Centeno looked like she wanted to rip your head off and eat it."

I run my fingers through my messy hair. "Carmen's twenty-five years old. Why does her mom treat her like that?"

"Traditional household," Vanessa says. "When you're a daughter, that's just the way things are. If you live at home, they'll treat you like a little girl until you get married, end of story. She's an only child too. They're probably extra hard on her."

Sal and Vanessa drop me off at the garden. I want to crash, but watching Rafa work in the garden makes me feel lazy. I clean the trailer. I vacuum, dust, and sweep. I find Carmen's blue lace panties under the sofa. I put them in my pocket like a classic pervert. I take all the laundry in the trailer to the Laundromat a couple blocks away. No one else is there, so I stay quiet with my thoughts as I wash and fold.

Rafa makes us an *ensalada de nopales* for dinner. He also hands me a weird concoction of juices made with beets and carrots that makes my mouth look like a vampire.

"Drink it all."

"But it's gross."

"Be quiet." He chuckles to himself. "She'll thank me later."

"Who?" I ask.

"You know who."

I wash the dishes while Rafa puts on his hat and jacket.

"Where are you going?" I ask.

"To see my *compadre.*" He means his pot-growing partner in Hacienda Heights. "I'm going to be gone all night." He laughs a little. "Call your lady over. Have at it, *mi'jo.*"

After Rafa leaves, I wait until dark. I watch TV, but nothing holds my interest. I take out my phone and stare at it.

Carmen and I were together all night. You'd think I'd be

satisfied, that I'd need a break, but the opposite is true. My hunger is double, triple what it was before.

I'm sitting on the sofa in the dark, alone. I look around the living room. My hand rests on the armrest of the sofa where she bent over as I took her from behind. I look down at the carpet. That's where she lay on her back with her long legs wide open, her hands gripping my hair as she came.

As soon as the sun goes down, I call her. I listen to my own breathing as the phone rings. I'm already hard.

"Hey," I say when she picks up.

"Hey."

She sighs. I want to kiss her and swallow the sigh.

"Are you alone?" I ask.

"Yeah, I'm in my room." Her voice is tired and a little ragged.

"Is everything okay? With your mom?"

"Yeah. It's fine." When I don't say anything, she adds, "Listen, don't worry about me. I'm used to it. I'm okay."

I don't believe she's okay, but I know a way to make her feel better. "Can you come out and see me? Rafa's gone. All night."

"I can't. They took my keys."

"What? Really?"

"I know. They changed the alarm code too. If I leave the house the alarm will go off."

She's on lockdown. I adjust my dick in my pants. "Jesus. Is that even legal?"

"I don't know."

"Will the alarm go off if I come in?"

"Pretty sure it will."

"What's a little breaking and entering?" I say. She laughs softly. I want to kiss her so bad my chest aches. "So, what are you wearing?"

She snorts. "Are you serious?"

"Tell me."

"Um, a T-shirt. And panties."

Goddamn. "Are you in bed?"

"Yeah. Under the covers."

"I wish I were there with you."

She's quiet for a little while. What is she thinking? "I wish you were here too," she says.

I turn off the TV. "I can be, if that's what you want."

"What do you mean?"

I turn off the lamp. "Want to try something with me?"

"What?"

"Go lock your door."

"Lock my door? Why?"

"Trust me."

I hear her footsteps and a click. "Okay."

"Is it dark in your room?" I ask.

"I've got a little nightlight on."

"Turn it off."

"What? Why?"

I undo my shorts and take my dick out. The cool air hits my skin. I run my palm gently down the shaft and over the head. It jerks, getting harder. "No questions, Carmen."

On the other end of the line, I hear another click. "Okay."

"Which hand is holding your phone?"

"My left hand."

"With your right hand, I want you to touch yourself."

She pauses for a moment. "How?" Her voice is so soft. She wants me to take care of her.

Five years—that's how long I was locked up. Over time, I learned how to live without sex. But sometimes, my body wouldn't listen to me. The urge to fuck would overcome me like a demonic possession.

Inside, some inmates found relief—and sometimes love—in

each other. Others, the predators, forced themselves on their victims. Because of my gang affiliation, I was lucky. I was never assaulted. But the loneliness—that was mine to face.

I masturbated twice, sometimes three times a day. I survived by living inside my head, by diving into whatever romance novels I could get my hands on, by creating fantasies so real they held me tight all those long, long years when I was alone.

"Okay, baby girl," I whisper. "Listen carefully."

SEVENTEEN

"After we slept together for the first time," I say, "I would dream of you. I would dream of that long black hair. So straight and beautiful." I take a deep breath. Like a ghost in the memory of my senses, the smell of her fills my lungs. "Undo your hair for me, Carmen. Make it loose."

I hear the phone rustle against the bedsheets. Against her hair.

"Now run your hand over it. Imagine that's my hand. Touch your hair like you're touching it for the first time. You've never touched anything so soft in your entire life. How does it feel?"

"Slippery," she whispers. "Cold."

"Why is it cold?"

"I washed it and it's not completely dry yet."

"Comb your fingers through it."

I let a few seconds pass as she strokes her fingers through her hair.

"Imagine I'm sitting on a couch and you're sitting on the floor. You're resting your head against my knee. And I'm petting your head. My sweet, beautiful girl. My good girl." I pause. My cock twitches and gets thicker. I give it a stroke. "Are you imagining it?"

"Yes."

"Does that picture turn you on?"

"Yes."

I lean back on the sofa and slide my hips forward. I'm fully hard. My cock lifts off my abs. Gently, I grasp it and slowly jack off the first few inches, back and forth.

"Your door is locked, right, baby girl?" I ask.

"Yes."

"Take off your T-shirt and drop it on the floor. Lie back down on your bed. On top of the covers."

She does it.

"Imagine you're here in the trailer with me," I say. "Now you're lying on the floor in front of me, where you were last night. Run your hand over your throat. Slide it down the center of your body, between your tits. Down your stomach. Now back up again—but slowly. So slowly. Let me watch you touch your skin. Let me feel it."

I let the quiet spread out between us. I imagine her long, brown body on the floor in front of me, beautiful and smooth. I imagine her breast brushing her forearm as she touches herself. "How do you feel?"

"Good." She pauses. "Cold."

I grip my dick harder. I want to run my tongue over the goosebumps I imagine on her skin. "I'm in front of you, looking down on you. Will you put on a little show for me?"

"Yes," she whispers. She's breathing a little faster.

"Slide your hand down over your panties. Rub yourself, slowly, up and down, over the fabric." I wait. I strain to listen, but all I can hear are her soft breaths. "What do you feel as you touch yourself, baby girl?"

Her words come slowly. She likes my dirty talk, but she

doesn't feel comfortable talking back. "Lace. It's rough. Underneath that, I'm soft."

"What's soft?"

I hear her lick her lips. "My body."

"Use the word, Carmen. Say it."

Her voice is barely a whisper. "My pussy."

"Good girl." I smile to myself. "I can imagine it. The soft mound of your pussy—that's under the palm of your hand. Press down on it. Press the flesh against the bone. Fuck. I can imagine how it feels, Carmen. So good. Your fingers rest against your pussy lips, don't they? I can see everything. Your middle finger rests against your pretty little clit. It's getting harder and harder. I'm not even there and your pretty pussy is aching for me—keep rubbing. Don't stop."

Quietly, in the dark, I jack off slowly. A minute passes as we touch ourselves, alone in our rooms, linked only by our phones and the same desperate thirst that makes my cock hard and her pussy wet.

A drop of precome forms on the tip of my dick. I swipe it away with my thumb and lick it off. Sweet. Familiar. I wish I could put that taste in her mouth.

"I'm watching you. From where I'm sitting on the sofa. You're my beautiful girl. So sweet and dirty and perfect. Lying there on the floor, putting on a show just for me," I say. "Now open your legs. Nice and wide. Keep rubbing yourself. Make the fabric wet. I want it dripping."

As she touches herself, I pull her panties from my pocket. I close my eyes and hold them against my face. I breathe in. Her scent fills my lungs. Blood pounds through my body. My dick stands straight up, electrified by the candy-sweet, narcotic scent of her cunt. With her panties in my fist, I grab my dick and jack myself off harder. The lace is rough against my skin. I tighten my grip. Pleasure shoots through me like fire.

"Slip your fingers underneath the panties." My voice is hard. There's an edge to it now that my orgasm is in clear sight. "Now slowly stroke those swollen little lips. Up and down. So wet. So perfect. Tell me, Carmen. Tell me you were made to be fucked. Say it."

Her voice shakes. I can hear her panting. "I was made to be fucked."

"Say it again. Say my name."

"I was made to be fucked, Eddie."

"Say you were made to be fucked by me."

"I was made to be fucked by you, Eddie."

My jaw tightens. An orgasm threatens to rip through me but I put a strangle-hold on my dick and push my release back down. My stomach clenches. It hurts—physically hurts—to deny myself. But I do it, because pain tastes good with pleasure.

"Take off your panties," I grunt. "Open your legs as wide as they go. Show me everything, baby girl."

I hear the rustling of bed sheets and cloth. I hear her throw herself back down on the bed. She picks up the phone and waits for her next instructions. I listen to her breathing, quick and soft, and I swear I can feel it against my skin.

"Are you doing it?"

"Yes," she says.

"I know how wet you get. I know how much your pussy likes my dick. Put your fingertips against that little opening. Feel how wet you are."

I jack off as she does it, clenching my abs whenever I get too close to the edge of my orgasm.

"Are your fingers wet?"

"Yes."

"Are you aching? Are you aching for me the way I'm aching for you?"

"Yes, Eddie."

Hijole. "Tuck the phone against your ear," I say. "While your wet fingers play with your clit, I want you to slide one finger deep inside that tight pussy for me. Will you do that for me, Carmen?"

"Y-Yes."

"Do it now."

She's silent. I imagine her long fingers working away at her pussy, plunging deep and massaging her pink clit as she gets wetter and wetter.

"How does it feel?" I say.

"Tight."

I fling her panties away and wrap my aching dick in my rough, familiar fist. I grip myself without mercy, imagining how tight she feels around me.

"Put a second finger inside." My voice is shot, deep and ragged. "Fuck yourself hard. As you stretch your pussy, I want you to grip your fingers back. Push and pull." I take a breath. "Make it hurt a little, baby girl. Just like it does when we're together."

A few seconds pass. My ears strain to hear signs she's getting close. Her soft breaths turn to whimpers. "I'm gonna come."

"Now?"

"Yes."

I throw my head back on the sofa and close my eyes tight.

There in the dark, I know we're not alone—we're together.

She's underneath me, hot and real and alive.

I'm above her, slamming my dick deep, hammering away at her sweet spot until the whole world disappears around us. An orgasm vibrates at the base of my spine.

As soon as I hear her desperate gasp over the phone, I explode. A pained and strangled yell escapes from my chest. Pure ecstasy slams me. I shoot come all over my abs and the sharp, clean smell of it blends with the scent of her. The orgasm roars through me and I think, desperately, this is what it means to lose control. This is what it means to lose yourself.

"ARE YOU STILL THERE?"

I blink in the dark. I clear my throat. "Yeah. Yeah, I'm here."

I lift my head and take stock of my situation. I still have my dick in a death-grip. It's still hard. Come cools in little puddles on my skin. Quickly, I clean myself up. I pull my shorts back up and stretch out on the carpet. All of my muscles are relaxed, and I'm feeling mellow as hell. I'm trashed on sex—trashed on Carmen.

She makes a sound like she's stretching. "That was amazing."

"Fuck yeah." I rest an arm over my eyes and take a deep breath. Curiosity gets to me. "Ever do anything like that before?"

"No," she says.

A bubble of pride swells in my chest. "So I popped your phone-sex cherry?"

"Popped it? You pitted it, swallowed it, and tied the stem in a knot with your tongue."

I laugh a little. "You did good."

We stay on the phone together and say nothing. The silence is not awkward. It's far from awkward—it feels right, almost like holding each other after making love. I listen to her breathing and imagine wrapping my arms around her as we drop off to sleep, just like we did last night.

"Hey, listen," she says.

"What's up?"

"I really want to apologize to you. For my mom."

The last thing I want to talk about right now is Carmen's mom. So I say, "You don't have any reason to apologize. And anyway, we found a way to be together tonight. Sort of."

But Carmen wants to continue apologizing. "I hate that you had to see us like that. It must have been really uncomfortable for all of you."

"Yeah, *really* uncomfortable." I smile to myself. "You know, my dad once threw me out of a moving car for tossing a switchblade at Sal. The tip stuck in his leg. His calf, to be specific."

That makes her pause. "Are you serious?"

"Did you forget who I am? My last name? I'm a Rosas. We invented family dysfunction. What I saw today at your house? That was nothing." I rub my forehead. "Let's see. Okay, imagine I'm your mom. My only beloved, beautiful, precious daughter Carmen is living at home. She loses her job because of some dishwasher at her work. In spite of the fact that she's a total babe—"

"Oh my God, stop."

"Shh," I say. "Don't interrupt my scenario."

"Okay."

"Are you going to interrupt my scenario?"

"No." She laughs softly. "Go ahead."

"Good. What was I saying? In spite of the fact that she is a total babe and can get any man she wants, she continues to see him. He's a formerly incarcerated gang member with neck tattoos and a black eye. She spends the night with him and sneaks in the next day with messed-up hair and wrinkled pajamas. Does that sound right?"

"Sounds about right."

"If I were your mom, I might be a little upset. Just a little."

She doesn't say anything.

"Do you get what I'm saying?" I ask.

"That gangster—he's pretty cute, though," she whispers.

"He *is* pretty cute. Handsome. Fucking gorgeous, really."

"I wouldn't go that far." She laughs again. It's music to my ears.

We talk a little more, about nothing, about everything. Time slows down. I want to stay like this, talking to her, forever.

I don't really want to ask her this next question, but I have to know. "So what are you going to do now?"

"About what?"

It feels strange to say *us*—there isn't really an *us* yet. "About me. About hooking up."

"I don't know yet," she says slowly. "But...I want to see where this goes."

I lie there on the floor of the trailer and look up at the moon-light shining on Rafa's paintings of the saints, his bouquets of flowers and medallions and good luck charms meant to ward off the evil eye. I wonder if all of these things are finally having a positive effect on me. So I test my luck.

"You sure you can't sneak out tonight?" I ask. "I'm good to go again if you are."

She groans a little. "Don't you ever quit?"

"No," I say. "I don't."

"I'm sore, you know that, right?" she says quietly.

I feel a little flash of guilt. "I didn't want to hurt you."

"Don't worry. It's a good hurt."

We talk a little bit more. In between, we flirt with each other, both of us giddy about this new thing we've discovered. I'm hungry to know—to feel—more.

She yawns. She slurs her words. "I'm falling asleep," she says. "I have to hang up."

"Will you call me tomorrow?"

"Okay."

"Good night, baby girl."

"Good night."

My dumb heart is all hot and achy. I stay on the phone until she hangs up.

I'M SQUASHED between my brother and the door of the old truck. We've just finished our delivery run and are on our way to the bakery where Carmen's parents want to meet us to share their decision.

Vanessa is in the driver's seat, chatty and animated. She's confident that they'll say yes, and she's excited about the first steps we'll take to open the brewery. Sal as usual is reserved. He's waiting to see what their decision is before he expresses any emotion.

Vanessa parks in the small lot next to the bakery. This is where Slim was beat up. I try not to think about that as we get out of the truck and slam the heavy doors shut.

"Ready?" Vanessa's high heels click over the sidewalk. I wish I had her confidence. I can fake it, though, so I follow behind her and my brother with my head held high. I employ my gangster lean, just for the hell of it.

Inside, Carmen's mother stands behind the counter with her arms folded. She has turned on all the lights of the bakery, showing off the empty cases. The machinery is still covered in clear plastic. She's turned on the fans to ventilate the place. Air rushes above our heads, swirling under the high ceiling.

Carmen isn't here. Neither is Slim.

Not good.

Carmen's mother shakes hands with both Vanessa and Sal. When I hold out my hand, Carmen's mother looks me in the eye and drops hers.

Okay, then.

That's how it's going to be.

Sal and I exchange a look as I step back behind Vanessa.

"I'll get right to the point, Ms. Velasco," says Carmen's mother. "The terms of the lease are acceptable to my husband and me. Pending the building inspection, we will make any necessary structural changes, but you will be responsible for any improvements or changes on top of that."

Vanessa looks at the documents the Centenos have prepared for her. "This looks good. And the term of the lease?"

"We agree to the lower monthly payment provided you agree to a three-year lease with an option to renew."

Out of the corner of my eye, I see my brother take a quick breath. Three years—that is a serious commitment. Neither of us have committed to do anything for three years before, except hang out in prison. But that wasn't exactly our choice.

"Excellent." Smiling, Vanessa looks over the paperwork. "I'm so happy you've decided to move forward. This will be a great addition to the neighborhood, and I'm glad we're able to keep this transaction in the community. I'll call the broker to draw up the lease today so that we can—"

"Wait," says Carmen's mother. She looks at me. "There is one more thing."

EIGHTEEN

Vanessa's smile doesn't move. "What's that?"

Directly to me, Carmen's mother says, "We will agree to sign the lease if you stop all contact with my daughter."

Vanessa's smile disappears and she stands straight up. She's little but there's something about her body language that makes her look bigger than she is. Before she can get a word out, Sal steps in front of her.

"Mrs. Centeno." His voice is calm. "Can you explain what you mean by that?"

Carmen's mother is cool. Her face is expressionless. I'm trying to figure out how someone could throw such a big monkey wrench into the machine without even blinking.

"My daughter's happiness is of the highest importance to me," she says. "I'm sure you understand that I want to protect her. My husband was beaten by gang members. Horribly. A fact you know."

Sal says, "It makes me sick that this happened to Slim. But my brother and I—we had nothing to do with that."

Carmen's mother continues to stare at me. For a moment, I

think about my own father and my inability to protect him when he needed me most.

"Gang members did this," she repeats. "Whether this gang or that gang doesn't matter to me. They were gang members just like you."

Without hesitating, Sal takes the folder out of Vanessa's hands and puts it back on the metal counter. "Mrs. Centeno, thank you for agreeing to meet with us. Send my regards to Slim. But there are other properties in this city. And our family doesn't do business like this."

"Stop," I say.

"Eddie," Sal says. "We're done here."

"No, we're not." I look at him. He's a goddamn hero. But I need a chance to be a hero too, and if that means removing myself from the equation, I will do it. I turn to Carmen's mother. "What exactly do you want?"

"Stop calling her. Stop seeing her. Leave her alone."

I stare her right in the eyes. "Those three things?"

She blinks. I can see her mind racing, covering her bases. "Delete her number from your phone."

I take out my phone and show her the screen as I erase Carmen's number. My anger almost—almost—eclipses the ache in my heart when I do it. "Anything else?"

"If you break any of these rules, we take back the lease."

Vanessa says, "But there's no legal precedent for—"

"Done." I put my phone back in my pocket. I look at Vanessa's confused expression. "Listen, I won't be the reason you and my brother can't get this business off the ground."

"But what about Carmen?" Vanessa asks. "Isn't anyone going to ask what she wants?"

"This is what Carmen wants. She just doesn't know it yet." Mrs. Centeno's eyes burn into me, dark like her daughter's but cold instead of hot. "Remember, Eduardo. I'll say it again. If you break any of these rules, we take back the lease."

She's tall, but I'm taller. I weigh two times what she does. But she doesn't budge, and now I see where Chef Centeno gets her steel backbone.

"Understood." I adjust my hoodie and put my hands in my pockets. I'm so worked up I could put my fist through one of the cinderblock walls, but I won't let this woman see my anger. I avoid looking at Vanessa or my brother as I head straight out the door.

FIVE MINUTES.

That's all it takes.

Regret hits me like a Metrolink train.

I'm pacing back and forth by the lake in the park, staring down at the dirty water and wondering what the hell I was thinking.

How could I let that woman set me up? I'm Trouble Rosas. I know all the scams and cons and get-downs. Nobody fools me. Right?

But I just fell for one of the oldest tricks in the book. It works because it's simple. Cops use it all the time. Look your mark in the eye and tell them they have two choices, A or B. Make the decision dramatic, life or death. The key is to stress the other person out so bad they forget there's a whole fucking alphabet of letters after A and B.

The reality? My choices were not limited to A. Stop contacting Carmen Centeno or B. Ruin Sal and Vanessa's chances of opening the brewery. There was also C. Tell that dictator to kick rocks, D. Steal a car, pick up Carmen, and take off for Mexico, or E. Ignore Carmen's mother's ultimatum completely and do whatever the hell Carmen and I want.

What have I done?

I make fists but I've got nothing to punch, so I shove my hands back in my pockets and keep walking around the lake as if the solutions to my problems are going to rise out of the pond scum.

When Carmen finds out, will she be angry? I want to think she'd be furious as hell that I sold us out to her mother.

But there's that word again. There is no *us*. Not yet. We've been hooking up for a couple of days. And yes, it's good.

More than good.

It's fucking amazing.

I think of Carmen, her hardness and her softness, the way she sets her sights on something and just goes for it. Her ability not just to do shit but to do it well.

In the last few days, I've learned so much about her. Behind Chef Centeno is Carmen. Carmen knows how to be kind to little kids even though she pretends not to like them. She's a woman who knows how to connect with others, to make them feel welcome and safe. A woman who came to visit me when she was worried about me. A woman who isn't afraid to get close to me, who isn't afraid to see me as more than a warm body on a Saturday night, or as a tatted stranger she wants to fuck once and throw away.

And underneath that, even deeper—a woman whose body I want to hold tight and never let go, from the moment the sun goes down to the moment it comes up, skin to skin. I want to hide inside her, my hunger matched to her hunger, to take the pleasure she gives me and return it to her times ten, times a hundred, times a thousand. I've never had sex like this before. I'm not the man I was before her. Wherever this thing with her goes, she's changed me. I never knew it could be like this.

Fuck.

For reals. What have I done?

There's a chunk of loose concrete on the edge of the sidewalk by the lake. I kick it hard and it flies into the water with a small splash.

More regret.

Why—Jesus, *why*—did I say yes to Carmen's mom?

Carmen told me I needed to think before I speak. That I was a grown-ass man and I needed to work on that aspect of my personality. I know. Shit.

For once I wanted to play the hero. The martyr. For once I wanted to get out of everyone's way.

A group of middle school kids in PE uniforms crosses the street from St. Amaro's. They start a game of flag football on the grass while their coach stands by. I watch them for a second, their little serious game faces and the way the scoring team cheers, as if there is no greater happiness than a day in the park doing exactly this.

Takes me back.

I was around the same age as these kids when my life went completely to hell.

So long ago.

My phone buzzes in my pocket and surprises me. I answer it. "Hello?"

"What were you thinking?" Women have a special talent of whispering in such a way that makes you feel like they're screaming at you at the top of their lungs. "Is this what you really want? Never to see me again? Are you tired of me already, Eddie?"

Carmen is angry, but I can tell from the desperate tone in her voice that she's more hurt than mad. Her hurt becomes my hurt. I want to reach through the phone and hold her, because I don't really have the words right now to explain why I did what I did.

"Answer me," she says. "Is this what it was going to be? Because...I thought"—she sniffles—"actually, I don't know what I thought. Fuck."

I watch the kids running up and down the clearing. A screech of the whistle. The smell of torn-up grass, green and rich.

An ugly truth rises up inside me.

Something I've been trying not to think about since I saw Carmen standing in the kitchen at Giacomo's.

What can I honestly offer her?

I flinch at the truth.

Any guy would be better for her than me. I don't want to admit it because I want her for myself, but that wanting is selfish. I'm the reason she lost her job. I'm the reason she's fighting with her mom. I'm unemployed, and I don't have any money. I'm nobody.

Maybe it's better to break up with her now, before I've had the chance to let her down for reals.

"Since I came into your life," I say, "I've caused you nothing but trouble."

She's quiet.

"It's true," I say. "You know it's true."

"Are you being serious right now?"

"Think about it."

"What did she say to you? What did she do? I swear to God—"

"You have a career. A good one. You have a family who loves you. I mean, in their own way, they do. What can I be in your life but a problem? It's only been a few days and I've turned everything upside down."

"You..." She's quiet for a second, trying to gather up her

thoughts. I imagine her hiding out in her room. "You are full of shit."

I don't say anything, because she's right. I am.

"What was all that talk about 'let's see where this goes'? Were you lying to me?"

"No, I wasn't. That was the truth," I say. "But I see things now that I didn't before." Even though I want her so much I hurt, a woman like her is not for me. One-night stands. Booty calls. That's what my love life is supposed to be. Nothing bigger or better than that. That's the only way not to disappoint someone. And breaking up with her now is a hundred times better than the alternative—bouquets of red roses. Fake apologies.

Wanting something more from Carmen is only going to lead to disaster for her. She's already had a taste of it.

"Eddie, please," she says quietly. "Talk to me. Don't be like this."

My patched-up heart breaks in a completely new placc it's never broken before. I hold steady. "You know it's better this way."

We're quiet for a long time.

"That's all you have to say?" she asks.

"What else is there to say?"

"I don't understand you." Her voice is bitter as black coffee.

"Carmen—"

She hangs up and I stand there holding the phone to my ear as if the silence will turn back into her voice.

I put the phone back in my pocket and let it all wash over me—the pain, the anger, the regret. The hot, thick tar of self-hatred. It is always there, inescapable. A worse prison than prison.

The coach on the field blows his whistle. The kids run to him and gather around, panting and sweaty.

My phone rings. I take it out. My heartbeat roars back to

life. It's a sign—I can fix this. She's letting me fix this. She's letting me undo the enormous damage I've just done.

"Carmen," I say. "Please, just listen—"

"Hey, *mi'jo.*"

At this voice, I'm completely speechless.

"What, you ain't got nothing to say?"

Ghosts are supposed to appear at night, in your house, slamming doors and flickering the light switches. They're not supposed to appear in the middle of the day, in the bright sunlight, while you're standing in a park watching a flag football game.

My voice cracks. "Dad."

NINETEEN

Dizzy—I'm going to fall over. My stomach seizes up like I've been punched.

The last time I heard my father's voice was over the prison phone more than two years ago. Between then and now, the rumors of his disappearance, his death, and his goddamn resurrection have brought me and my brothers to hell and back, again and again and again.

"So who's Carmen?" he asks.

My worlds crash together and I can't get my balance. I sink down on the grass and rub my face with my hand.

My father is alive.

"She's—she's just a girl," I say. I shove all thoughts of Carmen away, out of Dreamer's reach. I clear my throat. "Where are you? Are you okay?"

"I'm okay, mi'jo. Just fine."

I glance at my phone. His number is blocked.

"So, did you miss me?" He laughs.

To miss someone means that they're gone and you want them back. My feelings for my father are more complex than that. "Where are you?" I ask again.

"Somewhere safe. Somewhere far away," he says. "I'm not supposed to be talking to you, as a matter of fact."

"Witness protection?"

"Are you kidding? No one wants to protect me." He laughs. When I don't say anything, he says, "Breathe, Trouble. Take a breath. In, out."

I do it. My dizziness subsides a little bit.

"Now tell me. How are your brothers?"

My throat is dry. Somehow I find the words to answer him. "I haven't talked to Angel since Christmas. He's probably okay. Abuelita and Tío Rick would tell us if he's in trouble."

"They have him on the short leash. He's probably a little altar boy by now. Praying morning, noon, and night."

I want to tell him that the short leash is what's keeping Angel from following his older brothers' footsteps, and that all of us are lucky our relatives in Salinas could take him in. But now's not the time. "Sal—he's in school," I say instead. "College."

"No shit?"

"Yeah. He got a big scholarship."

"That's tight. What's he studying?"

"Brewery science."

"What the fuck is that?"

"Beer making. He's learning how to brew beer. He's selling it too."

"Who knew? That's wonderful." I can almost see his crinkle-eyed smile. "And you, mi'jo? How are you doing?"

Without thinking, I take little handfuls of dry grass and rip them out of the dirt. What do I tell my father? That I can't hold down a job? That I hurt a girl who is worth a dozen of me, or that I'm broke, no better off than on the day I got out of prison? "I'm okay, Dad."

He grunts. "You don't sound okay."

"Naw, I'm fine. Great. Going straight. Figuring it out."

"Good. That's good. You know, this kind of thing, it takes time. You've gotta just take it one step at a time. Each day is a new day."

He rolls out his usual dumb sayings. I've heard them all before. As he keeps talking, I pull myself up and brush the grass from my pants. I get my balance and start a slow walk around the lake.

I'm trying to get my emotions locked down, but it's a struggle.

When I heard my father had been killed, I felt empty. Hollowed out. See, he's called Dreamer for a reason. He doesn't think things through, and he follows his weird ideas wherever they take him. This time, they took him down a dark path, and I wasn't there to protect him.

He finishes with his lecture, a mixture of twelve-step standbys and New-Age self-improvement quotes. "I'm worried about you, Trouble. You always wanted to be the one in the middle of everything, the one in the middle of all the action. You're just like me. Isn't that what I've always told you?"

"Dad," I say, suddenly tired, "just tell me where you are."

He's quiet for a long time, making his decision. I hold my breath. Then he says, "Where are you staying?"

"What?"

"Where are you sleeping? Who are you staying with?"

"With Rafa."

"In the garden?"

"Yeah."

"Okay. Go there tonight. I'm going to send you something. Wait for it."

"What are you sending me?"

"Instructions. And a bus ticket."

He knows I'm on parole. I can't leave the county. "Dad—"

"You won't get caught, if you do what I tell you," he says. "I promise you'll be okay."

I know what Dreamer Rosas's promises are worth. I say nothing.

"Do you want to know what really happened?" he says.

More than anything. The mystery has been eating me alive. "Yes."

"I know you do," he says, "but I'll only tell you in person, *mi'jo.*"

Why does he have to do this? Test my loyalty to him, knowing I'll do whatever he asks, just like when I was a kid?

"Are you still there?" he asks.

"Yeah." My voice is rough.

"Whatever you do, don't tell anyone where you're going." He pauses. "Don't tell Sal."

Fuck. Secrets—again. "I won't," I say.

"Promise me."

"I promise."

"Okay. I'll see you when I see you."

He hangs up without saying goodbye. I snap my phone closed. I stare at it.

Two cops park their cruiser in the lot on the other side of the lake. They walk up to a homeless guy who's enjoying a private date with a bottle of cheap vodka. While one cop gives him a talking-to, the other stands there with his hand on his gun, surveying the park. The kids have all returned to school. That leaves me, sitting on a hillside by myself doing nothing but looking suspicious.

I put my phone back in my pocket, stand up, and head back to Rafa's.

AFTER DINNER, Rafa and I share a bowl. I know I should be clear-headed tonight but I can't face the ugly feelings rising up inside me.

We're sitting in the living room. I tell him about my father's phone call. I watch as Rafa lights a shitload of candles, he says, to protect me. I try to ignore the real danger he might burn the place down.

I hear a soft knock at the door. When I open it, no one is there. Quickly, I run into the garden and search the rows and the shadows. Still, no one. Annoyed, I head back to the trailer. A thick envelope sits on the top step. With one last look at the empty garden, I pick the envelope up and go back inside.

"Who was it?" Rafa asks.

"I don't know. But they left this."

I open the envelope and empty it onto the coffee table. There's a debit card of some kind plus a fat wad of cash, twenties and fifties, more money than I've seen in weeks.

Rafa whistles. "Not bad."

A California driver's license matches the debit card. I don't recognize the name, but the face looks like mine. Rafa picks up the last thing in the envelope. It's a piece of white paper, folded in half.

"It's a bus ticket for a private bus company." Rafa squints and points at the downtown address. "I guess that's the station." He reads the information quietly. "You leave at eight o'clock tomorrow. Los Angeles to Wenatchee."

"Los Angeles to where?"

"Wenatchee." He shrugs. "Wherever that is." He gives me the paper.

I run my fingers over the paper. I'm buzzed—the lines of the bar code begin to blur. I rub my eyes.

"Are you going to go?" Rafa asks.

I nod.

Rafa knows all about my quest for my father. He's stood by and watched silently, but I know he's worried about me. "I don't understand. Why? Why go?" he shakes his head. "Why risk going back to jail?"

"Because he's my father. Because I have to know the truth." Dreamer is a shitty father, but he is still my father. I can't abandon him, even if that makes me an idiot.

"Are you sure, mi'jo?" Rafa asks.

"I'm sure."

"What about your girl?"

I say nothing. She's not my girl, but I don't want to hear those words aloud.

He shakes his head again. "Fine, fine. Be stubborn."

As I sit there on the floor of his trailer stoned as hell, Rafa lights some sage. Then he lights some copal. I breathe in the sweet, heavy smoke. He says some prayers in Spanish, in English, and in Nahuatl, a native language that I recognize because homies in prison used to study it to communicate in secret. The words mix together to become one language. Rafa's voice leads me to a place between waking and sleeping.

Slowly, I slip down into my subconscious.

I walk through the familiar museum of regrets and painful memories, my many embarrassments and my bottomless pit of shame. I tiptoe past all of these things, trying to avoid the pain that always surfaces whenever I visit the past.

But talking with my father has brought all the pain back.

So tonight, instead of avoiding it, I face it.

THE WASHING MACHINE.

It's simple, white, with three dials. It sits in the basement of the house where I grew up.

I'm twelve. Sal's thirteen. Angel is hanging on me—he's eight, bug-eyed, eager to please. Sal's holding Esperanza, and she's hugging his neck, confused and fussy. She's wearing her pajamas. Our little sister is only three years old.

It's the middle of the night.

Our parents are fighting upstairs.

Sal looks at me as he closes the top door of the washing machine, starting the water to hide the sound of the yelling. I hear the cold water pouring into the empty tub. I'm sleepy, so for a second, my hazy brain thinks, we're going to get in trouble. Our mother is going to get angry that we're playing with the washing machine, that we're wasting water. In our household, everything has a price. We turn off lights. We finish every bite of food. Every penny counts, especially since my dad lost his job at the slaughterhouse.

These days, my father doesn't work. My father drinks. Three beers in, he begins to tell us his favorite stories about his past, his glory days in the neighborhood, his days in the game. Six beers in, he gets quiet—the angry kind of quiet my brothers and I know to avoid.

Our mother doesn't drink. Instead, she prays for our souls, says endless rosaries for her husband and her children. In her eyes, we live on a thin line, in constant danger of temptation.

She tries to scare us with stories of hell and the devil, but at twelve, I'm terrified listening to my mom and dad fight.

Tonight, they rip into each other in English and Spanish, letting loose all their frustrations on each other. They say all the bad words. They yell and break things. I hate it.

Usually, by morning they're back in the bedroom, the door closed. Everything is quiet, as if nothing has happened between them.

But this time, something is different.

Our mother is screaming at our father because he's back to

hanging out with his friends in East Side Hollenbeck—ESHB, the letters tattooed on his knuckles.

He's told us he was a gangster before he married our mother. But it's hard to see the gangster inside of the grumpy working man we've known all our lives.

"*Pinche* Ruben!" our mom yells. "That piece of shit. You want to go be with him? Go be with him. But don't you dare come back to this house."

"This house?" Our father laughs, low and slow. "This house? You think this is your house? This house is not yours. Every nail and board and window in this house is mine. I paid for it."

He's bullying her—using her insecurities as weapons against her. Her lack of education. Her lack of work experience. Her complete financial dependence on him.

"Every penny in your purse," he spits. "Every thread on your back. I clothe you. I feed you. I pay for everything. What are you going to do, Amalia? Get a job? You didn't finish school. You've never worked a day in your goddamn life."

Sal and me exchange a look. Anyone can see how hard she works for this family. She runs the household, cooks, cleans, looks after four kids, and serves our father hand and foot.

"You have no idea what it's like out there. Without me, you'll starve to death." To make his point, my father switches to Spanish. "I give you everything. You are nothing without me. So stop pretending you're somebody. You're nobody. Absolutely nobody."

When the washing machine starts spinning, my mother snaps.

I hear her footsteps moving around the house. I hear the jingle of keys and I can guess she's grabbed her purse.

"You ain't going nowhere," my father says. He's slurring now.

We hear our mother open the door of Esperanza's bedroom. She curses to herself. The basement door bangs open and we see her at last. She's wearing sweats and a coat. She's put on tennis shoes without socks. Her familiar face is clouded with anger. We are all scared of her when she's like this. Her eyes latch on to our little sister. Sal realizes what's going to happen before the rest of us do.

"*Amá, no, por favor.*" He tightens his grip on Esperanza, who begins to cry. "Calm down."

I'm too young and stupid to understand until I see my mother wrap one arm around my screaming sister while trying to push Sal away.

The little girl is terrified. She's not sure what to do. She loves her brothers. She loves her mom. She loves her dad. I can see it on her face. Why is everyone yelling? What is happening?

I stand with my hands on Angel's shoulders, holding him back so he doesn't get hurt. In the middle of the confusion, his face collapses too, and he starts crying. His screams mix with Esperanza's screams and I have to tighten my hold. "Don't cry," I tell him, even though I want to cry too. "Stop crying. You have to stop crying."

He looks up at me with his wet eyes and sniffles. He rubs his face and tries to stop but new sobs keep breaking loose.

"Stop being such a baby," I say, which is stupid, because that's what he is. That's what we all are.

Our mother shoves Sal so hard he almost loses his balance and has to catch himself against the spinning washing machine. She uses this moment to pull Esperanza away from him. She embraces the girl tightly and runs up the wooden steps, where my father is standing, looking at everything with a mixture of bitterness and anger on his face.

"Don't," he says. "Don't you dare."

He pulls his arm back to smack my mother's face but I'm too

fast. I bolt up the steps and stand in front of her. The blow glances off the side of my head, hard. My ears are ringing. Blood drips down into my right eye. He's cut me with his wedding ring. I'm bleeding down my collar and my face is burning hot from the blow.

Taking advantage of the distraction, my mother runs outside. She jumps into the car and locks the doors. My father pounds on the windows as she straps Esperanza into the car seat and climbs behind the wheel. I can hear my little sister's muffled screaming. I run toward the car but Sal grabs me. Behind us, Angel is sobbing.

"Are you going back to your mother?" my father yells in the driveway. "Good. Go back to Salinas. Don't bother coming back. Bitch. Trash. You were trash when I met you, and you're trash now. *Puta. Vete a la chingada.*"

She puts the key in the ignition. Full of rage, my father smacks the windshield. He's a big man—strong from years of manual labor—and we hear a crunch. His fist leaves a huge crack on the safety glass, white like a spiderweb.

Dizzy, I sway on my feet. Sal grabs my arm and helps me keep my balance. Silently, my brothers and I watch as our mother starts the engine. My father plants himself behind the car, daring her to run him over. She puts the car in reverse and taps the brakes, lurching back inch by inch, pushing my father out of the way.

Lights in the neighbors' houses are coming on. Dogs bark.

My father, overcome with anger, loses his footing and at last, falls onto the lawn. She hits the gas and peels out of the driveway. She shifts gears and speeds away before my father can get to his feet and chase after her.

Sal, Angel, and me—we stand on the front porch. We don't know what to say. Our parents fight all the time. But not like this. Not like this.

Our father walks back to the porch just as the neighbors open their doors to see what's going on.

He looks at all three of us, the rage hot and deep in his bloodshot eyes. "Your mother—she's trash. Human garbage. We don't need her." He turns to the street. We can see the brake lights of her car at the stop sign.

"You're trash, you hear me?" he yells. He spits on the ground.

We watch as the car disappears around the corner, and the neighborhood gets quiet again.

TWENTY

Back in Rafa's trailer, I draw a breath, pulling the smoke as deep as I can. My buzz wears off slowly, melting like butter. My pain has a sharp, hot edge.

Because this is a memory, I know what will happen next.

Sal will put Angel to bed. He'll sit me down in the bathroom and clean up the cut on my forehead. He'll make sure we stay quiet so that our father in his drunken rage forgets about us.

While we lie awake in bed, our father will trash everything downstairs. We'll listen to the crash of dishes, glasses, and empty liquor bottles. He'll overturn tables and chairs. He'll rip our mother's clothes from the closet, taking the rod down with them. He'll shred the curtains. He'll destroy our television and rip the telephone from the wall.

The next day, like a storm that's passed, he'll be snoring in the bedroom.

As our dad sleeps, Sal and Angel will clean the kitchen. I'll fix the living room, sweeping up the broken glass and putting it in the trash.

At noon, the police officers will arrive at our door.

Our father will stand in the half-destroyed living room. I'll be embarrassed for him with his stained T-shirt and wet, red eyes.

One of the officers will say, "I'm very sorry to tell you this, Mr. Rosas. Your wife and daughter passed away in a car accident just south of Salinas early this morning."

Silence. After a long time, my father will manage to say, "What happened?"

"A drunk driver swerved into their car from the southbound lane. It was a head-on collision. Your wife—she died instantly."

My father's face will turn to stone. He will show no emotion, either to us, or to these strangers, these cops in our living room. "And my little girl?" he asks.

"Paramedics tried to stabilize her," the officer will say slowly, with a robotic voice. "They did everything they could. She passed away at the scene of the accident."

The darkness will close in on me, both then and now. It will swallow me whole until all I can see, breathe, feel is pain.

Pain.

So familiar.

It almost feels good.

HOURS LATER, I wake up on the floor of Rafa's trailer.

He's blown out all of the candles, put a blanket over me, and gone to bed.

My buzz is long gone. I take off my shirt and go outside into the dark. I wash my face and brush my teeth with the ice-cold water from the hose. I go inside and put on another T-shirt. I sit down on the sofa and check my phone. Two in the morning.

My head aches, but so does my chest. Once the memory surfaced, the pain rushed me like a flash flood. It's been more than ten years, but I can still see my sister in the back seat of that car. I can still hear her wails. I can still see her fear.

I cope by burying that memory as deep as I can—but sometimes it just breaks loose, and there's nothing I can do but let it have its way with me.

That night, everything changed.

Our family's story ended, and the story of four separate men began.

After the accident, my father threw himself back into the gang. He made just enough money to pay the bills. Bottles turned to balloons, spoons and needles.

With no one supervising us, my brothers and I ran loose. Sal tried to look after us, but soon the lure of East Side Hollenbeck was too strong even for him. He was jumped into the gang a few months after the funeral. Soon, he was sent away to youth authority for busting up some kid's jaw. That's when I got jumped in. I sold whatever the older homeboys gave me, held corners, broke into houses. When my brother got out, we teamed up and got really, really fucking good at stealing cars.

When Sal and I were sentenced, we made arrangements for our little brother to live with our uncle and grandmother in Salinas. Angel was starting to get into trouble, so we pulled him out of the life. If one of us was going to make it out, it was always going to be him. But he hated us for sending him away—he still resents us. I know it.

Without my mother, my father has been a walking disaster, one bad decision after another after another.

Suddenly, another fear grips me.

I'm alone.

Is that what I'll be too? Like him?

I take three deep breaths and let each one out slowly.

It's time to go.

Chest still aching, I stand up and put the few belongings I have in my backpack. A couple of shirts, clean socks, and *chones*. Two pairs of pants, one pair of shorts. I swap my real ID card out of my wallet and slide in the fake driver's license. I hide my real paperwork under the sofa. Carefully, I place the bus ticket and most of the cash back inside the big envelope. I tuck the envelope into the bottom of my backpack where it can't fall out.

One more step. I head out to the avocado tree in the garden. The knife Spider gave me from the failed gun robbery is still in the hole. I pull it out of its leather holder and inspect the blade— still sharp. I slip the knife into the outside pocket of my backpack and zip everything closed.

I leave Rafa a fifty-dollar bill for food and beer. In the dark, I write him a note.

Rafa,
See you in a few days.
Dios te bendiga, viejo.

I put on my hoodie, pick up my backpack, and leave.

As I walk, I keep my hands in my pockets to stay warm. The streets are empty except for two stray cats who chase each other into the bushes to fight. Cold wind blows down the gutters, stirring up little whirlwinds of trash.

After a long walk, I turn onto Carmen's street and head slowly to her house. The porch light is on, but all of the lights inside are off. Quietly, I creep alongside the house. No motion lights, no barking dogs. I hop the low wall into the backyard and count the windows to the one I remember is Carmen's. I wonder if the house alarm is on, but then I see the window to the bathroom is cracked just an inch. I take a chance that the system is off.

I crouch down low against the wall, set my phone to silent, and cover the lit screen with my hand as I punch out a message.

u awake?

I send the text and wait. The Centenos's backyard is neat and tidy. There's a lawn, and some patio furniture. A single date palm tree. A statue of La Virgen de Guadalupe sits next to a single rosebush.

My screen lights up, and I can almost hear her angry voice in my head.

What do you want?

My fingers feel too big, too slow on the buttons of my fucking flip phone.

im here

Carmen texts back, *What? At the door?*

no ur window

She doesn't respond for a long time.

I'm sitting right underneath her window, but I'm not a hundred percent sure it's hers. I want to peek inside but I'm afraid I'll see her mom pointing a Glock at me. I tell myself to calm down, take a deep breath, and let it out. I promise myself that I will sit here until the sun comes up, until someone sees me and calls the cops, or until Carmen decides she wants to open her window, whichever comes first. I fold my arms and wait.

It's quiet. The cold penetrates my sweatshirt and my T-shirt. I try not to shiver.

Will she let me in?

I wouldn't. Not after what I did.

But Carmen is a different kind of person.

Lucky for me.

After a minute or two, the window above my head clicks and slides open. I was right—the alarm is off. I stand up. As silently as I can, I snap the screen off the window frame and lean it against the wall. I raise my backpack up over my head and Carmen's pretty, dark hands pull it inside. It takes a hot minute for me to haul my big body in through the window but I manage to do it without making a noise, even though my heart is booming inside my chest.

I land on a fuzzy pink rug. An old heart-shaped nightlight is plugged into the wall. It gives off just enough light for me to see Carmen's beautiful face. She's kneeling next to me. Her hair is pulled back into a messy bun. She's wearing a little white T-shirt and pink panties—and yup. There it is. My boner. I sit cross-legged, hoping my pants will hide it.

"Are you fucking crazy?" she whisper-shouts.

I reach out to stroke her face but she leans away from me.

"No, don't touch me," she says. "I should call the cops. No, worse. I should get my mom."

"Jesus. Kick back," I whisper.

I look around her room. It's pretty bare—a twin-sized bed, a kid-sized desk. There are no decorations at all, no posters on the walls, no clutter. No makeup, no clothes or shoes scattered on the floor. I imagine her at eighteen, moving out of here, hoping not to return. But she's back, and even though she's lived with her parents for a few years now, I can tell she doesn't want to get comfortable. She doesn't want to stay.

She sits on the bed and stares hard at me. "You smell like weed."

"I'm not high," I say. "Well, not anymore, anyway."

"What do you want?"

"To see you."

"Why?"

"Because I made a mistake. A big one."

She folds her arms. "And what mistake is that?"

"I hurt you."

"How?"

"By being a dumbass."

"You're going to have to be more specific than that."

"I panicked," I say. "Your mom said she would agree to the lease if I agreed to stop seeing you. I know how much my brother and his girlfriend want this. I've seen how they've been planning together, how much they want things to work out for their business. I didn't want to be the reason why it didn't."

"I get that," she says. "But why didn't you talk to me about it? It was like you had made the decision for both of us, and that you...you seemed to believe it was the right thing to do. To stop seeing me altogether. I thought we..."

I wait for her to finish the sentence. She looks down at her feet and doesn't say anything else for a long time.

"Let's leave my mom out of this. I can handle my mom," she says quietly. "What I want to know is, do *you* think we could be something? More than what we are right now?"

"I don't know," I say. With my history, I honestly don't.

"Do you want to be with me?"

"Yes, but—"

"But what?"

"But I don't know how."

"What's there to know?"

"Being with you," I say slowly, "would require me to be a good person. I'm not a good person, Carmen."

She shakes her head at me but holds back her criticism. "You ever have a girlfriend?"

"No."

"Why not?"

"Girlfriends are hard to come by in the state pen."

"Don't joke," she says sharply. "Before that. Or after that. Did you?"

"No."

"Why not?" she asks again.

"Never appealed to me."

"How about now? Does it appeal to you now?"

"I don't know."

"So why are you here?"

She wants me to say something heroic, but I'm not a hero. "I don't know," I say again.

"Really?" She stands up. "I know why." She takes off her shirt. Even though this is what I had hoped would happen tonight, it feels wrong. I want her to put it back on.

"Carmen," I say. "Wait."

Her voice is hard. "But you want this, don't you? *This* you can understand."

She's not wearing a bra. I try not to stare as she slides off her panties and kicks them away. She lies down on the bed, leans back on her elbows, and spreads her legs wide.

My heart and my head and my dick are all aching, and I don't know which hurts the most. I look away from her. I look at the nightlight. I look at the carpet.

"No, look at me," she says. "This is what you want. Anything else is too complicated, right?"

Out of the corner of my eye, I watch her slide a hand up to her breast and squeeze it. I suppress a groan and run my hands through my hair. "Carmen, please," I say, but my voice is quiet. Weak.

"Sex is all you'll give me, so sex is what I'll take." She shakes out her ponytail. I can smell her from here, the flowery scent of her shampoo, the soapy scent of her skin, the sweetness between her legs. In the soft glow of the nightlight, she's like a hallucination I can feel with all of my senses.

"Tell me something," I say.

"What, Trouble?"

I don't like it when she calls me that. The name doesn't belong in her mouth. "Why are you fucking with me anyway?" I say. "A girl like you? You know I'm a piece of shit. Why try to change me?"

Her dark eyes glitter at me like arrowheads. Rafa has a shiny black stone on his shelf. *Obsidiana* he calls it. Volcanic glass, razor-edged. Dangerous.

"I'm not trying to change you," she says quietly. "I'm trying to make you see what I see."

"What do you see?"

"A good man."

"How do you know I am a good man? What evidence do you have?"

"From the way you treat your family, your friends. From the way you treat me, when you're not scared," she says. "I'm not stupid. I know you have your secrets. But I'm hoping one day you'll be brave enough to share them with me."

We lock eyes. Both of us are breathing hard. I stand up slowly and take the three steps to where she lies on the bed. I tower over her, my big shadow blanketing her body in darkness.

"You know I'm only going to let you down." My voice deepens. Goosebumps rise on her skin.

She says nothing. I watch her as she reaches down between her legs and slides her middle fingers up and down the sides of her pussy. She rests her heels on the edge of the bed and spreads her legs wider, teasing me. One finger plunges inside. The other circles her clit. I can almost taste her on the tip of my tongue.

"I'm going to break your heart," I say. "I'm not the knight in shining armor you think I am."

"Fuck you," she whispers, "you don't know what I'm thinking."

I lunge forward, grab her wrists and pin them to the mattress next to her hips. High on the scent of her, I lie down between her legs. I close my eyes and kiss her sweet, hot pussy. I lick open her lips and plunge my tongue inside her, drinking her in. She squirms but I hold her down. The more she thrashes and tries to kick me, the tighter my grip gets. I tongue-fuck her and lap at her clit without mercy. Her back arches and her thighs flex. Right before she comes, I flip her over, fast and rough.

"Don't fucking move." I pull down my pants and ram my cock into her trembling cunt.

"Oh God," she whimpers. "Yes."

My sweet, dirty Carmen. When I bend down to kiss her neck, she struggles against me. I fuck her bareback, deep and slow. She balls up the sheets in her fists.

"You're right. I don't know what you're thinking," I grunt. "But I know what you're feeling, *mi reina*. My dick. Stretching that tight little pussy. Fucking you like you've never been fucked before. And you think I'm a good man? You know I'm not. That's why you like this. You need someone bad to reach the bad inside you."

"No," she says. "That's not true. You're not bad."

"You said all I want is *this*." I thrust hard. She whimpers. "That *this* is all I can understand. But maybe, Carmen, the truth is the other way around. Maybe *this*"—I thrust again—"is all *you* can understand. All you want from me."

"I want to see you." She tries to turn around but I hold her in place with my hips.

I'm raw and hurting—I can't look at her like this. "No."

"Eddie, I want to face you."

"I said no," I growl.

I slide my arm underneath her stomach and drag her closer to my body. She's hot and dripping, and I know from our time together she's getting closer and closer to her orgasm. She's so turned on I can feel her wetness against my abs, my balls. Quickly, I stick my thumb in my mouth and suck on it. When it's wet, I reach down and stroke her slick little asshole. She shudders and her muscles grip my dick.

"You like this?" I trace the tip of my thumb back and forth.

"Yes."

"Ever had it here?"

She shakes her head.

"You want it?" I ask.

"I don't know," she whispers. "I'm scared it will hurt."

I don't want to hurt her—I never want to hurt her. "Can I try something?"

She nods.

Carefully, I pop the first joint of my thumb into her tight opening. She gasps but spreads her legs wider.

The beast inside me surges forward, but I beat him back. I lean down to whisper in her ear. My voice softens. "That's as far as we'll go tonight. Tell me if it hurts and I'll stop."

She looks at me over her shoulder. "Okay." Her dark eyes are wide, trusting, and unafraid. A part of me wonders why—how—she trusts me. No one else does. Not really. In return, I'll give her what I know she wants.

I harden my voice again. "Now close your eyes."

When she does it, I slowly pull out of her completely.

TWENTY-ONE

"Please," she whimpers, but I ignore her.

My life has been a long cycle of have and have not, of fists and empty hands, of freedom and lockup. I want her to feel me, but I want her to feel the absence of me too. Fullness and hunger. With and without.

I look down at us in the faint light. My cock is wet, standing straight up. I put my hands on her hips and slide my shaft along her opening. Her pussy is hot velvet against my dick. The sensation of skin against skin is powerful. Back and forth—each slow stroke drives us wild.

"What if the good man you're looking for isn't me?" I brush her hair off her back and slide my palm over her spine. "What if you look inside me and there's nothing? What then?"

"You're wrong."

I wrap my hand firmly around the base of her neck and pin her to the mattress. She moans. She's trembling.

"Tell me I'm wrong again," I whisper.

"You're wrong."

I take my dick in my hand and jam the tip into her pussy. She's feverish all over, on the edge of climaxing.

"Say that again," I say.

"You're wrong."

I grab her wrists with my free hand and hold them against her lower back like I'm arresting her. I get my balance and thrust my big dick deep inside her. Her dark lips strain around me. Pleasure floods my gut, my torso, my chest. Even my fingers and toes tingle. I strangle back the groan in my throat.

"What do you want, *mi reina?*" My voice is barely audible.

"I wanna come." Her voice is muffled by the bedsheets. "Please."

She's so wet we're both covered in slickness. I let go of her neck and hook my thumb back into her ass. I'm not gentle. When she flinches, her pussy flexes at the same time. She almost makes me come—we're playing with fire. Irresponsible. Guilty, I pull back. But when she gasps, can't help myself. I thrust again, harder, and once more, even harder.

"What do you want?" I ask again.

"You."

"The real me?"

"The real you."

She wants a thug, she'll get one tonight.

She wants to get fucked into the sweet hereafter by a gangster with a dirty conscience, I'm here. I'll deliver.

My hand tightens around her wrists. Will she have bruises tomorrow? Maybe. But tonight she'll have pleasure—more of it than her body can handle.

I switch from fast thrusts to slow, deep ones, tapping her spot again and again. Her ass tightens around my thumb and I feel the tremors inside her a split second before she explodes.

"Now, Carmen," I whisper.

Her hips buck against me and I hold her steady, fucking her until she falls over the edge. Her whole body flexes. She buries her face in the covers and swallows down her screams. Her toes curl and her fingers clench and the pleasure wells up inside her until it vibrates inside me. We're in sync. I feel what she feels. My body sends signals to my brain. I'm close.

I lean my head forward and close my eyes. In the darkness, the orgasm takes me. I can hear our bodies slapping together, muscle against muscle, flesh against flesh. Just when I begin to come, I pull out, take my wet shaft in my fist and let go. Ecstasy grabs me. I open my eyes and watch my come shoot all over her smooth, brown back. Like some kind of fever dream, Carmen reaches back and wraps her hand around mine, tightening the grip as I jack off the last drops.

The pleasure—it's a monster. Sweat covers my torso. I can't breathe.

I'm drowning.

Drowning in her.

AFTERWARD, Carmen stands up and takes my face in her hands. She kisses me—slow, tender, openmouthed kisses that bring me back to myself. We're a mess. I take her in my arms and that's when I realize I'm still wearing my pants and shoes, like a burglar who forgot why he came here. I sway on my feet.

"Are you okay?" She strokes my hair. "Eddie?"

"You should get security bars," I manage to say.

"Security bars?"

"Yeah." I blink slowly at her. My brain isn't working right. "For your windows."

With a smile, she kisses me again before she cleans up, puts her T-shirt and panties back on, and straightens the sheets. I take off my shoes and the rest of my clothes and stretch out on the tiny bed. She climbs on top of me.

"Bars." She smiles to herself. "Thought you might be tired of those by now."

I kiss her forehead, pull the covers over us and wrap my arms around her. She snuggles against my chest and her soft breathing grazes my skin. I want to relax, but we've spent so much time together, I think she can feel the tension in my body, the truth I'm holding back from her.

"Just tell me," she says. "Just tell me what's going on with you."

I want to, with all of my heart. But I can't.

"Do you know," I say slowly, "what it feels like when everyone has given up on you?"

Carmen says nothing. I place my hand on her head and slowly stroke her smooth, cool hair.

"I hate that feeling. I hate it because I can't blame them. When I think of the decisions I've made, the people I've let down, I know I'm trash. I don't deserve anyone's forgiveness."

"Stop it—"

"But you." I squeeze her. "You haven't given up on me yet. Why not?"

She's quiet for so long I'm afraid she's fallen asleep. But she lifts her head and looks at me in the dark. "Because you're much more—so much more—than the bad things you've done, Eddie. They don't define you."

When she kisses me, the touch of her lips is sweet and cool. We kiss slowly, a gentle good night unfolding between us along with the first flashes of something I've never felt before. Something deep and real. Something I'm still too afraid to name.

BY THE GRACE OF GOD, my internal clock wakes me up before Carmen's parents do.

As gently as I can, I slide out of Carmen's arms. She's a heavy sleeper. To be honest, she snores like a hibernating bear, but this doesn't bother me. I think it's kinda cute.

Yawning, I get dressed. I tuck the blankets around Carmen and take one last look at her before I go. I memorize what I see. Messy hair. Dark lashes. Full lips, swollen from kisses. There are creases on her cheek from the wrinkled bedsheets. On her wrists, faint bruises blend into her dark skin. They're barely visible, but I can see them. They burn themselves into my memory.

God.

She is so beautiful.

I hesitate. I should wake her up. I should tell her the truth about everything—my trip, my dad. She would understand, wouldn't she?

I reach out to touch her cheek.

My hand stops short. I can't.

"I'm taking a trip, *mi reina*," I whisper. "Goodbye."

Without looking back, I climb out of the window. Outside, the sun still hasn't come up, and the sky is bluish-gray. Quietly, I snap the screen back in place, hop the wall, and walk down the silent street.

After paying my fare with a handful of change, I take a bus filled with bundled-up nannies and factory workers on their way to work. I step off the bus downtown and I walk through a homeless encampment set up on the sidewalk in front of a row of warehouses. A block away, I see the flower district, brightly lit and open for business. I see plastic buckets of roses, and my thoughts go immediately to Carmen.

I imagine she's still in bed, waking up alone.

I should be there.

I'm sorry.

The gray sky, the gray asphalt, and the gray buildings make the red roses look even redder, as if they're lit from the inside out. I can smell them from here. I imagine the strange velvety petals, so easy to crush and bruise.

I grip the straps of my backpack and walk down Sixth Street, sliding past the shadow of LAPD's Central Division. The bus station is a big garage next to a small ticket office with a glass storefront. Next to the door, there's a neon sign that says *Cinco Estrellas*. I walk inside. It's run-down but clean. There is a bench with a half-dozen passengers waiting with backpacks and rolling suitcases. In the back, I see a glassed-in booth with a speaker. The prices of the bus tickets are listed on a big menu above the window: Las Vegas, Phoenix, San Diego, Tijuana, Nogales, Kingman, Fresno, Bakersfield, Barstow, Gilroy, Sacramento, Redding.

The clerk eyes me with suspicion but says politely, *"Buenos dias. ¿En que puedo ayudarle?"*

I show her the ticket. She reads it through the glass.

"They're boarding your bus right now." She tips her head toward the door connecting the lobby with the garage. "You should hurry."

I enter the garage and join the line of people waiting to get on a charter bus. It's nice but not new. The sign in the window says *Wenatchee*. I've never heard of this place before, but to be honest I haven't traveled much outside of Los Angeles. My family went to Salinas a couple times when I was a kid, but I don't remember too much besides my grandmother's house. I served my time in Delano and Vacaville, but I wouldn't include those locations in a list of exotic places I've been.

As much of a hardass as I pretend to be, I'm nervous. All of this is new. Where am I going? And what happens if I get caught violating my parole? My heart beats fast. To steady myself, I take a deep breath and let it out silently.

I watch the passengers put their bags in the cargo hold and board the bus while a clerk checks their tickets. When the clerk scans mine, his machine beeps and he welcomes me on board along with everyone else.

I find a seat toward the back of the bus and put my backpack on the seat next to me to signal I want to sit alone. It's not an issue. This bus to Wenatchee is barely a quarter full. Almost all of the passengers are Mexican or Central American. Farm laborers, I think. They're silent or talk quietly to their neighbors. I can't hear what they're saying.

While we wait to leave, I study my new identity.

I'm now Hector Villalobos. I'm from Santa Ana, and I'm twenty-six years old. I memorize the address and birth date. The stranger in the picture looks a lot like me when I was sixteen. Like Hector, maybe I never renewed the photo on my card. It's a strong enough resemblance that I don't think this would make anyone look twice.

The driver stows the last of the luggage and closes the hatch. He climbs into the front seat and shuts the door. The big engine turns over and comes to life with a shudder. We reverse slowly out of the garage into the street.

On my flip phone, I begin to tap out a message for Carmen. I second-guess myself and delete it. It's still early—I don't want to wake her up. I turn off the phone and put it back in my pocket.

I lean back in the seat. The bus is warm and comfortable. Even though I want to stay alert, last night catches up with me. My eyelids begin to droop.

As sleep overtakes me, the bus crawls out of the city limits and leaves everything I know behind—my family, my neighborhood, my gang. My girl. Even my name.

TWENTY-TWO

When I open my eyes a few hours later, the sky outside is blue and bright. I turn on my phone.

One message, from Carmen.

classy way to take off this morning

I smile to myself as I type. *ha ha classy thats me*

I send the text and wait for a response, but nothing comes. Disappointed, I turn off my phone again to preserve its battery.

The man on the other side of the aisle is dressed in jeans and work boots. He's wearing a Seattle Mariners cap and a fleece jacket. He's not tall but he's bulky. I think he's about forty.

We talk. His name is Memo, short for Guillermo, and he's from Sinaloa—a long way from home. We speak Spanish, but talking to Memo, I feel the limits of my ability with the language. My words are mixed up, more Spanglish than Spanish. He's not a dick about it so I manage to get by.

"What's waiting for you in Washington?" he asks me.

I blink. Wenatchee is in Washington? What the fuck?

"My grandma," I say.

I don't add more. We leave it at that. Memo sees my appearance and doesn't ask me more questions. To pass the time, he lets me ask him as many questions as I want. I learn he's a farm worker on a guest worker visa, just like the other passengers on this bus. He has a wife, a son in high school, and a daughter in college. His wages from working in the United States have paid for a car, his children's school expenses, and a brand-new house in his hometown.

"I worked as a history teacher for many years, but we couldn't get ahead," he says. "With the money I earn here, we are now middle class. I can support my family. We can even afford luxuries we couldn't afford before."

Memo shows me photos of his family. He's so proud of his kids. I can tell he's a good dad. As I stare at his phone, my eyes lose focus and I see my own face in the reflection on the screen. For a second, I feel something like sadness for my own father and the years we could've had together. I shake off the feeling and remind myself I'll see Dreamer soon.

I ask Memo, "Isn't the work hard?"

"Sure. But I'm still strong. I can do it."

"Are the farmers fair? Do they treat you well?"

"Well enough." He shrugs. "Most of the time."

Outside, the Central Valley spreads out to the foothills and mountains like one big farm. Many of the state's penitentiaries are out in the sticks. Because of this, I associate big open spaces with being locked up, with loneliness and frustration. Instead of looking out the window, I stretch out my legs, fold my arms, and try to take another nap. But a few minutes later, Memo taps my shoulder.

"Hector, look at this."

I open my eyes. The other passengers are staring out the windows. On either side of the bus are rows of white trees.

"Almonds," Memo says. "They're in bloom now. This lasts one week, maybe two."

I rub my eyes and look outside into the bright sunshine. Against the clear blue sky, the trees seem to glow. Each one is covered with pale pink and white flowers. Petals cover the ground like snow.

"It's nice, isn't it?" Memo snaps a few photos with his phone. "I will send these pictures to my wife."

The orchards go on and on. As I stare, I start to drift off.

The black branches of the trees remind me of Carmen's hair. The white flowers remind me of her bedsheets. The brown earth, of her skin.

I fall asleep again, dreaming of her.

More hours pass. When the driver takes a break, I visit the truck-stop restroom and use my new wealth to buy Cokes and some halfway decent tacos for both me and Memo. After lunch, one of the passengers takes a soccer ball out of his gym bag and we play a quick match in the empty lot behind the gas station, using traffic cones and an old *Piso Mojado* sign for goals.

Overhead, the sun is bright and clear. The dry wind smells a little like cowshit. I let a goal get past me and my new *compas* go crazy with delight. Memo grabs his head and falls to his knees in fake despair.

My life is work, hustle, sleep, and sex. But play? I haven't played anything in a long time. I'm laughing. I feel like a kid.

Back on the bus, I turn my phone on to check my messages.

No voicemails, but three missed calls and one text, all from Carmen.

Where are you?

I call her but she doesn't pick up. Slowly, I tap out a text and send it to her.

takin care of some shit but i wish i was with you i'm sorry

I turn off the phone again. We have a long road to travel, and there are no outlets on this bus.

Every few hours, we make stops at gas stations and empty

parking lots, twenty minutes to stretch our legs and get a gulp of fresh air. The air gets colder. More trees fill the landscape. The sun goes down. Memo points out the town of Weed. He laughs as he takes a picture of a sign by the road. In Redding, I brush my teeth and splash warm water on my face. I change my T-shirt. Back in the bus I slip off my shoes and stretch out as best as I can on my row of seats.

I turn on my phone again. Nothing.

My chest feels hollow. I imagine being there in Carmen's bedroom again, lying in her arms instead of here in a dark, creaky bus that smells like armpits.

I text her again.

good night mi reina

I turn off the phone and fall asleep imagining her soft skin against mine.

EARLY THE NEXT MORNING, I wake up in Oregon. I turn on my phone again. No messages.

At our first stop in Corvallis, I bite the bullet and call my brother. As usual, he doesn't answer. I hang up and call Vanessa. I hear the sound of dishes. She's with Muñeca. I can hear the little girl singing in the background.

"Hey, what's up?" Vanessa says. The connection crackles a little.

"Hey," I say. "Is my brother there?"

"No, he already left for work." To Muñeca, Vanessa says, "Just one more bite of waffle. Please?"

"Listen." I clear my throat. "I'm going to tell you something, but I don't want you to trip."

Vanessa's voice goes hard and impatient, the result of living with gangsters and putting up with our *pendejadas*. "What's wrong?" she demands.

"Nothing is wrong."

"Where are you? What's going on?" Even though I expected it, Vanessa's anxiety both annoys and comforts me. "Trouble, tell me."

I spit it out. "I'm not in LA."

"Okay," she says slowly.

"I can't say where I am. But tell Sal I'm okay. And I'm not planning to be gone more than a couple days."

"When do you check in with your PO?"

I appreciate how practical she is. I'm breaking the rules, but she knows I might be able to get away with it if I don't skip any meetings with my parole officer. "Don't worry about it. I'll be there."

"Trouble—"

"Just tell Sal everything is okay. I'm on the road. I'm safe."

"You..." she starts to say, but halfway through she realizes how useless it would be to lecture me right now. "Do you need us to wire you money?"

I grip my backpack closer to me. I feel the thick envelope of cash inside, and it makes me feel warmer and safer than any blanket. "No, I'm good. I just wanted to let my brother know what's up."

In the background, Vanessa's daughter asks, "Is that *Tío* Eddie?"

Instead of answering, Vanessa says, "Finish the egg now."

The little girl whines, "But I don't like it."

Vanessa sighs, I suspect at both me and Muñeca. To me she says, "Sal's gonna be mad."

"I know," I say. "But it's for a good reason, I swear."

"Whatever." Her voice softens. "Be careful. Please."

"I will."

We hang up. My conscience is both heavier and lighter after talking to Vanessa—now the rest of my family's involved. I have to stay on my toes. I have to keep them all in mind.

There are showers at this truck stop, so I pay a little money to quickly wash up and change my clothes. After a hot cup of coffee, I almost feel human again.

Back on the road, Memo folds his arms and snoozes. The world outside the bus grows colder and grayer. Thick trees fill the landscape and we cross bridges over rivers that look like actual rivers, deep and green, not like the dried-out LA River with its tall concrete embankments and abandoned shopping carts.

South of Seattle, we finally branch off from the interstate. Rain starts to fall, first a mist, then a heavy downpour. Fat drops smack the windshield and the temperature in the bus drops even more. Mist rises up, thick and white, hiding the view. We crawl our way into the mountains and the highway is jammed with cars and trucks. When the fog breaks for a moment, that's when I see it.

Snow.

Actual snow.

Piled on the sides of the highway. Covering the mountains ahead.

Holy shit.

I've never seen snow before. Part of me wants to run to the front of the bus and beg the driver to stop. I have to know more. What does snow feel like? Soft and fluffy? Or hard, like crushed ice? I know I'm not supposed to eat yellow snow, but what about the little drops of snow coming down? What do they taste like? Do they really look like snowflakes up close?

In my excitement, I feel something like a soft, wet rip in my chest.

It hits me—I'm twenty-three years old. A convicted felon. A

hardass, tattooed all over. Down for my neighborhood as long as I can remember. A survivor.

But right now, in the foggy window, I can see my reflection. My eyes are big, and I'm smiling. I want to say I'm happy but that word feels too simple for what's in my heart right now. It's a sad kind of happy, mixed in with a little flash of pride—I'm alive. I'm here.

Snow. Mountains. A new state. A new world.

Soon the highway opens up and the bus accelerates. My window fogs up again from the moisture of my breathing, and my reflection disappears.

Shivering, I put up the hood of my sweatshirt. I close my eyes, and soon, like Memo, I fall asleep again.

COLD.

That's my first thought when I wake up—I'm fucking cold.

I yawn and stretch. We drive slowly through a small town next to a river. No one's on the street. Even though the town is neat and tidy, compared to the streets of Los Angeles, it's a ghost town. The sun hasn't gone down yet.

We pull up behind a two-story brick building. The driver parks, opens the door, and fills the passenger compartment with freezing air and the sweet smell of exhaust.

I fist-bump Memo, but we don't have time for a long good-bye. There's a white van waiting for him. He gets in it along with the six other passengers left on the bus. The door of the van slides shut and I watch the van drive away over the empty, icy road. The bus driver puts on a heavy jacket and walks across the parking lot to the office. He goes inside and closes the door behind him.

And now I'm alone.

It's quiet. I hear the soft rushing of the river and every now and then, the wind through the trees. Cold snakes up my pants legs and through my thin hoodie. I pull out my phone. It's dead —I forgot to turn it off to save the battery. Annoyed, I shove my hands into my pockets and try not to shiver.

Now what?

The stores we passed in town are all closed. I saw one or two motels by the highway, but I'm not ready to test out my new fake ID. You need confidence to run a scam, even something as simple as that. Any shadow of doubt, any fear, you're out. You're done.

I stand there in the empty parking lot next to the bus. I dig my hands into my pockets. This is a different kind of cold than any I've experienced before. It's got teeth, and it slides under my clothes and soaks through my skin and muscle until it gets to the bone.

"Where are you, Dreamer?" I say to myself. My words evaporate into white steam.

Half an hour passes until the only thing keeping my frozen feet in that parking lot is my stubbornness.

A Ford F-150 from the 1970s pulls into the lot. It's more rust than truck. A white lady in her fifties cranks down the window. She's a big girl, with bright blue eyes and bleach-blond hair styled in the same era as her truck.

"Are you Eddie?" she asks.

She knows my real name. "Yeah." My teeth chatter.

"Your dad sent me. Get in."

When I slide in and slam the heavy door shut, the lady shuts her window and turns up the rattling heater. The hit of warmth feels so good, it's like a drug. I buckle the lap belt to show her I'm responsible, and she rewards me with a big smile. She's missing a tooth and the remaining ones are crooked. She's dressed in a faded winter jacket, jeans, and worn-out snow boots. Besides some homeless Vietnam vets on Skid Row, I've never actually seen a poor white person. In Los Angeles, in my mind, all white people are rich.

"All set?" Her voice is cheerful.

"Yes, ma'am," I say, polite as a Boy Scout.

"Okay. Off we go."

TWENTY-THREE

We drive out of town, which doesn't take long. Bumping down a country road, we pass field after field of bare trees and brown ground covered in a thin layer of snow. On the other side of the road is a thick forest. The sky is turning dark.

"I'm Lisa Jo," says the lady. "You like music?"

"Sure," I say.

She turns the knob on her radio. Static one way, static the other way. She finds a sweet spot and "Hotel California" comes up, which is a funny song to hear when you're in another state for the first time in your life.

Lisa Jo bops her head. "Oh yeah. That's a *good* one." She turns it up. The headlights of the truck are weak, but bright enough for me to see the curves and twists in the road. In a loud voice, Lisa Jo sings along to the Eagles, screwing up the lyrics with so much enthusiasm that I hide my smile with my hand.

"Do you speak Spanish?" she asks.

"Yeah, a little."

"Do you know what *colitas* are?" she asks. "In the song?"

I try not to crack up. "I'm gonna guess marijuana, ma'am."

"Oh. That makes sense."

In the fading light, we pull onto a long driveway that opens into a clearing. I see a double-wide trailer next to a river. Wood is stacked high on the porch. There's a Trans Am in the driveway but it looks like it hasn't been driven since dinosaurs walked the earth. We park behind it.

"Here we are," Lisa Jo says. "Follow me."

We walk around the trailer. Lisa Jo opens the back door and in a small laundry room, she takes off her jacket and her snow boots. Her socks are mismatched, pink and striped yellow. Following her lead, I take off my shoes but I'm still too cold to take off my hoodie.

When she stands up straight, she studies me. "That the warmest thing you've got to wear?" she asks.

I nod.

"Your dad might have an extra jacket somewhere for you." She looks at me with narrowed eyes. "Hmm, I don't know if it will fit you. We might have to borrow a coat from one of the neighbors, okay?"

"Okay."

She opens a second door and I almost shit my pants. Behind the door is a giant wolf with mismatched eyes.

"Eddie, meet Outlaw," says Lisa Jo.

I catch my breath and watch as the wolf takes a few slow steps forward and nudges Lisa Jo's hand with his nose. His eyes —one blue, one orange—are runny. His fur is thick in some places, patchy in others.

"Outlaw is thirteen years old." Lisa Jo pets the top of his head. "Very old for a Husky. He doesn't move so good anymore. Doesn't hear well, either. But he's a sweetheart." She pats his butt and kisses the scruff of his neck. "Say hello, Outlaw."

The dog raises his head slowly and his tail moves back and forth, once. Step by slow step, he comes over and greets me by sniffing my crotch. I pat him on the head. He limps back to the kitchen. We follow him.

"Are you hungry?" Lisa Jo asks. "Have a seat."

I sit down at the small table in the middle of the kitchen. She starts a pot of coffee and the smell fills the trailer. There's a crate taking up half the kitchen, ridiculous to call it a crate, it's the size of a Fiat. Outlaw crawls inside and rests his big head on his paws.

I have so many questions for Lisa Jo but I have no idea where to begin. Instead, I let her ask me questions. The ones she chooses to ask are all polite, as if she also knows we're treading water in a dangerous place. She has secrets on me, and my being here means she knows more than is probably good for her.

"Have you been to Washington before, Eddie?"

"No, ma'am. This is my first time."

"What do you think so far?"

"It's nice." This is not really an answer. "It's cold," I say.

"That it is. That it is."

Lisa Jo bends over and pulls out a banged-up pot from a cabinet. I watch her take out two cans of chili, open them, and tap the contents into the pan.

"So you have two other brothers, right?" she says. "Sal and..."

"Angel," I say.

"Are you the baby?"

"No, ma'am. I'm the middle. Sal's the oldest. Angel's the youngest."

"Three boys," she says. "I can't imagine. Your poor mother."

There were four of us, once. What has Dreamer told her about my little sister? Has he even told her about Esperanza?

"Do you have any children?" I ask her.

"Yes." She smiles again, but this time there's pride in her eyes. "One daughter."

There's something familiar about her face, about those bright, sad eyes that tip downward. I can't shake the feeling that I've seen her before.

Lisa Jo clicks on the burner on the stove and places the pot on the fire. There are dirty dishes in the sink, and the trash needs to be taken out. Everything in the trailer looks run-down except for two things: a new refrigerator and in the living room, a new TV. There are lace curtains on the kitchen window, but they're gray and torn. Through the rips I can see the darkening sky, the water rushing by behind the trailer.

"Your father," Lisa Jo says, "he's been living here almost a year."

I look around, trying to see any signs of Dreamer in the house. What would those signs be? Empty liquor bottles. Maybe, the smell of *Tres Flores* in the air. A pair of work boots by the door. I see nothing of him here.

"He works at the packing house."

"Packing house?" I ask.

"Yeah. Fruit. This place? All orchards."

The image of Dreamer playing the part of a *campesino* is too strange for me to accept. He used to make fun of my mom endlessly for being too country. "So my dad picks fruit?"

"No, he drives a forklift at the warehouse. Swing shift. You'll see him later tonight." The chili sizzles against the sides of the pot and Lisa Jo gives it a stir with a wooden spoon. She pours two mugs of coffee. "Cream and sugar?"

"Both, please."

I drink and the hot liquid slides down, defrosting me. I watch as Lisa splits the chili between two glass bowls and places one in front of me with a spoon and a napkin. She sits down, bows her head, and says a quick prayer.

"Amen," we say in unison.

Lisa Jo eats slowly, daintily, like a princess or a first lady, even though she's in sweatpants and a faded T-shirt. She folds her paper napkin and dabs at the corners of her mouth—good manners.

"Are you from here?" I ask.

"Not originally. I'm from Michigan. My boyfriend was in the army. We eventually moved out here. Things didn't work out between us, but I stayed. It's been almost thirty years now."

"Why did you stay?"

She shrugs. "I grew up on a farm. Work here's the same. I'm a country girl at heart. The big city—that's not for me."

The big city—and prison—are all I've known. I take a bite of the chili and wash it down with hot coffee. Carmen has spoiled me on gourmet food, but right now, I appreciate this hot meal. "So do you work at the packing house too?"

She nods. "I used to, for many years. Until I hurt my back. I sort mail in town now. It's not a bad job. Good benefits."

Lisa Jo has steady work and her own place. She's not wealthy, but she supports herself. She seems like a nice lady, and I'm worried about what affect Dreamer has had on her life. In my mind, he's pure chaos. Whatever is balanced, he unbalances. Whatever is peaceful, he disrupts.

We finish our meal. I tell Lisa Jo to take it easy and I clean up the kitchen. I wash all of the dishes in the sink. I clean out the coffeemaker. On the windowsill above the sink is a small figurine. An elephant holding a daisy. Inscribed on the base, it says *You are my sunshine.* I gather up the trash and head out the back door.

From the living room, Lisa Jo calls, "There's a special locker about a hundred feet down the driveway," she says, "to keep the bears out."

I zip up my sweatshirt and put on my shoes. Out there in the dark, the cold burns my lungs. I hurry down the gravel driveway. What a way to go out. I walk a little faster. Homeboy, eaten by a bear. That'd be fucked.

Lisa Jo and I spend the rest of the evening watching television while she knits in the light of a reading lamp. The television is so new, there's still plastic on it. We watch *Dancing with the Stars* and the local news. At eleven thirty, she yawns and looks at the clock.

"Will my dad be here soon?" I ask.

"He should be."

I help her as she makes up the couch with bedsheets and three heavy blankets. "Let me know if you need anything else, okay?" she says.

"Okay."

"Good night, Eddie." Even a missing tooth doesn't ruin Lisa Jo's kind smile—not really. Nothing can snuff out a light like that. "See you in the morning, kid."

"You too. Thank you."

Lisa Jo goes into her bedroom and closes the door. I plug in my phone and turn it back on.

No texts. No messages.

Wait, one message. My heart jumps up a little only to be smashed back down.

NO SERVICE

Fuck.

I snap the phone closed and lay it on the floor. With a groan, I stretch out on the couch and close my eyes in the dark.

I wait. Still no Dad, no Dreamer. I listen to the sound of the snoring ancient wolf in the kitchen, to the rushing river outside.

———

I'M LOCKED UP, pacing back and forth. I've just received the news. My cellie—I can't remember his name—tells me to calm down. I push him away.

"My dad's dead," I murmur, again and again. "They killed him. They killed my dad."

The pain is intense, but so is the confusion, the sense of uselessness. The anger and the love I've always carried for my father blend together into a wave that drowns me in my jail cell until I can't breathe.

I can't write him off.

Because that would be like writing myself off, and...I can't do that either.

Someone squeezes my shoulder.

I open my eyes.

Tears wet my cheeks—a souvenir from the dream.

I'm buried in blankets. The laundry soap smells different from the all-natural hippie stuff Rafa uses.

Shit, where am I?

I blink.

Wait—Carmen's bed?

No.

"Rise and shine." Another squeeze. "Come on. Wake up, kiddo."

I push the covers off my face. The small living room is filled with bright sunlight. I squint to see who's talking to me.

He's tall, but much skinnier than I remember. Sunken cheeks, bags under his eyes. His skin is rough and red. Still handsome, in spite of everything. Instead of a gangster's shaved head he's got a full head of black and gray hair. Instead of his khakis and white T-shirt, he's wearing a Bass Pro Shops sweatshirt, jeans, and wool socks.

Dreamer Rosas.

Back from the dead.

I sit up. "Dad."

"Mi'jo."

He gets down on his knees by the sofa and embraces me for a long time. In my grief, I see the old wolf crouching in the corner of the room at the feet of Lisa Jo, who drinks coffee and watches us with smiling eyes. My chest is tight and hot, like it is about to burst.

"I never thought I'd see you again," I say. "We thought you were dead."

He slaps my back and lets go. I watch as he wipes his eyes with the back of his hand. "Shit," he says. "Not even death can keep your old man down. Believe that."

Dreamer tells me to take a shower and get dressed. Lisa Jo has gotten me a warm fleece sweatshirt from one of her neighbors along with a long-sleeve thermal shirt. I come out to the kitchen. There's another cup of coffee waiting for me along with a bowl of cornflakes. As I eat, Outlaw rests his chin on my knee and looks up at me with those weird mismatched eyes.

"I've got to go to work now." Lisa Jo pats my back. "You catch up with your dad today, okay? Maybe we can all go out tonight and celebrate with a meal."

"Thank you," I say. "For everything."

She nods. "You two be good."

After breakfast, my dad hands me a puffy jacket. I put it on and follow him out with the dog. We walk down a path that runs next to the river. There are thin patches of snow here and there. The air is so fresh and clean, it seems to burn the smog out of my lungs. Thick trees grow on either side of the water, which is shallow and quick and makes me feel cold just looking at it.

My dad walks next to me, his boots crunching in the gravel. Outlaw limps slowly next to us, setting the pace.

"So," my dad says. "You have any trouble getting up here?"

I feel shy around him, so I tell him about my trip. I include all the details. I tell him about the bus, Memo, the almond blossoms, the snow. I thank him for the ID, the bus ticket, and the care package, but I don't ask where the money came from. Nervous—I'm talking too much. He seems to enjoy it, and laughs at my jokes. For the first time since I left Carmen's room, I feel a lightness in my heart.

We follow the curve of the river and the path narrows. After barely a mile, Outlaw slows down so much, we stop and sit down on some boulders. The old dog settles down in the dirt and flops on his side. His paws are muddy.

We toss rocks into the river. There are a million rocks in the middle. I can hear the water dragging them across the bottom of the river, slowly grinding them to sand.

I look at my father's face. It's been six years since I've seen him, and in that time he looks like he's aged twenty.

So I ask the only question I can.

"What happened?"

TWENTY-FOUR

Dreamer starts the story exactly where we left off—at the criminal courthouse downtown on the day of the sentencing hearing for my brother and me.

Car-jacking. With gang enhancements for our East Side Hollenbeck affiliations, we each got five years.

"I saw them take you both away. When I got home, the first thing I did was call my connect." My dad rubs his arms through his jacket. "I went on a bender, you could say. Then I went on another. And another."

Sal and I had heard the stories. My father had done heroin in his youth, but stopped cold turkey when he married our mom. He started up again after she died. I watched him through an open door once. I remember seeing the flash of the spoon. The smell. He found ways to keep his heroin addiction under control while we lived at home—shooting up just became part of his daily routine.

"I sat in the house. I looked around. I said to myself, in a little while, this will all be gone. Furniture. Truck. House. And I was right. I lost it all. Like some fucking *tecato*." He smiles to himself—smiles, as if he's proud of how badly he's fucked up.

"My case worker sent me to Narcotics Anonymous again. That's where I met Daisy. She was good for me. Cleaned myself up just enough for Ruben to put me back to work. Made myself useful again."

He makes it sound so simple, but I know my dad. This was probably years of back and forth, jail to the streets and back again, failure after failure after failure. I toss another rock into the river and watch the white foam swallow it up.

"So then what happened?"

My father rubs his arms again. Under his sleeves, I can imagine the old track marks tangling with his gang tattoos, the scars of his drug use snaking through the names of his children— Salvador, Eduardo, Angel, Esperanza.

"It's a long story, mi'jo," he says. "I guess something clicked for me when I moved in with Daisy. She is a good woman. She knows what it's like—sabes que, she understood. She gets the addict mentality, and she knows what it takes to change it."

I say nothing. Outlaw slowly gets to his feet and shuffles toward me. I pet his big fluffy head.

"So I started to take a little off the top. Here and there. Some milk money, nothing they'd notice. I socked it all away. Over the years, it added up. A little lifeline for me and for you and your brothers if you ever needed it." He takes off his hat and runs his hand through his thick hair. "God knows I have my regrets when it comes to you and your brothers. But maybe, I thought, maybe I could do something for all of you now."

I study his face. I'm not sure if I believe him, but he looks so sincere and defeated that I *want* to believe him.

"But something went wrong," I say.

"Your father's name is Dreamer Rosas." He laughs. "Of course something went wrong." He stands up and stretches. His clothes hang on him—he looks like Miguel, the groundskeeper at the church, his old buddy. I have trouble realizing that this scarecrow is the same guy who raised me, the same tough-looking muscleman who carried me on his shoulders when I was a kid.

We head back to the trailer. My dad tells me the rest of the story in a quiet voice, as if he's afraid there are people who will hear him here in the middle of the woods two states away from the neighborhood.

"Eventually, the big homies did the math and found out my payments were light. They were not happy. So Ruben had a talk with them on my behalf. We made a bargain. They took away my collections and I had to pay them back what I took plus interest. But your old man got to live another day."

"That's the story I heard," I said. "Sal and I—we thought you dodged a bullet."

"I did. Multiple bullets."

"What went wrong?"

"You know your dad enjoys a drop every now and then. La Sirena—you remember that place?"

"Your old dive bar. Of course I remember."

"I was there, celebrating my victory. *Estaba pedo.* I can't remember. Apparently I started mouthing off about the big homies. I can't remember that either. Some ESHB captains were in the room. Didn't like my attitude. Later that night, Ruben and his right-hand man Demon show up at Daisy's. They want to take me for a ride."

My blood goes cold. Ruben and Dreamer came up together. They were as close as brothers. But if there's a green light, friendships, blood bonds, promises, nothing matters. Ruben was tasked with the murder. He had to follow orders or get green-lit along with my dad.

"Where did they take you?"

"Angeles National Forest."

Graveyard for gangsters. ESHB has buried more bodies in that forest than anyone can remember. "What did you do?"

"I couldn't put Daisy in danger. So I went along with them. The whole ride up I talked. I bargained. I begged. I made promises. But Ruben said, 'Your time is up. Nothing personal, Dreamer. This is just business.'"

As my dad and I walk along the pathway, the clouds gather and hide the sun.

"We reached a trailhead. Demon shut off the engine and pulled a piece. Together he and Ruben walked me out into the trees. It was so dark. I thought to myself, 'This is it. I'm never going to see my boys again. Never tell them I love them again.'"

We're quiet for a moment. My dad gets hold of his emotions and continues the story. "They marched me to a ridge on the side of the mountain where they could push me over. I remember looking out and feeling nothing but sky, nothing but emptiness."

Ahead of us, Outlaw sniffs the air. When some squirrels get into a fight in the branches of a nearby tree, he lets out a big, steamy bark. The sound echoes in the forest. I feel it in my chest.

"At the last minute," my dad says, "Ruben takes the gun from Demon. 'I'll do it,' he says. Like some kind of hero. 'He's my responsibility.' He makes me get on my knees. I say my final prayers. Then he fires—two shots. Right next to my ear. The biggest sound you ever heard, *mi'jo*. My ears are ringing, painful. My heart is beating hard. I'm not really sure if I'm alive or not. In the dark, I throw myself over the ridge. Roll fifty, maybe a hundred feet over the rocks. I slice open my legs, my arms. I land in some kind of ditch. Every part of me hurts. But I don't move. I don't breathe."

I stop in my tracks. "Are you saying that Ruben...let you *live*?"

My father nods. "He found a way out for both of us. Faked the murder, and used Demon for a witness. Smart guy. I guess you don't get to be top dog for nothing." He laughs to himself. "Smart guy."

The story is too crazy to believe, but for that reason, I think it might be true. Dreamer Rosas lives larger than life, and this would be just one more unbelievable adventure in his unbelievable life.

"What did you do after that?"

"I waited there until morning, freezing my ass off, bleeding, praying to God there were no hungry bears in the neighborhood. Then I hiked until I had phone reception and called Daisy. She came and got me. That same day we cashed out my savings and I came up here."

"Why up here? Why Wenatchee?"

"Lisa Jo didn't tell you?"

I shake my head. "Tell me what?"

"Daisy's her daughter. This is where she grew up."

The puzzle solves itself in my head. I think of the elephant on the windowsill holding a daisy. *You are my sunshine.* Now I understand. Daisy's father was black.

I watch as own my dad plays fetch with Outlaw. It's not really fetch, more like my dad throws the stick once and Outlaw slowly goes to get it. They play a weak tug-of-war together, two old survivors who can barely grip the piece of wood between them. But the dog is wagging and my dad is laughing and I think, they're alive. Right now, that's enough.

THAT NIGHT, Lisa Jo drives us to dinner. She and my dad are both smiling big, joking, and elbowing me like they can't hold in their excitement. I get the sense they don't go out much, and I can't help smiling myself. My dad reminds me that tonight I'm Hector, not Eddie. I can call him Dad, but his name is Omar, which is the name they know him by at the packing house where he works.

We pull into a motel whose parking lot is full. Next to the registration office is a restaurant that looks like a truck-stop diner with the lights turned down to make it fancier. We take off our jackets and coats and hang them up inside the door. It's busy inside. The tables are full of families and big burly people in hunting camo. Almost everyone is white, including the hostess who leads us to a booth in the back of the restaurant by the kitchen.

My dad orders the most expensive thing on the menu and encourages Lisa Jo and me to get whatever we want. We order beers—just the regular stuff, nothing like my brother's beer. Dreamer tells Lisa Jo to get the sautéed mushrooms on her steak like he's just won the lottery and can't wait to spend the prize. He's loud and charming, like he wants everyone in the dining room to know he's a celebrity.

The diners look over their shoulders at us and for a second, I'm embarrassed for my dad. Sometimes he'd act like this when he worked at the slaughterhouse. He'd tell my mom to dress us all up. He'd take us to a restaurant and order enough food for an army. For a night, he got to play the big successful man he always wanted other people to see whenever they looked at him. He'd blow a week's food budget on one meal. My mom hated it. My dad loved it.

One round of beers turns into two. My dad's voice gets louder. "Lisa Jo," he says, "this kid, his nickname is Trouble. You know how he got it?"

She shakes her head. "How?"

"Tell her," my dad says to me.

For some reason, my dad loves this story. "I was ten," I say.

"It was the Fourth of July. Everyone was on summer vacation. All us kids stayed out late, watching the neighbors set off all their fireworks. At midnight, almost everyone had already gone to bed. But my brother Sal—I don't know how—got his hands on some illegal fireworks. We snuck out to light them. Sal handed me the lighter and a bottle. I had never lit anything before so my hands were shaking, like this." I'm already laughing. "I knew what to do because we'd been watching our neighbors all night. So I set up the bottle. I lit the rocket. But I didn't look up to see what was above us."

Lisa Jo starts laughing too. "Oh no."

"The rocket went off—hiss, pop, pop, pop! And it landed right in the branches of a palm tree."

"An *old* palm tree," my dad adds. "A *dry* palm tree."

"Apparently they're extremely flammable," I say. "So there's my brother and me, standing there, and the palm tree ignites like the Olympic torch. It's the biggest fire we've ever seen. The tree is four, five stories tall. Flaming branches are coming down. The little sparks burn holes in our T-shirts. You can see it from the freeway. You can see it for twenty miles."

"Three fire engines showed up," my dad says. "Everyone came out to watch."

"My brother was smart. He went back into the house and climbed into bed like he'd been sleeping the whole time. But I hid in the crawlspace under the house. My mother found me and dragged me out by the collar. She was yelling, 'You are nothing but trouble!' Everyone in the neighborhood saw us and started laughing and pointing. Then they started cheering, 'Trou-ble! Trou-ble! Trou-ble!'"

My dad is laughing so hard he almost knocks his beer off the table. "And this kid"—he slaps my back so hard I cough—"raises his hands like Rocky Balboa. Hyping the crowd up. 'Trou-ble! Trou-ble!' From that moment on, that's what we all called him."

TWENTY-FIVE

The restaurant is crowded and cozy. My steak tastes delicious. I see Lisa Jo's smiling face and hear my dad's big laugh. My heart is warm in my chest. For a second, I imagine I'm in some weird version of Dreamer Rosas's afterlife.

After he pays for our meal, my dad asks Lisa Jo to drop us off.

She hesitates. "You sure?"

He's got his arm around her, which seems weird, but I chalk it up to being squashed in the truck. Also, he's always been a touchy-feely guy, especially when it comes to women. "Sure I'm sure," he says. "A couple drinks with my son. No big deal."

"What time is your shift tomorrow?"

"We won't be out too late."

"But—"

Dreamer makes his voice soft, just like he used to when he needed to calm my mom down or persuade her to do something she didn't want to do. "Don't worry about me, *mi'ja*. I'm a big boy, okay?"

In the end, Lisa Jo pulls up behind a biker bar off the highway. It's nothing much—a brick building with a metal door.

Lisa Jo's face is worried as we climb out of the truck. "Can you call me when you're ready to come home?"

"Okay." My dad kisses her cheek and slides out of the cab.

"Look after your dad," Lisa Jo calls to me.

"Hey, I don't need looking after!"

"I will," I tell her and turn to follow Dreamer inside.

People crowd the dark, smelly bar even though it's a week-night. I figure this place is the only game in town.

My dad greets his friends with fist bumps and chest bumps. He's happy, loudly introducing me to everyone as his son. I shake hands with everyone, but inside, I'm worried. Who's in here? Who's listening? After the story he's told me, we should be laying low, not playing celebrities.

I follow Dreamer to a table on the other side of the pool table where a group of guys are already congregated. They've got pool cues, and their table is full of dead soldiers and empty pitchers. My awareness level goes up a couple notches. But the guys cheer when they see my dad, and he shows me off to them —"My son. You can call him Trouble. Takes after his old man."

My dad's friends are mostly coworkers from the packing plant. I can't hear what they tell me over the noise of the juke-box, but I nod and laugh when I can. I don't share anything about myself.

The beer in my hand goes warm as I keep an eye on my dad, like Lisa Jo told me to. Impatient, I take my phone out of my pocket. Still no service. I see a payphone in the back of the bar. I think about calling Carmen—but she'll see where I'm calling from. She'll ask questions.

I put my phone back in my pocket.

The less she knows about this part of my life, the better.

One round of pool turns into two. Three rounds of beers turn into four. Soon Dreamer has ordered a tray of tequila shots for his buddies. He's too trashed to notice I don't drink one.

He's buying drinks left and right, flashing his *feria*.

Where the hell is he getting all this cash?

More people come into the bar. It's so crowded I can't see who they are. I try not to show it with my body language, but I'm on alert. I squint my eyes. A shaved head? Tattoos? Did I see what I saw?

When I was locked up in general population, I could sense when a fight was about to break out. The energy in the room would change. I can feel the change now.

I keep my sights on the exit of the bar. I lean my back up against the wall. The knife I brought from LA is hidden in my sock. The weight of it makes me feel both anxious and calm.

Dreamer staggers over to me and throws his arm around my shoulders. He's leaning back and forth, unsteady on his feet. Even though he's skinny now, I can feel the strength in his wiry body. Indestructible—gangbanger, drunk, addict. He's like a piece of beef jerky that can't be chewed.

"How you doing, Trouble?" he asks. "Are you having a good time?"

"Fuck yeah." I fake a smile. "How about one more and we call Lisa Jo?"

Before he can answer, one of his friends grabs at his jacket. "Come on, Omar," Larry says. He's one of my dad's coworkers from the plant. He mimics smoking with his hand.

I follow them out of the back door. It's cold as fuck. I zip up my jacket and shove my hands into the pockets. One weak bulb lights up the alley. It's snowing, just a little. The flakes disappear when they hit the ground.

I watch as Larry, a guy with a gray beard and bony shoulders, sways on his feet and slowly pulls a pack of cigarettes from his pocket. I watch as the two *borrachos* struggle to light up. They almost cheer when they finally accomplish their goal.

I'm laughing when two shadows appear behind us.

SOMEONE WAS WATCHING us in the bar. Sent a quick text when we left—*easy money*.

They're big. White dudes, maybe bikers.

More importantly, they've done this before.

"Empty your pockets! All of it!"

One goes straight for me. He's counting on me being drunk, so when I rush him, he's not ready. We crash to the muddy asphalt and start whaling on each other. Adrenaline fills my veins. The smell of wet dirt fills my lungs.

I land a few blows, feel the satisfying impact against my knuckles. He gets in a few, and I brace myself to take the punches. He pops me in the face, same side where Lalo got me the other day. But I'm too amped up to feel any pain.

I get him in the side of the head. He's stunned for half a second, just enough time for me to get to my feet and pull the knife.

That ends things fast. When he sees the flash of the blade, he scrambles backward and takes off down the alley.

I turn around. My dad's friend is sitting on his ass, dazed. My dad is trading blows with the other robber, which I chalk up to muscle memory, not sobriety. The other guy is more annoyed than hurt.

"Hey!" I yell.

The guy looks up. I lunge at him. To avoid the knife, he trips backward over Larry's legs and falls. He looks like he's about to get up so I kick him, hard, in the side. Groaning, he struggles to his feet. His path is crooked as he jogs away, escaping into the shadows of the alley.

My dad is unhinged. He screams and hollers after the guy. "That's right! You better run! *¡Culeros!*"

"Dad, pipe down," I tell him. I put the knife back in its

hiding place before helping Larry up and leaning him against the wall. He's dizzy on top of being drunk. The side of his face is swollen where he caught a solid punch on the jaw. "You okay?"

"Yeah, yeah." He sways before getting his balance. "Thanks."

"*¡Pinches maricones!*" My dad is still yelling. Someone inside the bar might hear him, might come outside to investigate. We'd have to answer questions.

"Dad—"

Before he can answer me, my father bends over, braces his hands on his knees, and barfs up a tequila shot, ten beers, and a fancy steak dinner.

When he's finished, Larry hands him a handkerchief. "Good one, boss."

My dad wipes his face. They're giggling.

Fucking drunks.

"Give me your phone," I tell my dad. "We gotta get the hell out of here."

"I don't have it, *mi'jo*. They took it. My wallet too—all my cash."

I bite back my annoyance. I can't get a signal on my phone. There's a phone in the bar, but I don't want to go back inside and risk running into more trouble.

I look around, watching for witnesses or police or the robbers returning with bigger, angrier friends. There's no one. What do I do? We need to leave this place.

"I got a car," Larry says. "The guy didn't take my keys."

After a slow, drunken search, we find Larry's Bronco parked on the street not far from the bar. He gives me the keys. I start it up and run the heater. Larry climbs into the back seat and falls asleep, groaning and holding his jaw. I strap my dad into the passenger seat and slide back the driver's seat so that I can fit. I adjust all the mirrors. Because of my run-ins with the law, I've lost my license and driving privileges. I haven't driven a car in five years. When I turn the key, the roar of the engine sends tingles all the way up my spine. A rush. I grab the wheel. I missed this.

"We're going to have to take him home to Lisa Jo." I toss my head toward Larry, groaning in the back seat.

"She don't care," my dad slurs. "'S'fine."

I put the truck into gear. "All right. Tell me which way to go to get back."

"Sure, sure, mi'jo. Of course."

We pull onto the highway.

I'm a patient guy, more or less. You don't survive five years in prison unless you learn how to swallow your anger and wait patiently.

But not even time in the state pen prepared me for the night ahead.

Dreamer Rosas, drunk as fuck, telling me to turn right, then left, then right again. To make a U-turn because I've gone too far. To cross this bridge and make a left at the stop sign. To look for a gas station that isn't there, to look for a barn we already passed twenty minutes ago.

Forty-five minutes later we're lost in the woods in the middle of the night, and I'm gripping the steering wheel to keep from putting my fist through the windshield.

The heater in the Bronco sucks. I'm cold and wet and dirty from my fall in the mud, my eye is swelling up again, and my dad smells like vomit. Larry's passed out in the back seat, groaning in his sleep. I'm half anticipating that he's going to barf too.

In frustration, I pull over into a turnout and stop the Bronco a safe distance from the highway. I put the car in park and turn to my dad.

"Why are you stopping?" he says. "We're almost there."

"No, we're not." I let out a big sigh. "We're going to wait until you're sober enough to give me some decent directions."

"I *have* been giving you decent directions!" He throws his hands up in the air. "You just don't listen. You're just like your mom. Never listen. Think you know everything."

Inside, I flinch. I hate that he brings her up so casually. I was never my mom's favorite, but as I get older, I realize her intentions were always good. She tried to teach us to behave. She kept us safe and fed. She acted out of love.

So it makes me angry that my dad—the guy who was supposed to look after us and failed spectacularly, miserably— feels entitled enough to talk shit about her like this.

But what's the use of arguing with a drunk?

"Get some sleep." My voice is defeated. No fight. "When you wake up, we'll get going."

"We're going to freeze out here!" My dad bangs the dashboard. "Just go, go straight. It's up the road."

I ignore him. I just sit there, trying not to boil alive in my own anger.

Something has been bothering me since he told me the story of his run-in with Ruben. A suspicion has been tickling the back of my throat all day. Right now, my nerves are worn down. My head aches. So I decide to ask him, flat-out.

"Dad, what really happened that night with Demon and Ruben?"

The expression on his face changes slowly from angry to confused. "What do you mean? I told you everything."

"Bullshit."

"What? Why do you say that?"

I stop for a minute and think about what he's just said. Not, "It's all true," but, "Why do you think I'm lying?" As if Dreamer

Rosas can admit that he lies, but he can't believe he's been caught.

"The money," I say. "You told me you took some off the top and put it away. But I've known you my whole life. You don't have the discipline. You can't save for shit. Tonight, I watched you flash money left and right. You bought Lisa Jo a new fridge and a new TV." I save the biggest argument for last. The nursing home invoice was how Sal and I first discovered Dreamer was still alive. "You're even paying for our grandmother's nursing home back in California."

He laughs. "What, your old man can't work for a living? I was employed at the slaughterhouse for thirteen years. A union job. How do you think we got that house you grew up in? I earned it. Every nail, every board. I bought it."

I shake off the anger that rises inside me. "I know how a dollar spends, Dad. Driving a forklift? You're not making money like this. Not like this."

"That's your argument? I don't know how to make money like this? There's a lot you don't know about me, kiddo. A lot."

"I know enough." For example, I know my father's pressure points, so I use that knowledge now. "Sal and me, we're not kids anymore. You can't fool us into thinking you're a hero. You're not smart enough to figure this out. So what's the truth?"

"What? 'Not smart enough'?" He bangs the dashboard again. "'Not smart enough'? This is how you talk to your father?"

I don't like making him angry. I don't want to hurt him. But I need to get to the bottom of this. So I keep pushing. "You don't know how to run a con like this. You don't have the connections. You don't have the pull."

"*Mi'jo*, let me remind you of something you seem to have forgotten." He speaks slowly, deliberately. "I am an OG. You know what that stands for? Original gangster. I earned my stripes. I'm not some peewee, some foot soldier. I'm not some *pinche leva*. I've been running and gunning since I was in middle school and you have the *ganas* to tell me I don't have the connections to take care of me and mine?"

The answer to that question is a NO so big and obvious neither one of us has the heart to say it out loud.

"You and Sal were locked up," he continues. "I was getting clean, taking care of business. Then I saw some things that made me wonder."

"Like what?"

"Ruben. Going around town, talking to people he shouldn't be talking to."

Now we're getting somewhere. "Talking to who?"

My dad glances into the back seat. Larry's out cold. Still, my dad drops his voice and switches to Spanish. "Shot-callers from Las Palmas."

That surprises me. "What?" Hollenbeck's leader talking to a rival gang? This is some heavy shit. "Are you sure?"

"I didn't believe it at first either. So I followed him. Learned his patterns. Spent some money on a camera. Got all James Bond and shit. I wanted proof I wasn't crazy. And then I got it— Ruben having a conversation with some Las Palmas, out by the railroad tracks and the warehouses. Talking about setting up a joint operation with them, separate from his dealings with Hollenbeck."

"Do you mean what I think you mean?"

My dad nods. "Ruben wanted out of the Organization. He was going directly to the cartel."

TWENTY-SIX

The temperature of my blood drops several more degrees.

Forget the truth—shit, forget the lie.

The conversation my dad and I are having right now could get us killed.

"What did you do then?" My voice is dry.

"Me? Shit. I prayed. I got on my knees and prayed for guidance." He shakes his head. "I thought about not saying anything. There's power in having dirt on someone. You can play the card later if you need to. I thought I'd tell the big homies locked up in Pelican Bay. They'd order the hit out on Ruben to protect the gang's interests. And he'd deserve it too—fucking traitor." My dad rubs his arms again. It's a tic. "But what good would those two options do me? Nothing. So your dad did something smart."

"What?"

"I went to Ruben and told him exactly what I had on him. The recording of him talking to Las Palmas and selling out East Side Hollenbeck."

My stomach cramps up. I've never trusted Ruben when it comes to his dealings with me, but I never thought he'd roll on the gang. He's an OG, much more powerful than my dad. A leader.

On top of that, I can't believe my dad went toe-to-toe with him over this. "Why would you do that? And why didn't he kill you when you showed him the recording?"

My dad smiles. "I told you your father is smart. I made two copies of the file. I told Ruben I put the copies in safekeeping and if anything ever happened to me, my source would send one to Pelican Bay and one to San Quentin. All the big homies would see him dealing dirty. Ruben would be done. Green light."

I must be staring at him with my mouth open.

He laughs and taps his temple. "See, *mi'jo?* I know that man. He'll do anything to save his own ass. So I bargained with him. I said, 'Fake my death. I'll leave town. Pay me off and I won't say shit.' He agreed. Travel expenses, a nursing home for your grandmother, a monthly payment. It all comes from him. All for the freedom to run his business. And if you knew how much that motherfucker was making, you'd see that what I get is nothing." My dad whistles. "Drop in the bucket."

My dad kicks back in the seat and looks out the window at the dark forest. He laughs to himself. "Drop in the bucket," he says again.

I should be happy to learn the truth. Instead, I'm shaking with anger.

Dreamer Rosas is a sellout just like Ruben is, only worse— he's a dropout too, faking his death and hiding in the woods.

He didn't mention my brothers or me—it didn't occur to him to think of our safety when he did this. He took the money and ran, perfectly happy to let us absorb the pain, thinking our father was dead.

Who does that? To his kids? To anyone?

He didn't reach out to us until we sniffed him out like bloodhounds.

"What about Sal and Angel and me?" I snap. "Did you think about us at all when you did this?"

"*Mi'jo*, the three of you, let's be honest. You're better off without me. You even said so yourself—you're doing good. No more running and gunning. Staying straight. I was never able to do that. If I was around, all I'd do is fuck things up for you."

"So what?" I say. "So what? Do you know what hell it was to be locked up and learn your dad is dead? That you couldn't be out there to protect him?"

Instead of saying anything, my father shrugs at me. Shrugs—like I asked him if he wanted pizza or hamburgers for dinner.

"We all do what we gotta do. You know that." He folds his arms and settles into his seat. "And you and me—we're together now anyways. So none of that matters. Right, Trouble?"

MY FATHER—HE'S wrong.

It matters to me.

Soon Dreamer is snoring, like Larry. Exhausted, I put the car in drive and circle around until I find some landmarks that look familiar. After that, it takes me twenty minutes to find Lisa Jo's trailer. I am relieved and furious at the same time. We've been on a wild goose chase for no reason except my dad's fucking stubbornness.

I half carry Larry through the front door while Outlaw sniffs him. My dad shuffles in behind us. He strips off his dirty jacket and shirt and leaves them on the floor of the mudroom.

Lisa Jo comes out of the kitchen. She's wearing flannel pajamas. "Are you all okay? I was so worried."

"I'm sorry," I say. Lisa Jo doesn't deserve this. I turn my head to avoid Larry's death breath. "Things just got out of hand."

Lisa Jo looks between us. "I tried to call. Why didn't you pick up?"

"Everything is fine," Dreamer says. "What's the big deal?"

I'm laying Larry down on the floor and throwing an old blanket over him when a shadow appears in the kitchen behind Lisa Jo. I jump back, my nerves still on edge.

I blink.

What the fuck?

Maybe I got smacked in the head harder than I thought.

"I tried to call," Lisa Jo says again, "but I couldn't reach you."

Carmen stands in the doorway. She is wearing one of Lisa Jo's sweatshirts and holding a mug of hot coffee.

"My car almost didn't make it up here." She gives me a sad smile. "You should've warned me."

TWENTY-SEVEN

"Who the hell is she?" My father sobers up quick. His eyes harden as he looks Carmen over.

I push aside my surprise and try to ignore the warmth that spreads through my body. "She's a friend."

"What the fuck, Trouble?" he barks. "I said, don't tell no one where you're going."

"Calm down, Dad." I hold up my hands. "I didn't say nothing."

"Then how did she find you?" He frowns at Carmen before peeking out of the window at the empty street. "How do you know you can trust her?"

He talks as if Carmen isn't standing right in front of us.

I stand up straight. I know I look like hell. I ignore my father, take Carmen's coffee cup, and put it carefully on the counter. While everyone watches, I hug her tightly, pulling her body against mine. I know she's angry with me. I deserve it. But by some miracle of miracles, she's here. I kiss the top of her head and hold her tighter.

"It's good to see you," I whisper.

When she hugs me back, I can finally breathe.

My father is complaining, but I can't hear what he's saying.

Carmen pulls back to face him. "He didn't tell me where he was going. I followed him. My battery died two towns back," she says. "That's how I got delayed. The sign on the bus said Wenatchee, so I drove here after my car was fixed."

Dreamer seems satisfied, even though the story doesn't sound quite right to me. "Why would you do that?" my father asks. "Drive a thousand miles?"

"I was worried about him," she says without hesitating. She looks at me. "You—I was worried about you."

"Watch out, *mi'jo*." Dreamer laughs to himself and twirls his index finger at his temple. "She's already crazy."

Lisa Jo sees the spark of violence in my eyes and stands up between my father and me.

"Come on," she says to him. "You must be tired. Let's go."

He puts his arm around her and takes her into the bedroom.

I stand in the living room and stare as they close the door behind them.

It takes a second for the truth to hit me.

I think of Daisy back in LA, keeping my dad's secrets for him. I'm almost certain she's the one with the recordings. If Ruben finds her, she's in serious danger. He's ordered the killings of people for much, much less.

She's taking big risks for Dreamer, I'm guessing because she loves him.

But does she know that he's sleeping with her mom at the same time?

It's easy for women to fall in love with Dreamer. It's a disaster for them to stay in love with him.

Two women, both devoted and kind—how could he do this to them?

To my mother?

To any of us?

"Are you okay?" Carmen asks.

My stomach turns. I rush to the bathroom, shut the door, and puke into the toilet. Disgusted, I flush it. I take off my shirt and look in the mirror above the sink.

Trashed.

I look—and feel—like shit.

When I was a kid, I idolized my dad. Tough, street smart, good looking, always running one game or another. But now I'm a man. And nothing can keep me from seeing the flaws in his character. The carelessness. The self-centeredness. The addictive personality—for drugs, for booze, for women, for status.

He was willing to trade away everything meaningful in his life for shit that didn't matter.

An ugly truth rises inside me.

What am I doing here?

Am I chasing the real Dreamer Rosas? Or am I chasing my idea of what our story should be? What was I expecting up here? A happy ever after? A warm reunion with my long-lost father? For years I felt guilty that I couldn't protect him. Now all I feel is angry that I wasted those years on guilt.

I scrub away the dirt that's caked in my beard. In the light, I see my knuckles are scratched up and swollen. I wash my face and towel it dry. The cut on my eyebrow isn't big. It'll close up soon. There's some swelling, but it'll go down in a couple days.

Behind the mud and the blood, my face is still intact.

I am still intact.

I WALK out to the living room where Carmen sits on the sofa, waiting. Larry snores under his blanket, warm and oblivious.

"I need some air," I say quietly.

Carmen and I put on a couple old jackets hanging by the

door. Outlaw follows us behind the house and out to the river. The porch lights are just strong enough to light our path.

"You didn't follow the bus," I say.

She shakes her head. "No. I woke up at noon that day. You were long gone."

"So how did you find me?"

"Rafa," she says. "I didn't want your father to know, so I lied."

I shake my head. "That old *marijuano*. Jesus."

"To be fair, he wouldn't tell me, at first," she says. "I had to get him raging drunk. He was trashed."

"How did you find out we were staying with Lisa Jo?"

"I just asked around town." She pauses. "Speaking Spanish helps a lot. People open up, start sharing."

"So my father isn't the secret agent he thinks he is."

Carmen shakes her head. "Not up here, anyway." She tucks her hands into her pockets. Her nose looks cold. "Rafa told me half of the story. Lisa Jo told me the rest. But why did you keep all of this a secret from me?"

"Are you angry?"

"I was, at first," she says. "But more than that, I realized I was worried about you. Why didn't you just tell me about your dad? I could've helped you. I could've done something."

I pull her close. The air is so cold it stings my nose, but Carmen's soft breaths warm my neck and cheek. "I didn't want you to get mixed up in any of this." I pause. "I wanted to protect you."

"I can protect myself."

She is tough. A badass in lots of ways. But there are some dangers we can't protect ourselves from, as hard as we try.

"You drove a thousand miles," I whisper.

"More than a thousand," she says.

"Why?"

"I had to know you were okay."

I don't know what to say. No one has ever done anything like this for me. I stroke her hair and kiss her forehead and rub her arms. When we kiss, it's almost shy, as if we have an audience. As if the strange trees are watching us. As if the old dog cares.

"Eddie?"

"Yes, baby girl?" I'm caressing her cheeks.

"I'm fucking cold."

We start back to the house, but I forgot something.

"Wait," I say. "Hold up."

In the dark, I walk up to the edge of the water. I take the knife out of my sock and throw it hard. The river is so loud, I don't hear the splash, only the nonstop roar of water rushing over rocks.

"What was that?" Carmen asks.

I hesitate, but it doesn't feel right to keep secrets from her any more. "A knife."

She frowns. "Did you hurt someone with it?"

"No. But I could have."

We go back inside. With Larry and the dog asleep on the floor, Carmen and I keep our clothes on. We share the narrow couch and hold each other very close. I kiss her and stroke her hair. Soon she's drowsing on my chest and her gentle weight calms me down enough to fall asleep.

In the morning, I pack my bag, get dressed, and say goodbye to Outlaw. I don't leave a note, and I regret not saying goodbye to Lisa Jo. But I'm done here. There's nothing left to say.

When the sun comes up over the trees, we're on the road. Carmen's behind the wheel, and I'm at her side.

WE'RE WINDING down the mountain when my phone gets reception at last. I watch the message alerts appear. Three missed calls from my brother. One missed call from Vanessa. Two voicemails.

The first voice message isn't a surprise. It's from Sal. He's mad.

"Where the hell are you? Vanessa said that you skipped town. What the fuck—this is bullshit. Violating your parole? We talked about this. You can't have it both ways, Eddie. Forward or backward. You can't do both, you hear me? Call me. Just call me."

I hit the button. Next message.

"Eddie." It's Vanessa. "Listen. Something just went down at the bakery."

I freeze. What?

Vanessa's voice cracks. She's crying. "We're at the hospital. There was a shooting. Your brother has just been admitted into the emergency room here at County General. I'll call you when I know more. But...just...please call me." Her voice breaks. "We need you. Come home as soon as you can."

Carmen sees the fear in my eyes.

"What's wrong?" she asks.

TWENTY-EIGHT

Desperate, I call and text everyone, over and over again, trying to get answers. Vanessa, Sal, Chinita. No one responds.

A hard rain starts to fall. We're on winding roads and I feel like I have a hangover even though I didn't get drunk last night. Instead of alcohol, anxiety mixed with fear bubbles up in my stomach like a shaken bottle, ready to pop.

At our first stop, I make myself throw up again, just to settle my stomach. Afterward, I see myself in the mirror of the truckstop bathroom. I look like a dog turd smashed into the sidewalk. Bloodshot eyes, swollen face, stubble, bruises. I'm scaring people, even more than usual.

Carmen buys me a Seahawks cap and a pair of cheap sunglasses to hide my fucked-up face. Somewhere in the jumble of thoughts about my brother, I realize it's two more days until I have to check in with my parole officer. I pray to God the marks fade enough that he doesn't ask too many questions about what I've been up to.

We get back on the road. An hour passes. Finally—*finally*—Vanessa picks up her phone.

"Eddie," she says. "Thank God."

I stumble and skip over my words. "Where—what is happening? What happened?"

In a low, slow voice, Vanessa tells me the story. Yesterday, she and Sal drove to the bakery to check it out. As they walked toward the door, a car slowed down in front of the bakery. Sal shoved Vanessa inside, but not before the driver popped off two shots.

I want to cry, scream, break the windshield. Instead I force myself to sit still and say, "And then what happened?"

"I couldn't see." Her voice cracks. "Sal pushed me to the ground. The car drove away. There was shattered glass and blood everywhere."

Red fills my vision. I'm overcome with anger. I want—I *need* —to hurt the person who caused this pain.

"I panicked until I realized the bullet just grazed Sal's arm." Vanessa takes a deep, slow breath. "I swear to God, your brother bleeds like a bad horror movie. But it's a superficial wound. He's okay."

Carmen reaches over to rub my shoulders. The muscles in my back uncoil at last. I take control of my breathing. "Where is he now?"

"Upstairs."

"Can I talk to him?"

"He's asleep."

"Can you wake him up?"

"No." Her voice is sharp. "Come home and talk to him in person."

She's just survived a stressful experience, so her annoyance makes sense. I don't bite back. "I'm on my way now. I'm with Carmen. We'll be back tomorrow afternoon, okay?"

"Fine," she says, exactly the way women say it when things are the opposite of fine.

During the endless ride home, I try to close my eyes and

sleep, but the only thing I can think of is the anger swirling inside me, glowing and growing like a ball of fire.

Lady Chef is a warrior. She drives ten hours straight and refuses my offers to take over. She doesn't want me driving without a license and getting in trouble if we're stopped. As we eat up the miles, her car develops strange rattles and squeals. When we stop for gas, I check all the fluids, fix the tire pressure, and replace her windshield wiper blades.

"You're useful," she says, raising an eyebrow. "I might keep you around."

Again, I try to convince her to let me drive. I could drive us straight through without stopping. But she won't budge. Halfway to Los Angeles, we buy burgers at a roach coach and Carmen pulls into the parking lot of a roadside motel.

We eat and take hot showers. In bed, I hold her, trying to clear my mind. We try to get something started, but I'm preoccupied about my brother, and my body won't do what I desperately want it to.

She kisses me softly, again and again. "You need rest. We both do. We'll leave first thing in the morning, okay?"

This is fucking embarrassing. I look around the ugly motel room, the bright blue carpet, the orange striped curtains. "Do you know what I would've given in prison for a night in a room like this with a woman like you?"

Under the rough sheets, she snuggles close. "There will be more nights. Lots more."

With each action, she reveals more of herself to me. I know she's wild and tough and smart. And now I know this—she is kind.

I raise myself up on my arms and press our bodies together so that she can feel my weight on her. She moans very softly as I kiss her lips, her jaw, and her neck. I kiss the tops of her breasts and hold each one gently in my hands as I suck on her nipples, back and forth. Taking my time, I lower my body until my lips hover between her legs. I spread her legs and slowly stroke my hands up and down her inner thighs, again and again, until goosebumps rise on her skin and I can smell her pussy, wet and sweet.

I go down on her.

I take that first orgasm right off the top, nice and easy. She's amped up. She's been thinking about me for more than a thousand miles. That kind of dedication deserves to be rewarded.

I pull her onto my face. I close my eyes, losing myself in her softness, her smell. She balances on the headboard, arching her back, and when she comes a second time, I feel her thighs turn to iron on either side of my head. My face, my beard, and my neck are soaked. She rides my lips like the fucking goddess she is.

With a satisfied grunt, she collapses on the bed and stretches out. She's panting.

"Oh, my God," she murmurs.

"I'm not done yet," I say.

"What?"

Just to show her I can, I take one more orgasm from her with my fingers and tongue. She's holding her long legs wide open, watching what I'm doing to her. Her pussy is puffy and swollen from all my attention, and I can see inside her. She's dark pink. My chest fills with a painful sort of joy that I know this secret.

Carmen's mouth is open. Tears glitter in her eyes. "I'm coming," she whispers.

I hold her down while the climax rocks her body. She stares at me, and I tumble into her dark eyes, proud that I can make her happy like this. In a quiet part of my brain, I promise myself: I'll make her happy in other ways. As many ways as I can.

Afterward, I hold her. I rest my cheek against her head. Her cool hair is soothing on my skin. Her breathing becomes deep and even. So does mine. She's sound asleep in my arms.

"Sleep well, *mi reina*," I whisper.

EARLY THE NEXT MORNING, we hit the road. At our last stop before home, I toss the cap and sunglasses, wipe my prints off the stolen IDs and credit cards, and throw them into a Dumpster behind a gas station. We arrive in Los Angeles in the early afternoon. Carmen drops me off at Vanessa's house.

"Will you be okay?" I ask. "With your mom? With everything?"

"I've had four days to think about what to say to her." She shrugs. "She'll flip out. But everything will be fine."

I must have a doubtful look on my face because Carmen adds, "It'll be fine. I promise." She rubs my back. "Do you want me to come inside?"

"I think I should talk to Sal alone." I lean over and give her a slow kiss. She tastes like the red Gatorade she got at the gas station, sweet and a little salty. "I'll call you as soon as I know more, okay?" I kiss her again, for good luck. "Take care of yourself. Get some rest, if you can."

She looks at me carefully. "You too."

"Say hi to your mom for me."

Carmen rolls her eyes at me, and I watch as she drives away.

Taking a deep breath, I turn and walk up the steps to the house. Vanessa is at work, so her grandmother opens the door and lets me inside.

"He is so *pissed* at you," she says, shaking her head. She makes me a ham sandwich with pickles. There's pity in her voice. "Eat your lunch before you talk to him. You'll need your strength." I follow her advice and eat the sandwich.

Upstairs, Sal is in the bedroom. My anal-retentive brother is dressed in a crisp white T-shirt and basketball shorts. He's sitting on top of a neatly made bed—I'm talking neat, with military precision—his arms crossed, watching Jerry Springer on TV. One arm is in a bandage and there are a few scratches on his face, but other than that, he looks fine. The bedroom is spotless, everything in order. I'm guessing my brother doesn't like sitting in bed all day and burned off some nervous energy cleaning the room one or a hundred times.

"I'd beat your ass but it looks like somebody already did for me," he says instead of hello.

He turns off the TV while I sit down in the armchair next to the bed.

"Tell me everything," I say.

Sal tells the same story Vanessa told me, but there's anger in his voice, as if he blames himself for letting the shooting happen. He tells me cops arrived at the hospital to take a report since no one saw anything except for him.

True to gangster code, he didn't share what he saw with the police. Sal has been out of the game for a long time, but he knows the score. We both know this is something the streets have to take care of on their own.

"So who was it?" I ask.

"I didn't see the driver." Sal looks at the door to make sure it's closed. "But the shooter—I've seen him before. A dealer with the Hillside Locos, I think. Kid named Ochoa."

My heart stops beating.

Ochoa. The dealer Lalo and I jacked. The stupid kid who bragged about having an arsenal of guns that didn't exist. The one Lalo pistol-whipped again and again. The one who pissed himself, the one whose heroin we stole.

But why? Why would he take a shot at Sal?

I study my brother's face.

We're the same height. When I got home last year, I encouraged him to grow a beard just like mine. We both lift. He's only a year older than me. People have confused us for each other before.

Fuck.

What have I done?

Ochoa was retaliating. He thought Sal was *me*.

My brother frowns. "Are you okay? You look like you're going to throw up."

A drug dealer almost killed my brother. Because of me. Because of something I chose to do.

I have to fix this.

But how?

"I have to go," I say.

I stand up, like a robot. Numb, overcome with shame and anger.

"But you just got here," Sal says. "You haven't even told me where you went. Or why you were gone for four fucking days."

I can't even look at him. "I'll tell you everything. Soon. I promise," I say. "Right now I need...I need some fresh air."

Downstairs, I pick up my backpack by the front door and head out without saying goodbye.

Outside, teenagers are playing in the street, riding bikes or sitting on the front porches of their houses, talking and listening to music.

In the park, a couple lounges under a tree, kissing and whispering to each other while a homeless man picks through a nearby trashcan for cans and bottles.

Cars fill the avenues. The drivers are heading home from work.

A *paletero* pushes his cart down the sidewalk, jingling bells to catch the attention of school kids walking home with their mothers. He sells ice cream bars and plastic bags of *rueditas*, wheel-shaped chips flavored with chile and lime juice.

I absorb the neighborhood, every part of it. To calm myself down, I notice all the details. I let them fill me so that I don't overflow with the bad feelings gathering inside me. Anger. Regret. Self-hatred. All of the usual suspects.

I walk without thinking. I let the steady rhythm of my steps calm me down.

So much has changed in the last few days that I can't seem to get my balance in this new world.

I grip the straps of my backpack.

One step forward, then another. The pavement seems to pound me back, letting me know I'm still alive, that I still have the ability to do something about this fucking mess.

TWENTY-NINE

My mind drops down into its darkest, quietest place. There, I collect the threads of the things I know to be true. I try to tie up the loose ends, the half truths, the lies. I see my father's thin face in the darkness of that old Bronco, telling me the story of how he cheated death, how he backed away from the edge, alone and unarmed.

But he wasn't unarmed. He had a weapon—a big one. A weapon I can use too.

I stop. When I look up, I realize I've reached my destination.

Ruben's house.

Without giving myself time to change my mind, I walk up the steps, look straight into the security camera above the door, and press the button on the intercom.

"Look what the cat dragged in. How are you, *mi'jo?*"

Ruben's voice is scratchy and distorted by the speaker. Still, I can hear his deep annoyance. The East Side Hollenbeck shot-caller doesn't like unexpected guests, even longtime homeboys like me.

"I'm good, Ruben," I say, "but I need your ear."

The speaker is quiet for a second. I stand still, trying not to lose my nerve. I've faced down rival gang members, inmates who wanted to pound my face or worse. I've even looked down barrels of loaded guns without blinking. But to take a stand against Ruben, the closest thing to a kingpin that ESHB has, I need to pretend I have nerves of steel.

Okay. Balls of brass wouldn't hurt either.

I'm unarmed. Alone.

This is stupid.

My specialty.

The intercom buzzes. The security cage that encloses Ruben's front porch clicks open.

UNLIKE MY FATHER, Ruben is healthy and strong. Like a true OG, he's dressed in khakis, a warm flannel, and a pair of new Nike Cortez. His *bigote* is thick but streaked with gray, reminding me this old dog has survived at the head of the pack for a long, long time.

In the living room of his house, he gives me a hug.

"It's good to see you, Trouble," he says. His voice is flat.

I lift my arms and he pats me down like a pro. He checks me for wires, then searches my backpack. There's nothing in there but dirty clothes. He gives my wallet a lazy search but doesn't make a comment about all the cash. Every homeboy has his side hustle—that's usually his own business, no one else's.

When he's satisfied, Ruben says, "Let's take a walk."

I follow him out of the house and down the street to the park. We start a slow loop around the lake. This is Ruben's office. He conducts all his meetings here. It helps him control the situation and avoid any bugs or surveillance.

"So I heard your brother had a little trouble the other day," he says. "How's he doing?"

We both know this is bullshit. Ruben has his finger on the pulse of the neighborhood. He knows what happened, and he knows exactly how my brother is doing. But I still say what's expected of me. "He's doing good. At home, recovering. He'll be back at work and school soon."

"Good. That's good." Ruben glances sideways at me. "And you? Are you looking for work? Because I've been waiting for you."

I know he'd put me on the street. I'd deal for him just like I did when I was a kid, maybe even steal cars again. I'm all grown up now—maybe I'd graduate to muscle, a combat soldier. Beat the shit out of people. Put bullets in bodies and walk away. Ruben would know how to use me. He knows how to use all of us.

"I'm not looking for work," I say. "But I need your help."

"What do you need?"

We stop by the edge of the water. It's dark as tar. I swear, if this lake were ever drained, they'd find nightmares at the bottom.

I make my blood cold, cold as the icy river behind Lisa Jo's house.

"I know my father is alive," I say. "I know what he has on you."

Ruben doesn't react.

"My brother is starting a new business with his girl. Eastside Brewery. They're putting everything they've got into it. I know Las Palmas have been shaking down the businesses on the avenue, including the old bakery. I know they gave Slim Centeno a beat-down last year. I know you were aware of it and let it happen even though Slim's family has been paying protection money to ESHB since Jesus walked the earth."

"You know a lot of things, don't you?" Ruben's voice gets low and dangerous. "What are you planning to do with all this knowledge?"

"Nothing," I say. "Nothing at all. If."

"If?"

"If you fix a broken promise and put ESHB back to work protecting the businesses on the avenue."

Ruben says nothing.

"Put homeboys on the corners," I say. "Have them watch the bakery, but also the dry cleaners and the liquor store. Keep Las Palmas away along with any other knucklehead who wants to take a shot."

"Even, say, a little shit from Hillside Locos?" Ruben says with a sly smile.

I swallow down my anger. He knows about Ochoa. "Everyone."

"And if I don't?"

This is not a game I can lose. "If you don't, a recording gets sent to Pelican Bay of you dealing double with Las Palmas to get to the Cartel. The Organization will know that an OG shot-caller from ESHB is trying to cut them out." I pause. "They won't be happy."

We're both silent for a minute. Ruben isn't angry. He doesn't get angry. He's a calculator.

"You know," he says quietly, "if you keep this information to yourself and the Organization finds out you had knowledge of my dealings, you're complicit, *mi'jo*. You betrayed your loyalty to the gang. You'll be a dead man walking, just like me."

I nod. "It's a risk I'll take if it means my family will be safe."

We stare out at the water. After a long time, Ruben says, "All right. You have my word. Anything else, Eduardo?" He uses my real name, as if he knows what I'm about to ask.

I look him in the eyes.

As far back as I can remember, I always wanted to be a gangster.

I followed in my father's footsteps, then my brother's.

Every time a homeboy got in my face, demanding to know where I was from, I told him. Proudly. Defiantly.

In prison, "Where you from?" became a question to welcome, not to fear. I answered loud and clear. ESHB. East Side Hollenbeck.

But now I know—there's more to me than my *barrio*. More to me than the most obvious path. More to me than the terrible things I've done.

"Retire me from the gang," I say.

His smile is slow and sinister. "You sure?"

I've never been more sure about anything. "Yes."

Ruben shakes his head slowly. "Never thought I'd see the day. Trouble Rosas. Gone straight." He turns to me. "Okay. Consider it done." He studies my face. "You know, it's not going to be easy for you."

I look him in the eye. "Nothing ever was."

IT'S ALMOST dark by the time I find the kid. He's standing in the parking lot of a grease-burger joint, smoking and joking with one of his little friends. I didn't have to ask a lot of people to find out where he deals.

Ochoa is so green he doesn't see me walk up to him until I have him slammed up against the wall of the restaurant. I twist his arm behind his back, remove the gun from his waistband, and tuck it into mine. His friend takes off down the street, abandoning him.

"Remember me?" I say quietly in his ear. "Because I remember you."

"Fuck you!" He can't move, so the only thing he can do is insult me. "Let me go, you fucking faggot."

"Hey, be nice." I kick his legs apart and search him for another weapon. He's clean, except for a wad of cash and a few baggies of merchandise. I drop all his shit on the ground.

"Fuck you."

"I said, *be nice.*" I twist his arm at a sharper angle. "Now, tell me. Why did you take a shot at my brother? What did my brother ever do to you?"

"That was for you, bitch."

He's going to talk tough now. On top of his anger about getting jacked, he's embarrassed that I saw him on the floor pissing himself. Now he's embarrassed that he let someone get the drop on him. The embarrassment of a teenage boy turns to violence really fast—I've seen it. I've felt it. I have to needle him, break him, and make him listen.

"Do you see how fast I could've killed you? Killed you with your own piece? Do you know what kind of shit they would've said about you afterward? Everyone would be laughing at your funeral."

Again, Ochoa yells, "Fuck you!"

I look at him closely. Tiny tears are in his eyes. This is not from the way I'm holding him. It's from the embarrassment—a deep and never-ending embarrassment.

"Ask me," I say. "Ask me why I didn't kill you just now even though you tried to kill my brother." I shove him harder against the wall and press his forehead against the stucco. "I said, ask me."

He howls. "Why?"

"Because it isn't worth it." I let his head go. "They made me rob your house. I didn't want to do it. I don't give a shit who you are or what you have. I did it because they made me."

I look around. We're partially hidden by the Dumpster, but

there are customers just around the corner. I have to wrap this up.

"Listen to me. The Hillside Locos didn't green-light me or Lalo because they know a war with East Side Hollenbeck isn't worth three-hundred-dollars' worth of heroin and five minutes of your fucking pride."

Tears are running down his cheeks.

"I was like you." I drop my voice. "I had so much to prove to the world. That kind of thinking put me in prison for five years. Five years, dog. I just got out last year. I don't wish that on you. I don't wish that on anyone."

The kid has nothing to say. He struggles one last time and seems to give up, sagging against me.

"Your bullet missed my brother. That was a lucky shot. That was the universe telling you you're a fucking lucky man. If you had hit him, we'd be having a very different conversation right now." I loosen my grip a little. "I have no beef with you. If you let this go, we can both walk away. It ends here. You feel me?"

He doesn't say anything.

"Do you feel me?" I ask again.

I stand there holding him until he takes a deep breath and says, "Okay. Fine."

When he says the word, I let him go. There's anger in his eyes, but it's blunted—he understands me, even if he doesn't want to. We stare each other down. I nod, turn and walk away—just like I promised.

When I'm a safe distance away, I check to see if anyone's following me. I take the gun out of my waistband, wipe it down, and throw it in a storm drain.

BACK IN THE GARDEN, Rafa's just sitting down to his dinner. I've brought him a cold six-pack.

"What the hell's that?" he asks instead of saying hello. "Where's your brother's beer?"

"I wasn't able to get it," I say. "You'll have to drink this stuff for now."

Rafa makes a face. "But that stuff's no good."

"Tough." I make myself a bowl of hot *caldo de vegetales* and sit down next to him on the couch. "You didn't used to care what you drank."

The old man smiles and pats my shoulder. "Yeah, well, now I know better, don't I?"

THE NEXT MORNING, Rafa wakes me up by turning on the TV news.

"Hey," he says. "Watch this."

I sit up and yawn. This was the first good sleep I've had in days and I'm cranky that it's been cut short. "What the hell, *viejo*?"

"Just watch."

On the screen, a body lies on the sidewalk covered in a white sheet. It's nighttime, and red-and-blue flashing lights illuminate the scene. Police have set up a crime scene with yellow tape.

"Eighteen-year-old Jose Eduardo 'Lalo' Garcia was shot and killed last night near Hollenbeck Park. At about eleven o'clock p.m., Garcia was walking home from a party when a person approached him, pulled out a gun, and shot Garcia on the sidewalk before fleeing on foot. It's unknown whether the suspect knew Garcia but police believe the shooting is gang related. The shooter is described only as a Latino male, seventeen to twenty-one years old. Police ask anyone with information to contact the Hollenbeck Division homicide detectives."

Rafa turns off the TV. "That's your homeboy, isn't it?"

"Yeah." He was a dumb little tweaker who had watched *Training Day* too many times, but he was still a kid, and he didn't need to go out this way. I lie back down and sadness hits me hard. Ochoa couldn't leave this alone. If I had killed Ochoa instead of letting him go, Lalo would still be alive.

"Do you know who the shooter is?" Rafa asks.

I nod again. "HSL. Hillside Locos."

Rafa hisses between his teeth. We both know this means retaliation between HSL and ESHB. Unless there is an immediate sit-down between leaders on both sides, the violence is just getting started. And me—I had a hand in it, whether I wanted to or not.

"Bad times," the old man says. "Bad times ahead."

THIRTY

The next morning, I sit down in front of my parole officer's desk, take my usual unfair share of verbal abuse, shake his hand, and thank him for his support.

My bruises are faded. He has no idea what kind of *tonterias* I've been up to in the last few days.

If he'd caught just a whiff of the shit I've been up to, he would've sent me straight to jail.

But he suspects nothing.

After I leave his office, I make a halfhearted visit to my case worker, who gives me two job listings and tells me to call them right away. I put them in my pocket and look at the nameplate on her desk. Instead of calling her Sugar, I call her by her real name.

"Deanna Delgado."

She looks up from her computer in surprise. "Yes?"

"Listen. I know I'm not the easiest person to deal with," I say. "I really do appreciate what you've done for me." I pause. "Thank you."

She nods, a little suspicious.

"I'm serious," I say. "Thank you."

Back at Vanessa's, Sal is sitting on the back porch. Vanessa's daughter is on the far end of the backyard, dressing up her wiener dog in an old princess Halloween costume.

Today is Sal's last day stuck at home before he heads back to work and school. He's happy about it, like he can't wait. We pop open two bottles of Eastside Pride and I get down to business.

In a low voice, I tell him everything—jacking the imaginary gun arsenal, finding Daisy, going to Washington, learning the truth from our dad, blackmailing Ruben, and talking Ochoa out of carrying out his hit on me. Sal listens carefully, memorizing all the details.

When I'm finished, I take a deep breath and let it out.

I swear to God, I feel lighter, like I've dropped the invisible cuffs and shackles I've been wearing for weeks.

"Fuck," Sal says at last. "You know, you don't have to do everything by yourself. You're not alone."

"Yeah. I know."

"I'm always here."

I wince. "I know, but..."

"But what?"

"You've got a lot more to live for now. Vanessa. Muñeca. School. Your business. You can't go off and do the same reckless shit anymore. You have too much to lose."

"Yeah. I do. And one of those things is my younger brother. So shut your face and stop arguing with me." He kills his beer. "What are you going to do now?"

I take the two listings out of my pocket that I got at the employment agency. "I've got two numbers to call." I squint at the papers. "This one's for a factory. Maintenance at a frozen-food factory in Vernon. This one says, 'general warehouse worker' at a cold storage facility downtown." I shrug. "Either way, I guess I freeze my nuts off."

I hand the papers to Sal. He looks at them and then he looks at me. "You really want those jobs?"

"Not really. But it's work," I say. "I'm going straight like you, so I'll never see easy money again. Best get used to it."

In the yard, Vanessa's daughter picks up a wooden sword and hits a bush with it. It takes me a minute to figure out she's the knight in shining armor trying to save the wiener dog princess from a dragon.

"Listen," Sal says. "I've still got a couple years to complete this program. Vanessa's still full time at her firm. I'll be making the beer at Bay City Brews until we can afford our own equipment. Vanessa thinks it'll take us a year, maybe two to raise that kind of capital."

"What are you saying?" I ask.

"I'm saying, we need a full-time employee to take care of the business while we get it set up. Someone trustworthy who can run the taproom and get shit done." He raises his eyebrows. "Eddie, that's you."

I'm stunned. He'd trust me with this? "Are you fucking with me?"

"No, I'm not. Think about the last few days. The things you've accomplished. If we could use your talents for something good..." He shrugs. "What do you think?"

I think he's smoking something. "But...I don't have my driver's license."

"I was talking to my counselor at school. There might be a way to reverse that for both of us. We'd have to talk to a lawyer, but it's possible."

I think about all the tanks and machinery I saw at Bay City Brews. It was intimidating—Sal has to go to college for two years in order to run it, for fuck's sake. What do I know? "I don't know how to operate any of that equipment."

"You won't have to. Like I said, I'll make the beer offsite for now. You'll run taps. I'll show you how to change the kegs out and clean the lines. Vanessa will get you set up on a point-of-sale system."

"But—"

"Motherfucker, you've sold drugs, jacked cars, survived prison, and tracked down our no-good father. I think you can handle pouring a few beers."

Vanessa comes home from work. She's still a little sore at me, but her anger burns off like fog after we all have dinner together and Sal tells her his idea about hiring me on as Eastside Brewery's employee number three. I'm surprised by her enthusiasm, but then I'm reminded how much she loves and trusts my brother—his opinion of me means a lot to her, and I'm reminded of the value of family. Real family. They hire me on a handshake and that's it—the deal is done.

I decide right then and there to retire my jersey.

I'm no longer Trouble.

I'm Eddie.

Just Eddie.

BEFORE SUNRISE, I walk over the bridge from East LA into downtown. It's cold. Mist hangs over the shallow slick of river at the bottom of the concrete riverbed. The sidewalks are damp.

I take the long walk into the flower district. All the storefronts are brightly lit. Flowers fill the white plastic buckets that line the sidewalks. I see red roses everywhere, but I pass them by. I see other flowers too—pink, white, yellow, orange, purple. I see orchids and little cactuses in pots. I see lilies the size of umbrellas.

They're all beautiful.

But none of them seem right for Carmen.

The sun comes up as I walk emptyhanded back over the bridge. I head back into the garden. Rafa is hoeing some rows. I ask to borrow his shears.

"What for?" He hands them to me.

"I wanna make a gift for my girl."

With some garden string, I make little bundles of fresh herbs for her. Rafa reminds me of their names. Rosemary is *romero*. Marjoram is *mejorana*. Mint is *hierbabuena*. Thyme is *tomillo*. Sage is *salvia*. Some herbs Rafa knows by only one name—*toronjil*, cilantro, epazote.

I wrap everything in a clean towel and put the towel in a paper bag.

Rafa watches me. "Are you sure it was a good idea not to get the roses?"

I look at the crumpled paper bag in my hand. "I'm kinda regretting it now," I say.

Rafa reaches under his straw hat and scratches his head. "You know," he says, "if she's the kind of girl who likes someone like you, she's probably the kind of girl who thinks it's what's on the inside that counts."

"What's that supposed to mean, *viejo*?" I ask.

"It means, don't mention the roses. Just to be safe."

"Okay," I say. "I won't."

"I'll light a red candle for you. They're good for bringing people together. Maybe that will help."

"Couldn't hurt." I head for the gate.

"*Que dios te bendiga, mi'jo,*" he calls to me. "*Buena suerte.*"

God bless you, son. Good luck. With Rafa's words, I realize I *am* blessed. I *am* lucky. I wave at him and walk out into the street.

I'M ALMOST in front of Carmen's house when her front door opens. Carmen, her mother and her father walk down their porch steps. Carmen is barefoot, dressed in shorts and a T-shirt. She opens the passenger door for her dad, who climbs inside with her help. She shuts the door.

Carmen and her mother stand next to the car on the driver's side. I am close enough to hear their voices—they're arguing, too angry and caught up in the moment to notice me. I stop by the neighbor's fence, just out of sight.

"But how can you say that?" Carmen's voice is sharp and impatient. "The Rosas brothers did their time for crimes they committed years ago. Look at Sal. He's doing big things. He's gone straight."

"Salvador, maybe. But Eduardo?" Carmen's mom hisses, "He's trash."

"Don't say that."

"*Mi'ja*, listen to me. You have a good heart, but you're naïve. These people—they're ex-cons. They went to prison because they broke the law. They deserved to get locked up. They're felons. Your father and I signed the agreement for one reason, and that's Vanessa Velasco. I wouldn't trust either of those brothers. Not for one second."

"But Mom—"

"You never listen to me. That's why you always get into trouble."

"Here we go. Not again."

"If I don't tell you the truth, who will? Who? I told you, don't go to cooking school. It's expensive. It's wasteful. Did you listen? No. Are you enjoying paying off those student loans, Carmen? How many years will it be until you're finished?"

"I don't regret it, if that's what you want me to say."

Carmen's mom keeps going. "I told you, don't waste your time on useless men. The one last year—what was his name? Or the one before that? What did I say? They were no good. Losers. I was right. And now, the worst of all. Eduardo Rosas. Do you really think so little of yourself, so little of your family to carry on like this? To disappear for days at a time? It makes me *sick*."

I'm furious. I'm about to step in when I hear Carmen say, "Look, I know you're trying to protect me. I know you're worried about me. But you made your own decisions, Mom. You chose to marry Daddy, you chose to take on the bakery. You chose to have me. I make my own decisions, just like you made yours. And if I decide to spend time with Eddie Rosas, that's my decision, not yours. I like him. A lot. He's a good man. You're just too shortsighted to see that."

Carmen likes me. A lot. She thinks I'm a good man. I can't help it—I smile.

Carmen's mom snaps, "Go to him again and we will cancel the lease."

"No, you won't," Carmen says calmly. "Stop being so dramatic. I've seen Dad's medical bills. You need the income the bakery used to provide."

"We'll find another buyer. They're everywhere."

"You would never sell it to a stranger. You may act like you don't care, but I know the bakery means a lot to you. To our family."

After a long time, Carmen's mother says, "You think you know everything."

"Guess we're not so different, then."

Her mom says nothing. I hear a car door open and slam. The engine starts up. Carmen's mom pulls out of the driveway and passes by without seeing me, an angry frown on her face.

Holding the paper bag in my hands, I ring the doorbell to Carmen's house. A minute passes. I ring again. Nothing. I lean forward and listen. There's music playing.

I take out my phone. Carmen doesn't answer. I hang up.

After a quick look around to make sure the coast is clear, I decide to do something shady and reckless just for old times' sake. I creep around the side of the house and hop the same wall I hopped when I snuck into her bedroom.

The back door to the kitchen is open. I walk through the backyard. As I get closer, I hear Carmen—she's blasting "Bidi Bidi Bom Bom" and singing along. Her voice is awful. I like it.

I reach the back door and look inside. Carmen is there, singing with her eyes closed. She's wearing yellow rubber gloves. Her hair is tied up in a messy bun. All I see are her long, long legs as she dances around, mopping the floor and giving an imaginary Selena concert.

God.

She makes my heart happy.

I walk through the back door and give it two solid knocks.

"Hey," I say.

Carmen's eyes fly open and she jumps back, knocking over the mop bucket. Water spills everywhere.

"You motherfucker," she says.

"Wait, what?"

Carmen chases me out the door and around the backyard, whacking me with a wet mop and cursing me out in Spanish and English.

"You scared the shit out of me." *Thwack!* She gets me on the side of the head. Now I smell like purple Fabuloso.

We're laughing. I drop the bag, grab the mop handle, pull it from her grip and toss it on the ground.

Her dark eyes are full of that fire I adore. "Let's see," she says. "Breaking and entering. Trespassing."

"What?"

"I'm listing the charges I'm going to press against you."

I put my hands on her hips and pull her close. I press my

body against hers so that we both can feel how much I want her. "How about you kiss me instead?"

"Trying to cop a plea?" she whispers.

"Naw, I don't roll like that," I say. "I'm taking this to the box."

"The box?"

"Jury box," I say. "A trial."

"You'll lose."

"Not if I've already won."

I kiss her, right there in the sunshine. I've never felt more free.

THIRTY-ONE

Later, we're sitting on the steps of her back porch. She's holding my hand.

Just like I did with my brother, I let the story go. I tell it slowly and clearly. I tell her about my father's confession and my scheme to get protection for the brewery. I see fear in her eyes when I tell her about Ochoa and my cut ties with ESHB.

"But will Ruben keep his promise?" she asks. "How do you know?"

"He'll keep his promise because he's a gangster," I say. "That's how we operate. We balance profits against losses. Ruben thinks, will it cost him more to keep me in the gang or to cut me loose? In the long run, he wants to protect his profits. He wants to run his side hustle with Las Palmas, and he doesn't want me to get in the way of that by selling him out to the Organization." I look down and notice she's taken my hand. "These things I'm telling you, Carmen—they're dangerous. People die over information like this."

"Why are you telling me?"

"Because I'm done," I say. "Seeing my father again, I realized something. He lived so many secret lives, he got lost in them. Over time, he began to believe his own stories—his own lies. I don't want to be like that. I want one life. One good life."

It hits me—Dreamer liked to brag he was one step ahead of everyone. That he could beat the system and play by his own rules. But I'm old enough now to see the real Dreamer Rosas. He's living in his own prison, far from home, far from his family.

He can never come back.

I reach forward and touch Carmen's cheek. Her skin is so warm and smooth, it's unreal. "I'm so sorry I left without telling you why. I cut you off because I didn't know how much to share with you and how much to hide. I thought I was keeping you safe. But now I know. I'm telling you everything from now on. I will never keep any secrets from you."

She blinks slowly at me, falling under the spell of my touch but still not convinced. "But why me?" she says. "Of all the women you could be with, all the women who'd want to be with you, why me?"

For a moment, she sounds like the shy teenager she must've been once, a long time ago.

"Because you're real," I say. "The most real woman I've ever met. Smart. Fierce. Sexy as fuck. I can't pretend to want anyone else but you."

She stares at me, still wary.

"There's no one else for me," I say quietly. "No one else."

We sit together in silence for a little while. I feel shy, as if I've shared too much.

At last she asks, "So what did you bring me? In the bag?"

I reach over to where the paper bag lies on its side in the grass. I open it for her. The smell of fresh herbs fills the air.

She looks at me and I know what she's remembering—that first morning we met in the garden. The first morning we ever made love.

"Oh," she whispers.

"For you, Lady Chef."

She puts the bag aside and slowly, sweetly, climbs into my lap. Her legs drape over the step and she wraps her arms around my shoulders. I breathe her in. I swear to God, nothing smells as good as this woman. I rest my head against hers, close my eyes, and listen to her breathing. I keep waiting for the voice inside my head to tell me it's too soon. Much too soon. But there's no voice—only the truth I feel in my heart.

"I love you," I whisper.

She kisses my forehead and both my closed eyes. "I love you too, Eddie."

Our bodies want each other—always have, always do. They were just waiting for our hearts to catch up.

We kiss. For reals. We *kiss*. My thoughts stumble around, drunk on her. I want to go back in time and visit myself, stuck in a prison cell, reading romance novels and convinced that happy ever afters don't happen in real life—at least not for people like me.

I would say to myself, "Just you wait, fucker. Just you wait."

After a long time, I whisper, "Where are your parents at, baby girl?"

"My mom took my dad to physical therapy," she says quietly. "His therapist is in Santa Clarita."

"That sounds far." I kiss Carmen's neck.

She moans. "It's very far. She's the best, though."

"When do they usually get back?"

"Well, here's the thing. They don't like to drive in rush-hour traffic."

"Uh-huh. Go on."

"So they usually go to my Tía Yoli's house in Valencia and have dinner there. Then they drink coffee and talk."

"Uh-huh."

"They're not usually home until nine or ten at night."

"Shit. For reals?"

She smiles. "For reals."

That's it. I need her.

Now.

I pick her up. The back door has swung shut. I kick it open like a fireman and carry her inside.

In her bedroom, I sit down on her bed and she climbs on top of me, straddling me. We're both trembling, starving for each other. But Carmen holds back. Slowly, she strokes my arms, my neck, my face. Her fingers trail over the fading cuts around my eye.

She leans down and kisses me, one soft kiss, then two. I close my eyes to concentrate, but my hands can't stop touching her. They roam all over her body. I run my hands up her back and over her hips. I untie her dark, smooth hair. When it's loose I run my fingers through it. I can't get enough of touching her.

Our small kisses quickly melt into long, hungry kisses. She presses the tip of her tongue into my mouth. When I lick it once, she moans. When I lick it again, she starts to move her hips back and forth, grinding her weight down slowly on my hard-on.

It's hot—too hot. I push her back slowly.

"You know, this is what we are," she says.

"What?"

"Sweet and dirty."

"Who is who?"

She smiles. "We take turns."

Looking up at her, I slide my hands under her T-shirt and lift it up over her breasts. She's not wearing a bra, and her small breasts fit perfectly in the palms of my hands. I lean up and suck on her dark, perfect nipples, first one, then the other. She arches her back and grinds down again. I groan, high on Carmen, high on her body.

With a small smile, Carmen pushes me back on the bed.

She undoes my belt, takes off my shoes, and pulls down my pants and boxers all at once. I flex my abs and my cock stands straight up at her, hard and aching.

We take off our T-shirts at the same time. I stare at her beautiful tits. She stares at my chest. I lean up on my elbows so she can get a better look. It's all on display—muscles, tattoos, scars. My history.

"Be honest," I whisper. I grip my shaft with one hand and run my other hand over my abs. "What do you really see when you look at me like this? A gangster? A lowlife? A thug?"

She climbs onto the bed and kisses me again. "Shh." Her hand is cool as she strokes my chest. "I see a survivor. I see you."

I watch as the woman of my dreams kneels between my legs, takes my dick in her fist, and gives me a slow hand job while licking each of my balls. Her warm tongue glides over my sac again and again until the ache is so powerful I think I'm going to pass out. Then she pops the head of my dick between her lips and sucks on me like a popsicle. Again, she takes her time. Inside her mouth, she teases me with her tongue. When she takes me deep at last, I arch on her bed and grab the sheets in my fists.

"Okay, stop," I say, breathless. "Time out. Your turn."

I flip her on her back and kiss her deep, stroking her breasts. I slide off her shorts. Underneath, she's wearing pink panties. I rub her through the cloth until her pussy plumps up against my fingertips and her panties are soaked through. When I slide them down at last, I take a deep breath and fill my lungs with the sweet, rich scent of her body.

"Open your legs for me," I growl.

With a smile, Carmen parts her legs nice and wide. I look down at her. The windows are open. Sunlight fills the room. My eyes feast on her body, resting at last on the soft, sweet lips of her pussy. So fucking beautiful. Gently, I spread her open with my fingers, exposing her tight opening and the shiny bead of her clit.

Perfection.

I dive in. I lick her delicate lips, up and down, opening her like the pages of a book. I stroke her with the tips of my fingers while I lap at her clit with a steady, gentle rhythm. When she's dripping, I take a drink of her sweetness and slide my fingers inside her, pressing deep until she squeezes me back, moaning my name again and again and again.

"Please," she says.

With my fingers stretching her, I tease her clit lightly with my tongue, up and down, licking her until she's whispering curses at me.

"Please, make me come. Please. I want to come."

I press the tip of my tongue firmly against the root of her clit. I begin to fuck her with my fingers, back and forth, the wetness dripping down over my hand. I can feel her tension ramping up, higher and higher.

"Please," she begs.

I strum her hard. She bucks against the mattress, arches her back, and screams. Her muscles grip my fingers. I can feel the hard contract and release of her orgasm, her tight little cunt sucking at me, so beautiful and dirty and perfect.

I don't give her a moment to catch her breath. I withdraw, climb on top of her, and massage her hot, trembling pussy with the head of my cock.

I kiss her deep. I let her taste herself on my lips.

"I never want to leave your bed," I whisper against her lips. "I never want to let you go."

Breathless, she reaches for her nightstand and pulls a condom out of the drawer. She hands it to me. "Then don't."

We watch as I roll the condom on. The rubber barely stretches over my aching cock.

With a smile, she reaches down and rests the head of my cock against her pussy. I brace my arms against the mattress on either side of her torso. She rubs my back, pulling me close.

Eyes locked on hers, I slam my dick into her so hard we both groan. The aftershocks of her orgasm ripple against the head of my cock.

The pleasure I get from being inside Carmen is so powerful, I feel her in my soul.

She touches my face. "I want it," she says. "I want you."

I turn off my brain. I turn off the noise. I tune out everything that isn't her. My world sharpens to a single point of light, a single star—Carmen.

I fuck her for a long, long time. I alternate between slow and deep and shallow and quick. I lean back and spread her legs open wider to get a better look at my cock buried deep. The dark lips of her pussy are stretched tight around my shaft as if she can't take me—but she can, and she does.

I lick my thumb, reach down, and draw tiny circles on her raw little clit. She jumps against me but grabs my arms. Her nails bite into my skin.

"Eddie, yes. Oh God."

I take my time and make her come again, exploding like fireworks against my dick. I close my eyes and wrestle back my own orgasm. When her second climax fades, her eyes are glassy and sleepy. She's high.

"Use me," she whispers in my ear. "Use me to make yourself come."

I lie down on my back. Out of fear of wearing it out from too much fucking, we change the condom and roll another one on.

I watch, hypnotized, as this dream girl slides down over me, balances back on my thighs, and rocks her hips back and forth, squeezing me hard.

"After that first time in the garden, I never thought I'd see you again." She throws her head back and closes her eyes. "I gave up. I thought, it will never be as good with anyone else as it was with him."

I stroke her breasts and circle my thumbs around her nipples. My eyes are locked on the erotic show between her legs.

"I never thought I'd see you again either, *mi reina*," I say. "I thought you were lost to me. Like so much else."

I sit up, grab her, and flip her over again. She wraps her long legs around my hips.

"Now that we've found each other again," she whispers in my ear, "how about we keep holding on?"

I hammer her hard, fucking her the way we both like it. Our bodies slap together and the wet, obscene sound of my dick sliding in and out of her fills my ears. She locks her hands behind my neck, closes her eyes and smiles.

"You're going to make me come again."

"Damn straight I am."

We explode together at last, two rockets going off, lighting up the sky, setting everything we touch on fire.

In the grip of my climax I have a flashback of a torch blazing four stories high.

You can see the explosion from the freeway.

You can see it for twenty miles.

The night before the grand opening of the Eastside Brewery taproom, Rafa smudged the building with burning sage, adjusted the feng shui with mirrors and lucky bamboo, and said prayers calling on multiple gods and minor-league spirits to protect the new business and its owners.

The ESHB homeboys holding the corner also provided a good source of security.

Thanks to Carmen's contacts in the restaurant world, the grand opening got lots of attention. Food critics, beer enthusiasts, and other weird media people have fallen in love with the newest craft brewery in Los Angeles—started by former gangsters. Imagine that.

I saw some familiar faces in the crowd—Dino Moretti from Giacomo's. Rigoberto the chef and his family. Even Sugar from the employment agency came to visit—I mean, Deanna. I call her by her real name now. We're friends. She's happy I've found my way.

Anyhow, the line was out the door. Some of our customers had never even been to East LA before.

For opening weekend, Carmen fired up the ovens and

baked a batch of sandwich rolls. She set up a stove in the back room with three big pots: *cochinita pibil, pollo en mole verde*, and pork in red chili sauce for *tortas ahogadas*. For vegetarians, she made sandwiches of *queso fresco,* tomatoes, and ripe avocado, just like the colors of the Mexican flag.

Her sandwiches are beautiful. Works of art. And they went well with the four beers Sal and I served that weekend.

Eastside Pride, our signature brew, a *hefeweizen* flavored with the herb *hoja santa.*

Forever Mine, an amber ale Sal made just for Vanessa.

Esperanza, a malty, Mexican-style dark lager.

And my brother's newest beer, introduced just in time for our grand opening—Trouble IPA, a hoppy, crisp India pale ale. This one is my favorite by far. But I'm a little biased.

As promised, Sal taught me how to take care of the taps, clean the lines, and change the kegs. The cash register took me a little more practice, but I eventually got it. More or less.

My favorite thing to do is talk to the customers. I love learning about their lives, who they are, why they're here. Everyone has a story.

This taproom is a family affair. On opening weekend, it was all hands on deck. Vanessa stayed in the front of the house, welcoming everyone in and answering questions. Sal and me stood behind the counter pouring beers and providing an authentic thuggish atmosphere, obviously. Carmen worked in the kitchen, serving up *tortas* with the help of a kitchen assistant —my old buddy Boner, her prep cook. Chinita and Muñeca warmed up the crowd lined up outside by passing out cups of water and telling knock-knock jokes. Even our grumpy younger brother Angel came down from Salinas to clear glasses and load the dishwasher. I tried to give him some pointers, but he ignored me. That's all right. He'll catch on eventually...little shit.

At the counter, Carmen's mother and father sat front and

center, greeting old and new customers alike. The Centenos make our operation legit—the old generation standing by the new. Carmen's mother is very, very slowly warming up to me. Her full-blown hatred has died down to disgust. I can live with that for now.

I haven't heard from my father since I left Washington. I've been tempted to visit Daisy, but after talking to Carmen, I decided it would be safer for her if I just stayed away. I'm almost sure Daisy dropped off the bus ticket that night at Rafa's. She's probably keeping tabs on us for Dreamer.

For now, there's plenty to keep me busy and out of trouble. The taproom is open every day from four to midnight. Since Sal and I now have our driver's licenses again, we spend the mornings making deliveries. When he goes to school, I run the show. My job title? Sal calls me the "get-shit-done guy." The fixer. He says I'm essential to this operation.

Essential, believe that.

Awareness of the Eastside Brewery brand is growing. We feel the growing pains whenever vendors ask for kegs and cases we don't have. If we continue like this, Vanessa says Sal will be able to start making beer right here in the old bakery soon. We can't wait.

The sandwich idea was so popular and so lucrative on opening weekend that Vanessa invited Carmen to stay on full time. And Carmen said yes.

That's right. My girlfriend and I work together again.

Oh.

I forgot to say the best part.

Carmen's my girlfriend.

She still lives at home with her parents—her student loans will be paid off in a year and a half. I still live with Rafa. I'm working on saving my own money for the first time. When

Carmen says the word, I'll be ready to take the leap and find a place for us to live.

I can't speak for her, but I swear, the more time I spend with this woman, the more I want her.

I didn't know it could be this way, just like in those so-called trashy romance novels I used to read when I was locked up. I didn't believe I'd ever find it.

Love, I mean.

Sometimes after closing, Carmen and I lock the doors, clear the dishes, and sit at one of the tables in the dining room. We'll share a simple meal, maybe tacos, maybe one of the experimental *tortas* she's developing for the menu. We'll chat and laugh about the day.

At times like these, the peace I've been searching for my whole life finally settles over me. My heart and mind go quiet whenever I'm with her.

Tonight, by candlelight, I ask her, "Carmen, tell me the truth. Does this—all this—make you happy? Is this what you were looking for?"

She looks around the room, so different from the bakery where she grew up. "Yes. It's home." She nods to herself. "It's home, but better." She turns to me. "*Tesoro.*"

Treasure, she calls me. Trouble to trash to treasure—love has done this.

"*Sí, mi amor,*" I say.

"Now you tell me the truth. Do you ever miss the life?"

"No," I say. "That—that wasn't real."

She smiles. "So what is?"

"This life." I kiss her hand. "You, *mi reina.* You are my life now."

NOTE TO READERS

In 2014 and 2015, I volunteered at a gang intervention and reentry program. During my time there, I spent many hours conducting in-person interviews with trainees. Their stories of trauma and transformation inspired the characters in *Trashed*.

ACKNOWLEDGMENTS

To Jennifer Haymore, thank you for helping me breathe new life into Carmen and Eddie's story. Working with you is such a pleasure.

To Deidre Knight, for your unfailing kindness and faith in my writing.

To Lindsey Vargas, Oscar Ramirez, Zenobia Neil, Dorota Skrzypek, Jezz de Silva, and Michelle Barboza-Ramirez. Thank you all for sharing your time and insight. Next round's on me.

To Joseph Torres and family at Buena Vista. To Mark Alexzandr and Steve Boland at Holy Grounds. Thank you for your support and hospitality on an exceptionally rainy day in Los Angeles.

To Nickie Peña and Cinthya Cisneros for adopting me at the California Craft Beer Summit. Cheers to you both.

To Kristine Kobe, I raise a bottle to you.

To Brent Hopkins. Thank you for believing in us. I always knew you would be an excellent dad.

To the staff and trainees at Homeboy Industries, my deepest thanks always.

And most of all, to the readers, reviewers, bloggers, and amazing book people who took a chance on *Thirsty* and spread the word far and wide. Your enthusiasm has kept me afloat during a difficult year. Thank you for everything.

ALSO BY MIA HOPKINS

The Eastside Brewery series

Thirsty

Trashed

Tanked (coming soon)

The Cowboy Cocktail series

Cowboy Valentine

Cowboy Resurrection

Cowboy Player

Cowboy Karma

Cowboy Rising

The Kings of California series

Deep Down

Hollywood Honkytonk

ABOUT THE AUTHOR

Mia Hopkins writes lush romances starring fun, sexy characters who love to get down and dirty. She's a sucker for working class heroes, brainy heroines and wisecracking best friends. Her favorite form of procrastination is baking. She lives in Los Angeles with her family.

For more information...
www.miahopkinsauthor.com

@miahopkinsxoxo

Read on for an excerpt from
Tanked
An Eastside Brewery Novel
by Mia Hopkins

TANKED

ONE

No doubt about it. I am getting wing-manned.

Wing Man and his buddy Bad Haircut work in an office building downtown. I didn't catch what they do. I'm smiling and pretending to listen. Luckily, the loud music here in the brewery keeps me from having to pretend too hard.

Out of the corner of my eye, I keep a close watch on my coworker Ingrid. She is tipsy, and her girlish unguardedness makes her even more attractive to men than usual.

Bad Haircut is slightly older than Wing Man. At first, he was the introverted one of the pair. After three beers, this is no longer the case. He and Ingrid are dancing even though nobody else is dancing. He says something. She laughs and flips her hair. He says something else. She laughs and flips her hair again. Ad nauseam.

On the barstool next to me, Wing Man looks bored. He pulls out his phone. There's a photo of a young woman and a baby.

"That's my girlfriend. That's our little girl. She's seven months old. I love them so much."

The line sounds canned. If it's a trick, it's a good one, if not too subtle.

I can't believe I drew my eyebrows in for this.

Carefully, I adjust my glasses, look at the phone and back up at him. "Oh, they're beautiful!" I try to appear appropriately heartbroken that he is off the market. Satisfied, he smiles to himself and returns the phone to his pocket.

I take a long drink of my beer.

After a few more songs, Ingrid and I make quick eye contact. She touches her left earring. That means, "Let's get out of here." Right earring means, "You can go home. I'll text you the address where I end up for the night."

We tell the gentlemen we have to go—no explanations besides it's late and we weren't meaning to stay out. Bad Haircut protests. I have a feeling he doesn't get out much because when we apologize, instead of being cool, he gets aggressive.

"Aw, why you gotta go?" He leans too close to Ingrid. I slip between them and hold a hand up to help him keep his distance.

"Don't touch me," he growls at me.

"Dude, I didn't," I say. I look at Wing Man. "Come get your boy."

Wing Man shrugs and stays seated. "Don't make her mad," he tells his friend. "Big girl like that? She'll take you out, bro."

Bad Haircut stands between us and the door. "One more drink," he tells Ingrid.

She's too unsteady on her feet to do much more than smile and lean on me.

"We're done for the night," I say. I try to move Ingrid toward the exit, but Bad Haircut is in our way.

"How about *you* just go," Wing Man says to me. He waves his hand in my face. "Bye-bye."

His friend laughs and reaches for Ingrid.

I see a flash of the Eastside Brewery T-shirt before I know what's going on.

"Holy shit," Ingrid says in my ear.

I turn. The crowd has parted. By the front door, I see a large barback holding Ingrid's would-be lover by the collar. He uses the man's body to bang the door open. The patrons inside the brewery let out a collective gasp as he grabs Bad Haircut by the back of the belt, lifts him off his feet, and swings him forward in a perfect arc. Then the barback lets go. We watch as Bad Haircut goes sailing and lands face first on the sidewalk outside.

Wisely, he stays down.

The barback and the bouncer seated outside give each other a friendly little fist bump.

The crowd applauds and closes up like stage curtains.

I've never seen anything like this in real life. I am thoroughly impressed. Ingrid giggles. When I call for the check, I notice Wing Man is nowhere to be found.

Outside, the summer night is muggy and warm. Mercifully, there's no sign of Wing Man or Bad Haircut. As the bouncer keeps an eye on us, I wait with Ingrid for her ride. I notice she's glowing and she stands up straighter, like a plant that needed to be watered and finally got a drink. She loves it when guys lose their shit over her, and she thrives on drama like this. Also—and she would never say this—I know she likes going out with me because there's no way in hell I'd be her competition.

Her grumpy sister arrives at last. She's got rollers in her hair. I help Ingrid into the car, make sure she's buckled in, and shut the door.

"That was so much fun. Let's do this again?" Ingrid says through her open window. "Next Friday night?"

"Of course."

"You're such a good friend, Deanna."

I watch as they drive away, wondering if the thought ever crossed Ingrid's mind that I might get attacked and robbed on the way to my car, alone. Despite her lack of concern, I'm not afraid. Even though I live in Los Feliz now, I grew up here in East Los Angeles. This is home.

After a short walk, I reach my car. As I pull out my keys, I realize with a flash of annoyance that I've forgotten something. When I signed for the tab, I left my credit card on the tray.

"Son of a bitch," I mumble to myself.

Eastside Brewery closes earlier than regular bars. It's midnight when I arrive again. The bouncer is gone, so I let myself in through the unlocked door. The lights are on, but the place is empty and the music is off. I feel like I'm sneaking backstage after a show.

"Hello?" I shut the door behind me.

I know the owners, so I know a little of the brewery's backstory. I spot clues that this place used to be a bakery. There are marks on the polished concrete floor where display cases were once installed. I look up and see high ceilings, vents, and fans. In the refrigerators that used to hold birthday cakes, wedding cakes, and *pasteles de tres leches*, I see rows of cans and bottles filled and ready to take home.

I walk up to the bar. "Hello?" I say again.

No answer.

I creep behind the counter and through the swinging doors into the kitchen. A big, shirtless man stands by the mop sink in the corner. His Eastside Brewery T-shirt hangs on a nearby shelf. The water is running loudly into the bucket, echoing in the big space.

"Eddie?" I say.

The man shuts off the water, wipes his hands on his apron, and turns around. "Naw, Eddie went home." He has a quiet, deep voice. He steps out of the shadows. "Can I help you?"

I'm twenty-eight years old. My career as a social worker has ensured I've seen a cross section of humanity, a striated rainbow of highs and lows. I grew up poor, got scholarships, navigated the bullshit and institutionalized racism of the university system, got jobs, lost jobs. I've fallen in love and had my heart broken exactly three times. I have a big, loud, overbearing, flawed, beautiful family who makes my life both heaven and hell. They taught me that if life knocks me down nine times, I had better get up ten—otherwise, I'm not fit to call myself a Delgado.

All this to say...I think I'm a tough cookie.

I guess even tough cookies crumble in the face of nuclear hotness.

"Can I help you?" Shirtless asks again. His dark eyebrows furrow.

The barback—it's him. Up close, I see he is younger than me, and he's tall, stupid tall, maybe a foot above my five-foot-three. He's got wavy dark hair and the very first chapter of an excellent beard. Eastside Brewery owes a small portion of its popularity to its owners Eddie and Sal, two handsome brothers who are very much off the market but still make awesome eye candy.

In my opinion, they aren't even in the same league as this guy.

I struggle to keep my eyes on the level. This is not easy when there's a big naked chest in your face. Fit but not bulky, he is cut and carries his muscle well. Smoky gray tattoos enhance his shoulders, his chest, his abs, his—

"Miss?" He lifts one eyebrow.

I blink. "Oh, yes. Excuse me. I'm looking for my card."

"Your credit card? Did you lose it here?"

"No, I left it. On the tray, I think. After I signed my check.

About half an hour ago or so," I babble. "Eddie's not here?" I know Eddie—Eddie's safe.

"He went home," Shirtless says again. "But I can help you. Come with me."

I follow him out the swinging doors and stare freely at his smooth, muscled back. There are tattoos here for me to ogle too —skulls, roses, feathers, Aztec iconography, and the word *Fallen* in spidery, delicate script.

For the first time in a long time, I feel it.

Desire.

I want to touch this man so badly my fingertips tingle. Instead, I keep my arms straight down my sides and walk stiffly to where he stands by the bar.

He pulls a ring of keys from his pocket and unlocks a safe under the counter. Inside there's a wallet, a silver bracelet, and a small cardboard box of credit cards.

"Happens a lot here," Shirtless says. "People get drunk and forget they had a tab."

"I wasn't drunk," I say quickly. "I rarely get drunk. I think I was just in a hurry to get home after all that...stuff. Also it's late for me. I have to work tomorrow, pretty early, in fact. I have a special project and I'm eager to get started on it."

He nods. I don't think he's listening. "What's your name?"

"Deanna Delgado."

"Delgado," he mutters to himself. His long, strong fingers rifle through the cards and I notice—with some thrill—that he doesn't wear a wedding ring. "Benítez, Cortéz, Castañeda..." He finds my card and holds it up between his index and middle fingers like a magician. "Delgado. There you go."

For the first time, I look at him directly and our gazes lock together. His eyes are big and dark with long lashes. Heat pours through me. "Have we...have we met before?" I ask.

"I don't think so," he says, but he doesn't look away. "Eddie and Sal are my older brothers. I'm Angel."

Fallen angel. Apt.

"Nice to meet you," I say, like a dork. "My name is—"

"Deanna Delgado. I got that." He wiggles the card.

I take the credit card and slip it into my wallet. When I look up, Angel's eyes are waiting to meet mine again. My body temperature goes up a thousand degrees.

"All good?" he asks.

"Yes. All good." I fight to stay cool even though this staring game is making funny things happen to me. I clear my throat. "Also, I wanted to say thanks. For helping us out with that guy tonight. He was drunk, that's all."

"Maybe, but he was also an asshole," Angel says. "That kind of bullshit doesn't happen here. Not on my watch, anyway."

My lady parts tingle. "Well, um, yeah. Good," I manage. "Thanks again. Anyway." *Tingle tingle.* "Good night."

I turn. My feet are heavy as they take me away from the most gorgeous man I've ever met.

"Hey, hold up," he says.

I turn around. To my dismay, he's putting his shirt back on, but the cotton strains over his shoulders in the most delightful way. How could someone getting dressed be so sexy?

"Do you have a minute?" he asks. "I need some help." He opens up a big metal refrigerator and pulls out a clear pitcher filled with bright green liquid. "I'm working on something new. I could use some feedback before I let my brothers try it tomorrow. Interested?"

I look around and my urban woman alarms go off. I'm alone in an enclosed space with a stranger—albeit a very, very good-looking stranger—who is offering me what could be double-strength Rohypnol punch.

Angel sees my hesitation. He grabs two clean glasses and

fills them from the same pitcher. "What if we sit at the big table?"

It's like he's read my mind. The front door is still unlocked for an easy exit if I need one. The big table is right next to the front windows where people can see directly inside.

I look at the glasses in his hands. "What is it?" I ask.

"A new *agua fresca*. I've been working on it for a couple weeks." He studies my face. "There's no alcohol."

My alarms stand down, but I stay alert. "Okay," I say at last. "Sure."

I have a feeling Angel is not a smiley man. He nods and says, "After you."

I sit and he takes a seat opposite me. He puts the glasses down in front of us and waits for me to choose the one I want, further suggesting that he understands my justified fear of getting drugged by a stranger.

"The ingredients are lime, fresh ginger, mint, agave nectar, and spinach," he says.

I guess I make a face at the last item.

"You can't taste the spinach," he says. "It's just for color."

We clink glasses. "*Salud*," I say.

The drink is refreshing. Sharp and complex. I didn't realize I was thirsty until I had a taste. Now I want more. Which could be said of this entire experience with Angel.

"What do you think?"

"It's so good," I say. "Much less sweet than I expected. I like it."

"I made it for my sister-in-law. She's pregnant. She can't have beer, and she has bad morning sickness. I think the mint and ginger might make her feel better."

This is the squishiest, most adorable thing I've heard in a long time. Even though I'm sitting down, I'm in danger of swooning. I put my hand on the bench to steady myself.

He takes another sip and gives his bottom lip the tiniest of licks. "The more I drink it," he says thoughtfully, "the more I think we should sell it. As an option for people who can't or don't drink."

"That's a good idea. What would you call it?"

"I don't know. I haven't thought about that. But it should have a name—you're right."

A handsome man telling me I'm right. I can't think of better catnip.

We finish our drinks together. He asks me how I know Eddie. I tell him I used to be his brother's caseworker right after prison, before Eddie got his act together. That was about three years ago. I ask Angel when he started working at the brewery—I don't remember seeing him here before. I would've remembered if I had.

"On and off since it opened," he says. "I was living in Salinas...and some other places...for a while. I just moved back down here for good."

For good. I like the sound of that.

My lady parts tingle even more.

"So I know you have work early tomorrow and you have to get out of here," Angel says. "I need to lock up. If you hang out for five minutes, I can walk you to your car. You shouldn't be out there alone."

I wait as he turns off the lights, locks the doors, and sets the alarm. The last thing he does after we walk out of the front door is lower the security gates and padlock them.

We walk side by side toward my car. He's changed into a clean white T-shirt that smells like laundry detergent. The night air caresses my bare arms and neck. My skin feels extra sensitive. Even my hearing sharpens—I can hear his keys and coins jingling in his pocket. I can hear him breathing, slow and steady, then quick and shallow as we approach my car.

I unlock it. Angel opens the door for me.

"Listen, I don't know how to say this, so I might as well just say it." He hesitates before blowing out a breath. "You're very beautiful. I couldn't keep my eyes off you tonight. I could barely do my job."

To say my jaw drops would be an understatement. My jaw falls straight through the core of the earth and knocks out some poor woman walking on a sidewalk in China.

"Is this a joke?" I look around. "Did Ingrid set this up?"

"Can I kiss you?" Angel asks.

Definitely a joke. I roll my eyes. "Sure. Why the hell not," I say sarcastically.

Angel takes me in his big tatted arms and kisses me.

At first, I am too stunned to respond.

But then.

Dear God.

When he pulls back, I blink at him behind my glasses. "Angel's Brew," I say. My voice cracks.

"What?"

"You should call the green drink Angel's Brew."

He smiles, and of course, it's beautiful. "Angel's Brew. I like it."

He kisses me a second time. When he lets go, I realize my body temperature is so high, my good judgment, my inhibitions, and my hangups have all been completely incinerated. They're ash.

"Come home with me," I whisper.

"Yeah," he says. "Okay."

CPSIA information can be obtained
at www.ICGtesting.com
Printed in the USA
LVHW031526140720
660690LV00004B/771